All Arranged

Luella Linley
License
to
Meddle

BOOK 3

MEREDITH RESCE

All Arranged

Book 3 Luella Linley – License to Meddle

Golden Grain Publishing

PO Box 880 Unley SA 5061

The National Library of Australia Cataloguing-in-Publication Information:

A catalogue record for this work is available from the National Library of Australia

978-0-6489537-5-3 — Paperback
978-0-6489537-4-6 — eBook

Cover Art by Annie Millard Designs

Endorsements

"In 'All Arranged', a modern-day marriage of convenience romance, we see the indomitable Luella Linley at it again as she blends her fiction with the real lives of her adult children. This results in a deeply emotional and moving story that sees Pete and Carrie learning to trust, learning to love, and the healing power of forgiveness. Keep the tissues handy!"

Carolyn Miller – Author of the 'Regency Wallflowers' and 'Regency Brides' series

"If you love marriage of convenience tropes, you'll love this modern-day twist. Realistic characters, laugh out loud moments, and a deep emotional journey making 'All Arranged' a satisfying read. A stellar novel from Meredith Resce and the perfect ending to the series."

Lisa Renee - Author of the 'Single Again' series

"Imagine accepting a marriage proposal from someone you've never even met in person. Have you ever wondered what might happen if you let your family choose your spouse? Pete and Carrie take the risk, and the result is a blend of awkwardness, heartache and satisfaction that is always a delight to read."

Paula Vince – Author of 'Picking up the Pieces' and 'Best Forgotten'

"Meredith Resce has created a thought-provoking and emotional journey in 'All Arranged'. When Louise Brooker confidently organizes a happy-ever-after for her son, Pete, little does she know her meddling will lead the couple through emotions from humor, to embarrassment, to crushing grief before they finally land in happily-married land. Yet another read that is hard to put down from Meredith."

Amanda Deed – Author of the 'Jackson's Creek' series

A note for non-Australian readers: Thank you for deciding to read 'All Arranged'. I have set this novel in Adelaide, South Australia, and wrestled with the idea of whether I should adapt language and measurements to that usually understood by North American readers. In the end, though I have changed the spelling from Australian to US, I have retained the local Australian language. I hope you enjoy the local Aussie flavor. Below is a glossary of terms you may encounter that you may find unfamiliar.

Glossary of terms for non-Australian readers

Speed limit conversion - 60 km per hour = approximately 37 miles per hour

130 km per hour = approximately 80 miles per hour.

Fringe – In reference to hair styles, a fringe is what is sometimes referred to as bangs. Though I can never quite figure out why anyone would call a fringe 'bangs'.

Vegemite – Breakfast toast condiment loved by millions of Aussies, hated by anyone from anywhere else in the world. It's black and thick and salty, and perfect spread lightly with loads of butter. Warning— do not try it without an expert to show you how it's done.

Copper – Police officer.

Footy – Australian Football League.

Servo – Service station or gas station.

Esky – Portable cooler or ice box.

Mobile phone – Cell phone.

Celsius to Fahrenheit conversion – 38 degrees C = 100.4 degrees F.

Nappy – Diaper.

Smoko – Morning or afternoon tea/coffee break for workers.

Ute – Short for utility. A vehicle that has an open tray to carry a load but only requires a car license to drive.

Boot – In reference to a car, it is also known as the trunk.

Loo – Used in both British and Australian English to refer to the toilet or bathroom.

Tim Tam – Australia's favorite chocolate coated biscuit (and by biscuit, I mean cookie).

Ambo – Colloquial term for paramedic or EMT.

Medicare – Australia's national government health support system.

Agro – Australian slang for getting aggressively angry.

Chapter One

"She'd run away.

Rather than face him at the altar, she had taken her lady's maid, ordered a carriage and run away. Benjamin kicked at the small stones on the path in frustration. He was a suitable match for the likes of Kitty Coleborn. Just because she had independent money, an odd case where the estate had not been entailed away from the female line. This meant, of course, that she did not need him or his offer of marriage. She could survive well without him. But could he survive without her? He had loved her and was prepared to overlook her rather unladylike tendencies to speak of politics and business. She would have settled down and made a good wife—well she would have made an adequate wife.

But she'd run away to London where no one can be found if they do not wish it. And he was left with his large estate and manor house, left looking a fool ..."

Louise Brooker saved the document and shut her laptop. Her latest Luella Linley novel was sounding depressingly like real life.

Her son was too good for that woman and he deserved better. Thank goodness she was gone. Except Pete was in a mess. She'd never seen him this bad before, even after Rianne had broken off with him several years ago he wasn't so down.

As his mother, she had to do something. Standing by and watching him eat himself up with depression was too much for a mother to bear.

"Why are you moping?" Russell stood in the doorway of her office looking his usual sensible self.

"What makes you think I'm moping?" Louise asked.

"It's written all over you face."

And all over her latest work-in-progress, but her husband didn't need to know that.

"I'm worried about Pete."

"He's a grown up, Louise. He doesn't need us—"

"You don't know that! He might need us, especially now."

"I was going to say he doesn't need us drooling sympathy all over him. He's taken a blow but he'll get over it eventually."

Typical Russell. So logical and so insensitive. He just didn't understand a mother's concern for her children. It didn't matter that Pete was well into his thirties. He was her baby and she just wanted to coddle him.

"Leave it alone, Louise. You've got Chloe's wedding coming up and she's all for you putting energy into that. Pete will sort himself out.

***

Pete pulled down the roller door of the U-Store-It rental unit and turned the key in the lock. He sighed heavily.

"What now?" Pete heard the strained patience in Andy's question but didn't turn around. He just shrugged his shoulders and walked towards his car.

"I thought this was what you wanted," Andy shouted after him. "You thought it through, right?"

Pete didn't answer. He just opened the door of his ute and climbed into the driver's seat.

"Mate." Andy's tone was firm as he climbed in the passenger side. "You've got to snap out of it. How long are you going to pine over her?"

There was a pause. Andy was obviously waiting for him to answer but he had nothing.

"You said yourself it was better this way."

"I didn't say that. Why would I say that?" Pete turned and glared at his life-long friend.

"All right. I'll say it for you. It's better this way. She wasn't for you, mate. She would have eaten you for breakfast if you'd gone through with it."

Pete sighed again. It was easy for Andy to make judgements. It wasn't his heart that had been broken.

"Pete?" Andy's tone softened and Pete could tell he was trying to make amends. "Come on, mate, you know it's better this way."

"Why didn't I see any of this before we'd booked and paid for the wedding?" Pete said. "How come I don't ever see these things until it's on the verge of break-up?"

"These things happen to the best of us." Andy adopted that caring tone—the one he used when he was trying to play counselor.

"It didn't happen to you." Pete said. He pulled his seatbelt down and clicked it into place. "You've been married—happily married—for six years. You and Karen get on like a house on fire."

"We have our moments," Andy said as he fastened his seatbelt.

"I'm not stupid," Pete replied. "I know every relationship has ups and downs, but how come I can't seem to find someone who's willing to stick it out for better or worse—forever?"

That was the million-dollar question, and one that obviously had Andy stumped as he didn't seem to have an answer. Not that Pete was surprised. No-one seemed to be able to answer that question—

either that or no-one had the courage to tell him to his face. That was probably more likely. Pete started the engine and sighed again. He waited for Andy to call him on it—to offer more platitudes. But he didn't. He just faced forward and fell silent. What could he say that would help anyway?

Since primary school Andy had seen the best and worst of him, and knowing that didn't make him feel any better. Andy hadn't been jealous when Pete got his first girlfriend with ease. Or his second, or third. A long line of girls who fell all over him. Retrospect was laughing at him. Pete was the tall, good-looking one and, unlike his dorky friend, had not had any problems getting girlfriends. Keeping one was another issue. Then Pete watched Andy grow out of his awkward stage and was pleased for him when he met his one true love—Karen. They'd gone out together, got engaged, got married and now had 2.5 kids.

That's what I want.

"Look, let's not talk about women and relationships for a while," Andy broke the silence and Pete's reminiscence. "Let's just get you home, and we'll have a drink, play some x-box—"

"I don't have a home." Pete knew he sounded depressed. He was depressed. What a loser.

"Your parents' place then. This isn't the first time you've gone back home. There's plenty of room for you. They'll be glad to have you back for a while."

"I'm useless, aren't I?"

"You're not useless."

"How would you describe me then? I've just put all my worldly goods in storage, and I'm going back home to Mum and Dad."

"They won't mind."

"I'm thirty-five!"

"I know how old you are. Your age hasn't got anything to do with it. You were dumped two days before your wedding, and you're going to need some TLC. Who better than your parents to look after you? They love you, warts and all."

"I'm such a loser."

"Yes! You're a loser! Get over it."

Andy's words stung. Pete knew by the tone of his voice that Andy's patience was wearing thin, but he struggled to find something positive to say in response.

"I'm sorry, mate." There it was. Just as quickly as Andy lost patience, he'd turned around and apologized, even though it wasn't really his fault.

"I'm sorry too," Pete said. "I just need to pull myself together."

"Give yourself a bit of time."

Andy was right of course, but it didn't make him feel any better. He drove the car out of the storage car park and onto the road, heading towards the home he'd grown up in. He felt like an idiot going back to his parents again, but he simply couldn't face living in the house he and Collette had built together. Everything about it reminded him of what he'd hoped for—a wife, a family, a future together.

Andy fell silent beside him. There was nothing else to be said now anyway. It had all been said. Nothing his best mate could say would improve the way he felt.

***

"He was here! Everyone knew that he'd been jilted, and yet, here he was at an assembly. Charlotte could hardly breathe and couldn't tear her eyes away from his gaze even though she knew she should. One part of her wanted to turn around and walk straight out of the drawing room, but the other part ached for him to step across the small

distance between them and take her in his arms. What an idea! What sort of man did she take him for? Benjamin Hart was no rake. He was a gentleman in every sense of the word, and he would never breach propriety in such a bold and indecorous manner. And yet she longed that he would do so. She longed to be everything to him that Kitty Coleborn had refused to be."

Louise pursed her lips as she re-read the few pages she'd just written. She wasn't happy with the way her heroine was responding to the hero. She shouldn't be so flirtatious. Good heavens! This wasn't the 21st Century she was writing about.

"I can't deal with you at the moment," she said to the computer. She pressed save and closed the document. "I'll have to sort you two out tomorrow."

Her imaginary characters were not such a big issue. There were many times when she couldn't get her characters to cooperate, and usually she'd walk away and face them later when her own mind was clearer.

At the moment her real live drama situation was about to arrive back home. It wasn't as easy to manipulate real people as it was the fictional characters in her novel.

"Hey, Mrs B!" That sounded like Andy calling out. They were home. Andy had brought her dejected son home. She wanted to call back a cheery greeting but that didn't seem kind given how low Pete was. She stepped into the hallway and watched as Andy lugged the two suitcases inside.

"Hi, Andy." She returned his smile but was worried seeing her son's downcast expression, looking as if he had the weight of the world on his shoulders. "Brought him home to us, have you?"

Pete shook his head as he walked by her. Louise felt a jolt of guilt. She'd meant to make light of the situation but he didn't look cheered.

"Shall I put some coffee on?" she asked. Pete was already on his way to what used to be his bedroom, and Louise wanted to make amends.

"Not for me," Andy said. "I was going to try and cheer him up before I went, but I think it's a lost cause." Andy stood next to her as they both watched Pete disappear into the bedroom.

"You're still welcome to a coffee, if you want," Louise said.

"Karen could probably use some help with the kids."

"How is Karen?"

"She always struggles with morning sickness to start with, but she's nearly four months now so hoping we've seen the last of that. Exhaustion is the main problem at the moment."

"Well it would be with two little ones under foot. That will be three under four years old when the baby arrives, won't it?"

"We didn't exactly plan it that way," Andy grinned. "Had thought to wait another couple of years, but, hey…"

"That's what happens," Louise said.

"I feel bad about Pete and Collette." Andy changed tack now that Pete had closed the door.

"I feel bad for how he's feeling now, but I'm not sorry," Louise replied. "She was wrong for him, right from the start. She saw the world from a completely different point of view and wanted very different things. I tried to tell him."

"Well, he knows it now. He's pretty low at the moment."

"Yes, I know. Russell says we should just give him time. I hope he's right."

***

They think I'm deaf! Pete let himself fall backwards on the bed and tried to block out the sound of his mother and friend talking in the hallway.

When would he stop feeling like this? He did a mental calculation and figured it had only been two days since he'd last counted. One month and four days. One month and four days of emotional turmoil. Why did she do it? They'd loved each other. They were meant to be together forever. It had to be a mistake. She would change her mind and come back. He could change.

He sighed and bent his arm to press across his eyes. He was tired of feeling like he might break down crying. *Toughen up, man.* That was all very well, but he'd just lost the love of his life. She'd given his ring back and walked away on the eve of their wedding. Just like that.

He couldn't help the stupid tears that stung his eyes. He wiped them away and pushed himself up from his bed. At least they'd stopped talking about him in the hallway. *Stop thinking about her.* That was great self-talk, but it didn't work. Every detail of the break-up came back to him for a mental review, even though he'd been over and over it about a million times.

He knew Collette thought differently to him on just about every subject. But he'd loved her. Love would have sorted it out in the long run. Well that had been the plan. Except for the one crucial issue which brought it to a head, and on this, apparently, there was no sorting.

"What do you mean you don't want kids?"

Pete had asked the question the night before their wedding rehearsal. They'd just had dinner with Andy and Karen, and watched the frantic family pace their friends kept trying to get a two-year-old and a three-and-a-half-year-old fed, bathed and put to bed. And then the conversation had turned to the anticipation of the arrival of number three. Karen complained of morning sickness and Andy wondered how on earth they would survive, especially after he got up for the seventh time to return the younger child to his bed.

"Shoot me if I ever get to be like that," Collette had said when they'd left for the evening.

"Like what?" Pete had asked, confused.

"Pregnant, for one thing," she said, "and always talking about kids."

"I'm not likely to shoot you if you get pregnant." Pete smiled at her. "I'm looking forward to it."

This comment had met with an icy stare.

"What?" Pete had asked.

"You're not serious?"

"About looking forward to you being pregnant?" Pete asked. "Absolutely. I can't wait."

"I can't believe you said that." Collette's face told how incensed she was.

"If you want to wait a while, I can," Pete waivered in his enthusiasm. "But I don't want to wait forever. I am thirty-five, you know."

"Listen, Pete." Collette had the no-nonsense tone she used for difficult sales assistants. "You might want to play happy families, but that's not for me. I can't think of anything worse."

"Why?" Pete couldn't believe he was hearing this.

"Why? Because I don't want to tear my body apart to start with, and secondly, I have a career, and I don't want to be stuck at home with snotty-nosed kids."

"But it wouldn't be forever." Pete hadn't seen this coming and wasn't prepared for this argument. "Just until they went to school."

"No, Pete. I don't want kids. I never have."

"You've never said anything about it before."

"I have!" she glared at him. "I've told you over and over not to get your hopes up."

"But I didn't think you meant it."

"What did you think I meant?"

"I don't know. I guess I hoped you were just kidding."

"Well, you better not want it too hard because it's not going to happen, Pete. I always said that, and I meant it. I don't want kids."

Pete had slumped into silence. It was hard to hear what his future wife was saying, but she was immovable on it. He began to readjust his thinking, though his heart was disappointed.

The next day Collette dropped the bomb-shell.

"It's not going to work," she held her engagement ring out to him. "We're just too different, you and me. If we went through with it, you would always be hoping I'd change my mind and I won't. I've had my tubes tied anyway."

"What? Why?"

"So I don't get pregnant!" she said as if he was a dim-wit.

"But…"

"You are so ridiculously conservative. Did you imagine I'd never slept with anyone before?"

Pete felt a hot wave sweep over his head. Mentally, he probably knew, but he was conservative. Like the argument about having kids, he'd not allowed his mind to consider his fiancée might have been with another man before meeting him. If he'd been living in a cloistered bubble, it was fully burst now.

"You knew I didn't want kids, Pete."

Did he? How had he talked himself into believing something different?

"It's not going to work. You may as well face it now. Let's not make it any harder than it already is. Let's just call it off and save all the fuss of a divorce."

And that had been it. Just like that.

Pete sat, shoulders hunched, on the single bed that had been his when he was a teenager. He stared around the room. His mother, bless her, had left his giant posters still blu-tacked to the wall. Michael Jordan in full flight and a couple of autographed Crows Premiership posters. He wasn't thirteen anymore. All grown up and still an emotional wreck.

He'd just handed the keys of his house over to a real-estate agent after having signed a rental agreement, stored all his stuff, which wasn't that much after Collette had taken the things she'd bought for the house. He should have seen it coming, but he hadn't because he loved her. And now what? Thirty-five years old, broken-hearted and living with his parents. That was the complete summary of the situation.

Chapter Two

$\mathcal{C}$arrie held her two-day-old niece in her arms and felt all sorts of warm fuzzy feelings.

"We named her after you," Ellen said.

"I thought her name was Lucy," Carrie looked up surprised.

"Lucy Carolyn," Ellen supplied, "after her Aunt Carrie."

Carrie felt good about that for a few moments, until her sister continued. "Since you probably won't ever have any children of your own, we thought it would be nice to have someone to carry on your name."

"Who says I won't have any kids of my own?" Carrie immediately reacted to the comment.

"Right." Ellen smiled. "Have you finally found a boyfriend who's happy to play second fiddle to your career?"

Carrie didn't answer. She had always maintained that her job was first—well since Kevin, anyway. That whole fiasco had been an eye-opener. Since the day that had fallen apart she'd taken a long hard look at her chosen profession and decided it was a calling that was worth her full attention. She wasn't going to sacrifice it for anyone. But it hurt to hear her sister be so flippant about the subject, and the fact it hurt surprised her.

"You haven't found a boyfriend have you?" Ellen asked cautiously.

"Of course not!" Carrie snapped out of her moment of introspection.

"So what do you think of her? Lucy Carolyn?"

Carrie took a moment to absorb the soft warmth of her new niece before answering. "She's beautiful, El. I love her already."

"We're pretty wild about her ourselves," Ellen said softly, smiling into Lucy's eyes.

"Does the doctor think there'll be any more?" Carrie asked.

"I haven't asked just yet. She's such a miracle but if we beat the odds once, I guess there's always a small chance."

"Mum and Dad are thrilled, you know."

"Well they've been wanting grandchildren ever since you turned twenty," Ellen said. "That's like twelve years now."

"Don't go on about it, El," Carrie complained. "I'm glad I didn't get married when I was twenty. Kevin was a self-absorbed slob and a male-chauvinist."

"But in twelve years can you honestly say you haven't met another man who was further up the food-chain than Kevin?"

"I haven't even been looking. You know this, El. We've been over it before. I'm single, independent and happy. Leave it alone."

Ellen went quiet, but Carrie doubted it would end at that.

"Well, now Mum and Dad have their first grandchild—"

"Maybe their only grandchild," Ellen cut in.

"You just said there's hope you might have more," Carrie encouraged. "Or, you never know, I might have one."

Carrie watched Ellen purse her lips.

"Go on, say it."

"You have to have a man to have children, Carrie. I'm pretty sure that's how it works."

"Maybe I'll use IVF."

Carrie watched the predictable look of disappointment that crossed her sister's face and she laughed.

"I'm kidding, Ellen. I wouldn't dream of depriving you of your romantic hopes. And besides if I went to the trouble of having a child, I'd prefer to have a supportive partner to help me bring it up."

"To help get you pregnant in the first place," Ellen said.

"You have so much class."

"Just saying."

***

"You should marry, old man."

Benjamin inhaled slowly in an attempt to ignore his best friend's comment.

"Kitty Coleborn is gone. You should not give her another thought." Lord Spelford continued on. Did he not get the hint from Benjamin's silence that he did not wish to pursue this subject?

"I've heard Lord Featherstone is looking for a suitable marriage alliance for his daughter."

Benjamin paused at this comment and turned towards his friend. "Who do you mean?"

"You've seen her, surely. She has been out and at balls and assemblies for over a year now."

"Are you talking about Lady Charlotte Featherstone?"

"Of course. And she has a sizable dowry," Lord Spelford said, tipping back a small tumbler of brandy after he spoke.

"I'm not interested in money," Benjamin said. "I do wish you would leave this topic alone."

"You need to get over Kitty, old man. Consider Charlotte Featherstone. She would do you very well."

It was all very well for his friend to speak as if there was no feeling attached to it, but Benjamin had been in love. Kitty's leaving had left him bereft. He could not consider anyone else.

And that should be an end to it, except it wasn't. Not for Benjamin Hart and his well-meaning, intrusive friend, nor would it be the end for Pete. Louise sighed.

She'd continued to watch her son closely as he went through the motions of daily life—he was functioning, but he still had the air of sadness hanging over him. At least he'd gotten up each day and gone to work.

"How's your latest build coming on?" Louise asked Pete over dinner.

"Frame's up. Just organizing other contractors to come in to get the wiring and roofing done."

"How is your new apprentice working out?"

"Max?"

"Is that his name?"

"He's working out well for a kid just out of school."

"At least you have someone to talk to during the day."

"Actually, no. But that's what I like about him. He doesn't feel the need to be talking every minute of the day. We just have the radio to entertain us."

Louise shrugged. "I guess that's good, if that's what you want."

Pete didn't answer. He just kept on eating. Louise knew it wasn't what he wanted, but there wasn't anything she could do to retrieve the broken engagement. She wouldn't have even if she could. But she did worry about how Pete tossed and turned during the night. He'd get up and work on his computer and go to the fridge. She'd heard him because she was awake too, worrying about him. It was wearing them both down: Pete just drifting through life wounded and lost, and her watching him.

"Mum, you're hopeless." Chloe had said when she'd found out her mother wasn't sleeping properly.

"I hate seeing him so aimless and unhappy." Louise poured hot water from the kettle into the three cups.

"We need to run an intervention." Her other daughter, Megan, put the milk bottle on the kitchen table.

"And what do you propose we do to intervene?" It was a nice idea, but Louise had interrogated every possible scenario in her mind already and come up with nothing.

"Perhaps we could set him up with someone," Megan said. "That's your thing, mother, and you're good at it too." Megan waved her hand in Chloe's direction. True enough, the pair of them were settled in stable relationships because Louise had taken the initiative to organize a few details.

"Bad idea." Chloe brought her cup to the table and sat down. "The last thing Pete needs is to go into another relationship and then find himself dumped two months later."

"I guess." Megan sounded disappointed.

"I don't know what's wrong with the young women of this generation," Louise said, absently stirring honey into her tea. "Pete's nice looking, he's hardworking and responsible, he's polite and generous. What's with the girls? Why does he keep getting dumped?"

Louise saw her daughters trade a glance, both with raised eyebrows, as if they knew something she didn't.

"Well, I don't understand," Louise complained. "It doesn't make any sense to me."

"Mum!" Chloe adopted her no-nonsense tone. "It's not one of your romantic novels. Things don't always work out happily ever after."

"I don't see why they can't," Louise said. "Things have worked out very well for you two, haven't they?"

"I think Cam and I would have gone very well without your interference," Megan said.

"You would never have met him in the first place if I hadn't meddled, and you know it."

Megan smiled and reached for a piece of chocolate slice.

"Or you either," Louise said to Chloe. "Michael would never have called you the first time if I hadn't shown him your photo and made the suggestion."

"Yes, thank you mother," Chloe said. "However, in this instance I don't think we can arrange Pete's love life like you do one of your Regency characters."

"Or like you did for us," Megan added.

"I can't see why not."

"You're an idealist, mother," Megan said.

"Idealism is not such a bad thing—"

"Yeeess. We know. It provides us with something to aim for."

Louise could hear them parroting one of her favorite sayings and it was annoying. "Well, it does give us something to aim for."

"Idealism isn't going to help mend Pete's broken heart," Chloe also took a piece of chocolate slice.

"Maybe not," Louise replied, "but I still can't see why his girlfriends' insist on breaking up with him in the first place. He's such a nice boy."

"Mum! Pete is thirty-five. He's hardly a boy anymore," Chloe said.

"He's still my boy, and I can't see why things shouldn't work out nicely for him."

"I know!" Megan flicked her pointer finger up as if she'd had a flash of brilliance. "Why don't we use one of your arranged marriages?"

"Hah! Yes, perfect!" Chloe had a smug air. "A marriage of convenience would be just the thing for Pete."

Louise heard the sarcasm in her daughters' statements. They had teased her often enough about the number of times she had written novels using a marriage of convenience as a plot device.

"It works," she said. "It's a trope that sells, so get off my case."

"In Regency Romance, perhaps, but it's not something that works in real life" Megan said. "I'm sorry to tease you, but this is Pete we're talking about."

"But it does work in real life." Louise was suddenly fired up again. "It's only western culture that's abandoned the arranged marriage. Marrying for love has only been fashionable in the last two-hundred years."

"Actually, Ramesh and Meera—the Indian couple across the road—theirs was an arranged marriage," Chloe said.

"You're not helping," Megan said.

"How do you know?" Louise sat forward in her chair.

"They told us all about it when we had dinner there the other night," Chloe replied.

"You see!" Louise loved it when something came up to validate her point of view.

"Now look what you've done." Megan frowned at her sister. "She's got this thing in her head now and we won't hear the end of it."

"I'm just saying," Louise said, raising her eyebrows defensively. "Our Pete could do very well in a marriage, I know he could. He's a responsible, caring young man who has a great capacity to love, and I think he would make a wonderful father."

"You're impossible, Mum," Chloe said.

"And just so you know," Megan added, "I don't think you should pitch this idea to him at the moment."

"You were the one who came up with the idea."

"We were teasing you," Megan said.

"We were teasing, but in all seriousness, in Pete's current state of depression, he'd just as likely go for it." Chloe stood up and took her empty cup to the dishwasher.

Louise didn't say anything more but began to consider possibilities. Even if her daughters had been making fun of her romantic imagination, she was an author. Coming up with ideas was not difficult and she was used to manipulating situations and circumstances to make things work out in the lives of her romantic heroes. She'd had success meddling with her daughters' love lives. The idea of applying similar tactics to her poor broken-hearted son was appealing.

***

Pete knew he'd have to pull himself together sooner or later. It had been three months since the breakup yet his family were still hovering carefully in the background trying to protect his fragile state. He knew it and was becoming uncomfortable with that knowledge. And his best mate, Andy, was trying his hardest to cheer him up. Ironically, Andy was the worst person to help. He hardly ever came alone. He either had one or both of his toddlers in tow, or the whole family. Pete loved his mate but this continuous picture of domestic happiness didn't really help him in his present state of melancholy.

He should have been married by now, and Collette could well have been a couple of months pregnant with their first child. Well, at least, that was what he had imagined. *I'm as bad as my mother.* It was hard admitting just how idealistic he'd been in his hopes and dreams.

And while he was being honest with himself, he might as well recognize how he was behaving like a selfish clod. He'd been so caught up in his own emotional pain he hadn't given a thought to anyone else for months.

Andy and Karen were looking forward to the arrival of their third baby, and as Andy's best mate, he should show some sort of interest.

Chloe was planning her wedding. That was only a few weeks away and he should at least make an effort to go out and buy a suit for the occasion. Megan and her husband, Cam, had just started plans for a new house, yet Pete hadn't asked them anything at all about it.

His dad would always be his dad. Solid, reliable, unchangeable. Nothing much new ever happened with him. He was the dependable one. And then there was his mother. Pete wasn't sure if she had just released a new novel, or was working on one, or whether she'd given up writing romance altogether. He really should ask. She was admired worldwide by her fans and her own son had never read anything she'd written.

He had to do better. Three months was long enough. Collette was not coming back, and he needed to move past it.

"You look nice, Pete," Mum said, when he entered the dining room and sat down to the dinner table.

"Thanks."

"What's the occasion?" Megan asked.

"Well you're here for dinner for a start," Pete said. "Don't want to look like I've rolled out of the gutter since you've come to visit."

"You didn't dress up last time," Chloe said.

"Chloe."

Pete caught the warning in his mother's tone. She was in protection mode. This had to stop.

"I didn't Chloe, you're right. I've been in a bit of a funk lately."

"Like we didn't notice," Megan said.

"Megan." Mum's warning tone again.

"Have you got your suit for the wedding yet?" Chloe asked.

"Not yet," Pete answered, "but I was thinking I'd go out this Saturday and take a look at what's there. Which shop do you recommend?"

"Perhaps I'll come with you," Dad said. "I haven't got anything yet and I'm the father of the bride."

"That would be lovely, wouldn't it girls?" Now his mother was trying to encourage him. She wasn't very subtle.

"Don't overdo it, mother," Megan said.

They were still treading on eggshells because of his 'delicate' state.

"It's all right." He felt a flush of shame realizing just how self-absorbed he'd been lately. "I'm not going to sink into a puddle of tears. I'm sorry about the last few months. I know I've been out of sorts."

"It's all right, dear." Mum was still making allowances.

"It's not all right, Mum. So, I got hurt. Thank you all for being so kind and considerate, but it isn't an excuse for me being so selfish. I'm sorry."

"Well that's sorted then." Dad scooped up a huge chunk of roast potato and put it into his mouth.

"Thank goodness." Chloe didn't make any attempt to be tactful. "We were getting quite desperate there for a while. Mum was beginning to plan an arranged marriage for you—that's how desperate we were."

Everyone at the table seemed to freeze. Pete knew they were all looking at him afraid he'd relapse. The conversation stalled and if he didn't say something to reassure them, they would give Chloe a sound lecture the minute he left the room.

"Perhaps it's not such a bad idea," he said. "Mum usually has great success in her novels, doesn't she? Maybe I should let her take control of my miserable love life and see if she can't organize it any better."

Everyone laughed, but he could tell they were still uncertain. He had work to do if he was going to put his family at ease.

Chapter Three

$\mathcal{A}$s acting principal it was Carrie's job to organize a staff party for Josh and Laura. Laura was taking maternity leave at seven and a half months pregnant. Her husband, Josh, was head of the science department. Organizing a party was not among her usual responsibilities, but everybody was close to these two teachers.

Were there enough food and drinks ordered to be brought to the school staffroom? She hoped so, and she hoped that the streamers and balloons hung around the staffroom would not come loose and fall into the fruit punch. One could never tell how effective Blu-tac would be.

As she took the pen to write in the card, she sighed. Josh Hargraves. What a nice guy and she'd turned him down. Too late for regrets now. But that was easier said than done. She and Josh had started as junior staff at this school eight years ago. Carrie had only recently broken off her engagement to Kevin, which had been ugly, and Carrie had decided she was over men for life. So when Josh had asked her out, Carrie had been a little harsh in putting him off. Josh was a nice guy and hadn't taken the rejection too badly. Of course he hadn't given up so easily either. He'd tired several times before he got the message. What part of 'no, not now, not ever,' did he find difficult to understand?

Carrie sighed again. He'd got the message and given up around the same time Laura Sharp arrived as the new junior teacher.

Carrie wrote on the card: *Dear Josh and Laura.*

Laura hadn't been prickly and cold. She and Josh had clicked immediately and two years later they married. Now they were about to welcome their first child into the world. Regret was practically gnawing Carrie's insides to shreds. Not that she begrudged Laura her happiness. Carrie had had her chance—chances—with Josh, and she'd shut him out. Josh deserved happiness. Laura deserved happiness. It was ironic how now Carrie was the one to make sure the staff celebration happened.

She'd known Josh Hargraves that whole eight years and he'd never once proven to be like Kevin—self-centered, egotistical, rude and lazy. Not once. Despite her having rejected him, Josh was still friendly and kind towards her. Carrie thought about what to write on the card. *Good catch, Laura!* She was tempted, but instead she wrote the usual platitudes of congratulations and best wishes.

Another sigh. It was as it was. After the Kevin fiasco, Carrie had determined men were slobs and her passion for her job was enough. Time to stop sighing and accept the good with the bad.

But I wish I could have a great husband and kids too. The runaway self-pity broke its bounds again.

Don't be ridiculous. You have a great job, a great house, two great dogs. Get over it.

Self-talk was applied, but self-pity seemed to have the upper hand, especially as the party got underway.

All the girls on staff were clucking over Laura, and the guys drank a few beers and slapped Josh on the back. It was when Laura opened Carrie's gift that Carrie almost fell apart. She was thankful she was not the focus of attention at that point as she was sure her renegade feelings must show on her face.

"You OK?" Her long-time friend and colleague, Amanda Keenan, seemed to sense her low spirits.

Carrie swallowed the lump of emotion in her throat and fixed a smile on her face. "Yup. Good as gold."

"I thought I saw a tear," Amanda said.

"You know what a softy I am when it comes to things like baby-showers."

"Can't say that I do, Carrie. I wouldn't have picked you for a softy."

"Well, perhaps you don't know me as well as you think." Carrie forced a smile. Would her insightful friend buy it and leave her alone?

Amanda pursed her lips and shook her head. "I think I do know you, Carrie Davis, and I think you're a fraud."

Apparently, Amanda was not buying the facade. "What do you mean?"

"Never mind." Amanda took another bite of her specially cut, gourmet sandwich.

"I don't know what you mean, Amanda Keenan."

The trouble was, Carrie did know what Amanda meant. She was a fraud. Amanda knew how Josh had pursued her in the early days. They'd talked about it. Amanda had been the one to tell her she should give him a chance.

But this wasn't about Josh. It was about her. Single, independent and happy.

When she arrived home from school and put her key in the front door, her two dogs came bounding to the door to greet her.

"Hey, fellas," she said, pushing past them to get inside. They jostled around her feet, wagging their tails madly. They had been cute and easy to manage when they were puppies but now they were fully grown Labradors—big, clumsy and desperately wanting her attention and affection.

At least I have someone at home who wants and needs me.

The melancholy from the afternoon had followed her home and pounced. She put her school bag in her office, and her coffee travel-cup in the sink.

"All right," she said. "Let's sit and talk." She sat down on her favorite comfy armchair and allowed both dogs to come over to her. They both leaned their heads on her legs. Even though they were sitting, their tails were still wagging.

"You know I love you, don't you?" she said, fondling their ears. More mad wagging. "You're my best friends. So reliable. So affectionate. So caring."

And with that, she burst into tears.

It wasn't that she was crying over Josh. She was happy he'd married Laura and that they were having a baby. And she certainly wasn't pining over Kevin. But she suddenly felt this huge emptiness—longings for companionship and family; longings she'd furiously denied for years. And now she wondered if it was all too late.

***

"I really am a loser, aren't I?" Pete said as he watched the credits roll on the TV screen. He was sitting on the couch next to his mother, his father asleep on the other sofa adjacent, and they'd just watched one of his mother's all-time favorite movies. Pete didn't mind watching chick-flicks. Of course he liked a good action movie better, with plenty of testosterone and explosions. But spending a Saturday evening with his parents, watching an unrealistic romance movie, and feeling all warm and fuzzy at the end was not exactly the signs of a man about town.

"It's only for the time being," Mum said. "And I appreciate having someone enjoy a good movie with me."

"Could you do me a favor and not tell all your friends I 'enjoyed' the movie. I'm struggling here as it is."

"I won't say a word." Pete could tell she wanted to say more.

"But…" he prompted.

"But I'm intrigued to know why you enjoyed watching this story with me. Was it the story or the company?"

"Both, if you must know."

"You enjoyed all that romance and stuff?"

"I confess, I did."

"Didn't you think the plot a little unrealistic?"

"It was totally unrealistic. Nobody in their right mind gets down on one knee in front of a crowd of strangers and proposes with a microphone. That part of it was totally lame. But I liked the fact they managed to get over their differences and decided to commit to each other."

"Pete." Just by the way she said his name, he knew she was set to begin a serious discussion.

"Yes, mother? What's going on in that little head of yours?"

"Were you joking the other night when you said I should try to arrange a marriage for you?"

Pete didn't react, which surprised him. "I was joking."

He could feel his mother deflate right in front of him.

"But hey, you never know. Look at Megan's friend from high school. It worked for her."

"Really?" Mum perked up again. "Which friend? I don't remember."

"Can't remember her name. She was sent back to her home country, somewhere in the Middle East, to meet the husband her family had organized for her to marry."

"I think I do remember, now you come to mention it."

"Yeah. She came back engaged, and once the immigration department was happy with the paperwork, her fiancé came to Australia. She had enough time to finish her year twelve and then they had a big traditional wedding."

"How well did you know her?" Louise asked.

"I didn't really know her. She was in Megan's class. Don't you remember Megan going to the wedding fourteen or so years ago? She dragged me along as her date for the night."

"Yes, I do remember. Do you know how they got on?"

"You'd have to ask Megan."

Pete watched his mother, trying to gauge if she'd gotten over her disappointment.

"So have you thought about such an idea for yourself?"

Apparently she was over her disappointment and had taken courage instead.

"If you mean, do I want to send for an overseas bride? No."

"Well, I wasn't thinking of an overseas bride, actually."

"What were you thinking of?" Pete wasn't sure if he should be alarmed or amused.

"I was thinking of running an ad in the paper, and seeing who responded."

"Mum! For goodness sake. The desperate dating page! I'll have all sorts of girls wanting to hook up. Besides, if I wanted to advertise, I'd try one of those internet dating sites."

"No, I was thinking of something a little more difficult."

"I'm not sure I'm liking the sound of this."

"If I can find someone who meets the criteria—"

"What criteria?"

"The criteria you set, of course."

"Mum!"

"Just hear me out. If I can find her, and I put her through a stringent screening process with the whole family, and if we're all satisfied she would be good for you, would you be willing to consider it?"

"For a start with, no girl in her right mind would respond to such an invitation, and for a second with…" He paused.

"For a second with?" Mum prompted.

"Well, I don't know. But I sincerely doubt you'd be able to find someone to respond, let alone someone who would fit my criteria."

"Would you be willing to humor me and let me see how far I get?"

Pete was speechless for a moment, then was saved from having to answer when his father stirred from his sleep and sat up.

"Must be time for bed," Dad said. He had no idea of the conversation that had been going on right in front of his nose.

"Yes, dear." Mum also got up from the couch. "Sleep on it, Pete, and let me know what you think later."

***

It was Ellen's birthday and the whole family were going to meet at Mum and Dad's to celebrate. Carrie didn't go home often but she loved it when there was opportunity to visit. Along with Ellen, Brad and the new baby, Carrie's brother, Mark, was also expected—along with his new girlfriend.

Carrie braced herself. Following the emotional episode she'd had at Laura and Josh's baby shower, she was aware she was somehow extra sensitive. *I'm being ridiculous. Who'd have thought I could be so soppy and sentimental.* She checked her image in the bathroom mirror. Why? She had no idea. She wasn't trying to impress anybody.

"I'm single, independent and happy." And going slightly potty talking to herself in the mirror. Snapping off the bathroom light, she picked up her bag ready to leave. "I don't care," she told her two Labradors.

But by the time she was in her car, something sad rose up and sat in her throat. She *did* care, and the more she tried to deny it, the louder the thoughts shouted at her. *You're all alone. You're getting older. There's no one out there who'd want a self-made woman married to her job, especially one as old as you.*

"I'm not *that* old." *But you are talking to yourself.* "Cut it out!"

She had a house and two dogs. She had family, and they were all proud of her achievements in her career. And she was going to eat with them and enjoy the evening. That was all she needed.

***

"So, what do you think of Mark's new girl?" Ellen asked Carrie as they stacked dishes in the dishwasher.

"She seems OK. But she's very young. Do you think he's serious?"

"Well, you know Mark. He's ever the impulsive one."

"But she's only just out of high school and Mark's already twenty-eight. I don't think it's a great idea with such an age gap."

"Well luckily for us, we don't actually have any say in it," Ellen said. "Mark's a big boy. He can make his own decisions."

"I guess." Carrie couldn't help sounding resigned.

"You OK?" her sister asked.

"Yeah. Fine." The melancholy must show. Time to throw out her best imitation of control and calm. Ellen seemed to buy it. She had to pull herself together. There was no way she would let anyone in the family know the kinds of thoughts that had been running through her head the past couple of weeks.

But one hour with the family after dinner eroded away the best of these intentions. Mark and his new girlfriend, Shari, were so caught up making puppy-dog eyes at each other that Carrie wanted to shake them. Ellen and Brad couldn't talk about anything but baby Lucy, and Mum and Dad wanted nothing more than to dote on their granddaughter. They were gushing their delight in all the blossoming family relationships. Carrie was devastated. She didn't *fit*. Even in her own family. There was nothing about her life to dote over or delight in. She was the acting principal at a local high school, and the best she could do by way of family contribution was to show her mother a photo of her two dogs.

That hardly roused a moment's notice.

"Lucy will love to come to your house to play with them when she's older," Mum said.

Carrie was falling apart.

I want what they've got. Despite her heart screaming loudly, she managed to school her emotions until her brother and sister had left.

"Mum, can I talk to you?" She sat back down on the lounge chair instead of following her siblings out the door.

"What's wrong?" Mum asked.

"I want to get married." Carrie blurted it straight out. She couldn't think of any other way to say it.

"Are you seeing someone?" Mum asked, surprise written all over her face.

Her astonishment hurt.

"No. Not since Kevin."

"Kevin. We haven't talked about him in…what…ten years?"

"Something like that." Carrie said.

"I don't quite understand."

"Neither do I!" Carrie cried. "All of a sudden, with Lucy's arrival, and now Mark's girlfriend, I feel left out—as if I really am an old maid, and there's no hope left for me of having a family. I'm lonely and I want more."

"More than your teaching career?"

"I love teaching. I love my current position, even though it's temporary …"

"But you want more?"

"I don't understand it. I've never felt like this before. But … well … now I do."

"Well, there's nothing wrong with wanting a husband and family. In fact, if you recall, I've been saying that for quite some time now."

"Twelve years." Carrie supplied.

"But if that's what you feel now, then that's great. You know your father and I would have no objections."

"I know. But I don't know any great guys. I'm not even sure if there are any great guys out there or if it's all just a huge romantic fantasy."

"You like Brad, don't you?"

"Yeah. He's great, I guess. Of course he's married to Ellen, so he doesn't really count."

"There are heaps of men out there, you'll just have to wait."

"I hate to contradict you, Mum, but there aren't heaps of men out there—not eligible men, at least."

Her mother looked doubtful.

"There are heaps of guys who are either on their second or third marriage, who have kids from other relationships, or who have simply slept around throughout their twenties and thirties and have no notion of responsibility or commitment."

"That sounds more like the Carrie of twelve years ago," Mum said. "You don't have any faith in the male race."

"They are not a separate race, mother."

"Last time we discussed this, you decided they were a separate species."

"Yes well, we were talking about Kevin at the time."

"I think it would be best if you take some time to think about it. Look around at your male friends and just see if there isn't someone there right in front of you. Someone perhaps you haven't considered before because of your, how shall we say, 'Kevin complex.'"

Carrie raised her eyebrows. This conversation hadn't really been helpful. She didn't think she'd gotten through to her mother and she didn't feel any better.

"OK, Mum. You're probably right. Let's forget I said anything about it."

But even as she left to go home, Carrie knew her mother would be unlikely to forget the conversation. In fact, she would lay money on the idea that her mother was probably calling Ellen straight away to discuss the problem.

Chapter Four

"Pete, I've got to talk to you straight away." Megan's urgent tone coming through the phone made Pete straighten up and listen.

"Why? What's happened? Has some supplier not got our order on time?"

"When will you be home?" she asked. "I'll come around."

"We're packing up here now," Pete replied. "I'll be another hour by the time I drive home."

"On second thought, perhaps we'd better meet somewhere for coffee."

"Megan! For goodness sake! What's the matter?"

"I can't tell you on the phone. I'll meet you at our café in forty minutes. Can you be there by then?"

Pete wanted to insist on her telling him right now. She was his office manager. Was there something wrong with a contractor or client? But he knew his sister, and she had that determined tone in her voice. "OK. I'll be there in forty minutes."

He put his mobile phone back in his work-belt and continued packing up his tools.

"Girl trouble?" Max, Pete's eighteen-year-old apprentice asked, obviously unable to avoid hearing the phone conversation.

"You could say that," Pete answered. "It's my sister."

"The one who does our pay?"

"Yes, Megan. She's freaking out about something, hopefully not work related. But she wouldn't discuss it over the phone. You know what sisters are like?"

Max shrugged his shoulders. "Not really. Don't have any sisters. Hope she's all right."

"She's all right," Pete said. "She'd have been around here at the building site if it was really serious."

***

"So what's the emergency?" he asked the moment he'd slid into the café booth.

"Do you have any idea what Mum's up to?" Megan asked, her eyes wide, and her tone dramatic.

Pete didn't answer straight away. He was used to his mother being involved with all sorts of eccentric ideas. Nothing would surprise him.

"She's getting set to find you a wife," Megan blurted out. "What are you going to do about that?"

"Oh. Is that all?" Pete laughed.

"What do you mean, 'is that all'? She's going to place an ad in the paper."

"Calm down, Megan."

"Aren't you worried about it?"

"Not really. Just let her go through the motions. She won't find anybody."

"There will be hundreds of responses!"

Was that a compliment? Should he feel flattered? "I doubt it, Megan, and even if there were, she assured me they had to pass my criteria or she wouldn't consider them."

"You knew she was planning this?" The expression on Megan's face was full on disbelief.

"She's talked about it. I'm not really worried because I don't believe she'll find anyone who'll fit the bill. If someone like that existed they certainly wouldn't be scanning the paper in search of a matchmaker to arrange a marriage for them."

Megan sat back, a frown on her face. "So you're just going to let Mum go to all this trouble when you have no intention of cooperating with her?"

"I'll cooperate. I've been thinking about the criteria. When she's ready, I'll give her the list and she can go her hardest. But the chances of someone actually replying who fits the bill are so miniscule, I don't expect to ever have another conversation about it. Don't worry about it, Megan. If it keeps Mum amused and away from worrying about me, then let her go."

"You're really naïve, you know that?" his sister said. "You actually think Mum will give up if she doesn't succeed the first time?"

Pete thought about that for a moment as a shot of panic passed through his system.

"She's just trying to cheer me up," he said. "She'll get sick of it in a few weeks." *I hope.*

***

Ellen didn't usually read the newspaper, but since she was no longer at work and was finding parenting a lot easier than she'd anticipated, she found she often had time to kill while Lucy was sleeping. Carrie had suggested she take up a temporary hobby since Lucy was proving to be a perfect baby and Ellen found spare time on her hands. But Ellen hadn't found a hobby yet, so she took to reading the paper. Brad had signed up for a subscription to keep informed for work purposes, but he hardly ever read the paper.

Ellen knew she was bored as she sometimes amused herself reading the *searching for partners* page. She honestly didn't know whether to laugh or cry at some of the things she read.

But this particular morning, she came across a longer than usual ad, and it didn't read anything like other pieces she'd seen so far.

Wanted for a social experiment. A woman aged between 25 – 35 for an arranged marriage to 35-year-old, attractive, responsible man. Families of both parties to be fully involved in the engagement process…

"Mum, have you got today's paper?" Ellen blurted the words out as soon as her mother picked up the phone.

"Good morning to you too," her mother answered.

"Good morning. Do you have the paper? Check on page thirty-five."

"What's the rush?"

"Have you got the paper?"

"Just a minute."

Ellen heard rustling as her mother was obviously unfolding the newspaper.

"Page thirty-five, half way down the page, second column over – heading 'Arranged marriage.'"

There were a few moments silence and Ellen chafed with impatience as she waited for her mother to read it.

"What did you have in mind?" Mum eventually asked.

"You rang me a couple of weeks ago telling me that Carrie was all lonely and wanting a man. What do you think?"

"About Carrie responding to the ad?"

"Why not?" Ellen said.

"Because it sounds dodgy. Who puts an ad for an arranged marriage in the lonely hearts section of the newspaper?"

"Nobody! That's the point. This sounds different and it might be on the level."

"Ellen, you really need to get another interest."

"No, Mum, listen. This is the first time Carrie has shown an interest in anything other than her career. I think we should strike while the iron's hot."

"Are you thinking of Carrie or your own need for some romantic excitement?"

"Carrie, of course. She might not realize it, but she's been on that career train so long she might just pass the last stop to get off. Sometimes, I think the family should take an interest."

"My advice is to leave your sister alone. Don't go stirring up hopes in something that in reality sounds far-fetched."

Ellen finished the conversation with her mother but she was not half satisfied with the response. The idea was popping with romantic possibilities, and yes, she wouldn't mind a bit of excitement in her current routine. Still, she'd hoped her mother would take the opportunity and apply through the proper agency.

Just because Mum doesn't want to be involved, doesn't mean I have to stay out of it. Besides, Carrie doesn't have to know about it.

And just like that, Ellen decided to use her spare time doing a little research. She went to the website and sent off a query to the matchmaker. She wasn't going to let an eligible, responsible, attractive, thirty-five-year-old man go begging when it sounded just like what the doctor ordered for her sister, Carrie.

***

Father had promised. Charlotte had agreed she would allow him to search for a husband, but she had made him promise that the final choice needed to be properly scrutinised. She was not so desperate she would marry just any man that came along. Father insisted on money and title. She insisted the man must have a good character and was not a brute. There were too many of those about, masquerading as gentlemen, simpering and snivelling around prospective mothers-in-law, pretending to be worthy. Charlotte sniffed. Her cousin Amelia had married such a man. He was a rake! And more. Unfaithful to poor Amelia and not only demanding, but cruel about it too. Uncle Mortimer had made a grave error of judgement entering into an arrangement with that man. Charlotte would not allow her father to make the same mistake. There were criteria to follow. Conditions that must be met, and she would not be tempted to negotiate beyond them.

"Earth to mother."

Louise snapped out of daydreaming as Chloe brought the two coffee cups to their table.

"Sorry. I was just going through some ideas for Charlotte."

"So how is your matchmaking experiment coming along?"

"For Charlotte?"

Chloe laughed, and managed to get cappuccino foam up her nose.

"Charlotte is your imaginary experiment. I'm talking about your real-life character—Pete. How's it coming along for him?"

"Well I'm quite positive about it actually," Louise replied. "We've only got another week until your wedding, and then I can put some serious focus and energy into getting your brother sorted out."

"You have talked to him about it, haven't you?" Chloe asked.

"He knows all about it. He's agreed to cooperate."

"What, just like that?" Chloe sounded doubtful.

"Not, just like that. He's given me a fairly long list of requirements and apparently there is no room for negotiation."

"He's not cooperating. He's just making it hard so he knows you won't succeed."

"I'm not put off by it at all," Louise said. "I have high hopes that the perfect woman for Pete is out there, and even if it takes a little time, I'll find her."

Chloe gave another laugh.

"Don't you worry, my girl. You go off on your honeymoon and leave your brother to me. If we don't have a wedding for him within the year, it won't be my fault."

"No, I dare say not."

***

Pete was struggling to hide his emotions. This day was proving to be tougher than he'd thought it would be. Since he'd apologized to his family for his self-indulgent behavior, he'd been doing his best to at least act as if he was happy. But sitting next to his parents in the front row of the church, dressed in a very nice, charcoal-gray suit, and watching the minister perform the wedding ceremony for his baby sister and her new husband, Michael Sullivan, was harder than he'd thought. His heart was at war with itself. On the one hand he wanted to crumple in a heap and feel sorry for himself, but on the other he wanted to be as happy as everybody else in the family. Chloe was getting married. Mike was a great guy. His mother was ecstatic having had a second matchmaking success. She was a happy-ever-after specialist and to have both her daughters married was fulfilling her dreams. Pete felt that stab of something unidentifiable in his stomach. He hadn't made the grade. Though he and Collette had planned a beautiful wedding, it hadn't worked out. A happily-ever-after fail.

Michael was kissing Chloe as custom dictated, and all he could feel was turmoil, especially as his mother clapped enthusiastically. *I'm happy for her. She deserves to be happy and Michael will make her happy.* He kept reciting this mantra over and over to himself.

"Isn't she beautiful?" Mum whispered to him as the couple signed the register.

"Stunning," Pete replied.

And it was true. Chloe looked magnificent. Michael always appeared slick in his business attire, but the smile he wore today elevated that look to something else. This was a man deliriously happy. Mum and Dad were thrilled and Pete felt like a loser—again. Why did Collette leave? He had loved her. He had wanted to be with her and build a life together, and family. That's right—family. That's where it had all come unstuck.

A soloist was singing some romantic song and Pete allowed the strains of music to swallow him up. *I could have lived without kids.* Who was he kidding? Collette knew him better than he knew himself. He'd always dreamed of having a family. Despite Andy's rowdy and boisterous kids, Pete had been jealous of what his mate had. But Collette hated the very idea. *Would I have changed for her? Is that how much I loved her?*

There was the million-dollar question. Would he have changed for Collette on such a deep and dear dream? She had decided that he wouldn't. *I would have tried.* Perhaps, to be fair to Collette she had recognized that he couldn't change. Perhaps she'd done the right thing after all. Perhaps it was best.

The soloist finished and the bride and groom stood waiting to be presented.

"Would the congregation be upstanding?" the minister asked.

Pete stood with everyone else. He determined to pin on his most enthusiastic smile for his sister and new brother-in-law. Feeling sorry for himself was a waste of a perfectly good, happy day.

"Wasn't the wedding beautiful?" Mum said as they got into Pete's car following the reception.

"A lot of money went into it," Dad said. "It should have been beautiful."

"Well that's the last wedding you'll have to pay for, so you can relax," Mum said.

"What about Pete's wedding?" Dad persisted. "The father of the bride doesn't always foot the bill these days, especially when weddings cost so darn much."

"I don't think you'll have to worry," Pete mumbled from the driver's seat. "I'll probably have saved enough to pay for the whole thing by the time I find someone who's willing to go through with it."

"Now, don't you be like that, Pete," Mum scolded from the back seat. "Give me a week or two, and I'm going to take a serious look at some of those responses that have come in from my ad."

Pete nearly choked. "Are you serious? You've actually had some responses?" He didn't quite know what to think, whether he should be amused, excited or alarmed.

"I've had six, to be precise, but with Chloe's wedding I haven't had time to give any serious consideration to any of them."

"Were you ever going to tell me about it?" Pete asked.

"Certainly not! You've left it in my hands to find the right one, and I mean to do just that. Let me sort out the wheat from the chaff and I'll let you know when I have someone who meets the criteria."

"Mum, don't you think I should sort of be involved?"

Mum sighed. "The idea of an arranged marriage is that the parents do the hard work of finding the right person and making sure she is first of all willing, and second of all suitable. It takes the whole risk of rejection out of it for you. I think you've had enough rejection for one life time. Just leave it to me, Pete. I'll sort it out."

Pete wanted to argue, but she had made a valid point. He really wasn't ready to make himself vulnerable to any girl at the moment. Perhaps, if she did find one who fit the criteria, and who was willing, he might be willing to have a meeting.

Then he relaxed. He remembered how many unreasonable things he'd listed as non-negotiables on his list. No-one would give him a second thought if they went by that list. There was very little chance they'd ever get to the meeting stage, and that was how he preferred it. Wasn't it?

<h1 style="text-align:center">Chapter Five</h1>

Now that Ellen had done it, she didn't quite know how to bring the up subject with her sister. She thought perhaps she'd better apply to her parents as allies before she dropped the bombshell.

"You didn't!" Mum said once Ellen had told her what she'd done.

"What didn't she do?" Dad asked.

"I did, actually. And it's done now, so our next step is to decide whether we will respond."

"What did you do?" Dad pursued, still in the dark.

"She's responded to some nonsense advertisement for an arranged marriage." Mum sounded frustrated.

"But she's already married," Dad objected. "You're already married, Ellen. Don't tell me you and Brad are having trouble already?"

"Brad and I are fine." Ellen said. "I responded on behalf of Carrie."

"You can't do that sort of thing, Ellen," her father complained. "It's dishonest."

"They asked for the family to be part of the process. In fact, as far as I understand it from this last email, his family are having a go at the old-fashioned family arranged marriage. Like they still do in some countries."

"We are not from one of those countries for a start with," Mum pointed out, "and Carrie is going to have a fit when she realizes what you've done."

"Why don't we go to this first meeting before we tell Carrie about it?" Ellen suggested hopefully. "This woman, Mrs Brooker, says that is how they're approaching it at this stage."

"What do you mean?" Dad asked.

"Apparently the guy's family are doing the interviews and not even bringing him into it until they've found someone they think is suitable. Let's not tell Carrie, and what she doesn't know won't hurt her."

"Carrie will have a pink fit." Mum said. "I don't think it's a good idea, Ellen."

"I wouldn't mind going along for the meeting," Dad said. "It sounds like an interesting idea."

"Would you, Dad?" Ellen sounded eager. "If we meet up with the Brookers, and they turn out to be nutters, then we don't even need to tell Carrie."

"Nothing ventured, nothing gained." Dad returned to flicking the channels on the TV.

"If Carrie finds out, and if she blows a fuse, you make sure she knows I put in my objection," Mum said.

"I'll take full responsibility." Ellen smiled at her mother and kissed her father on the top of his head.

***

Carrie was bored and loneliness was creeping in again. She'd already rung Amanda to see if she wanted to go out, or come over to watch a movie, but Amanda had been busy. Carrie had all her school work up to date and it was Saturday night. Desperate and dateless. Those were the words that floated through her mind. Stupid words, because she'd never felt desperate or dateless once before in her life. What was going on with her lately?

She picked up her phone and hit Ellen's number. It rang several times and then went through to voice mail.

"Don't you ignore me, Ellen," Carrie said. Because where else would Ellen be but at home with her baby and husband? Carrie pressed her number again. "Come on. I know you're there. Brad can do without you for five seconds."

Finally the call connected.

"What's wrong?" Ellen asked.

"Nothing's wrong."

"Well, why do you keep calling?"

"Because you were ignoring me and I knew you were there."

"I wasn't exactly ignoring you, sis. I'm going out for dinner."

"Oh." *She's going out for dinner, and I'm sitting at home on my couch, alone.*

"Did you need me to come and babysit for you?" Carrie asked.

"No, Brad's taking care of Lucy for the night."

"Who're you going out with?" Carrie asked. *She has a husband, and she still gets to go out on a date.*

"Me and Dad are going out for dinner."

"Oh." What on earth? "Can I come?"

"What? No. Not this time. Dad and I are …"

"Are what? Why can't I come?"

"We're just sort of bonding. You know father, daughter thing."

"I'm his daughter too, you know."

"Sure. Of course. He'll probably go out with you next week."

"Ellen, what's going on?"

"Look, I've gotta go. Sorry I can't talk. Will catch you later, OK?"

The line disconnected. She'd asked if it was OK to hang up, but didn't wait for an answer. Actually, it wasn't OK. Ellen had a husband and a baby, and yet she was the one going out for dinner with Dad. *While I'm still desperate and still dateless.*

She glanced at her two dogs who were sitting at her feet staring lovingly into her eyes. Carrie sighed and got up from the couch.

"All right. You win." She walked over and grabbed the two leashes from the hat-stand by the door. "Let's see if we can be like those characters in *101 Dalmatians*. We can find another dog lover and you can tangle us together, and we can live happily ever after."

***

"Well, young man, what do you say?"

Benjamin took a moment to consider the proposal that had been laid before him. Despite Lord Spelford's urging him to pursue this possibility, it was Lord Featherstone who had approached him with an offer—a healthy dowry which would go a long way in shoring up his estate's needs.

"Your reputation precedes you," Lord Featherstone continued, "and it was one of my dear Charlotte's stipulations that I approach only a man of fine character."

Benjamin allowed a small smile. Fine character? He wasn't one to boast, but he'd avoided dissipation and scandal as a matter of course. He had friends who'd managed to find themselves at the mercy of rich wives because they'd allowed the lure of the gaming table to blind their good sense. He had no intention of being shackled to a woman he did not love. A pang tore at his heart. Who was he kidding? The woman he loved was gone. Now, any woman he married would be less than he'd aspired to.

"My dear Charlotte is a good girl." Featherstone continued to drone on. "She has an easy temperament, and she is beautiful as well."

"I suppose I must have met her at one time or another, but I am afraid I do not recall what she looks like."

"No matter," Featherstone said. "I have her portrait hanging in the gallery. I do not think you will be disappointed."

"Does she know that you are making this arrangement?" Benjamin asked.

"She does, sir, and so long as you treat her with kindness and respect, I should say you will do very well together."

"Does she not wish to interview with me first?"

"There is no need. She trusts my judgement in the matter."

Was that wise? Trusting someone else to negotiate on their behalf? Louise took a deep breath. Forget Benjamin and Charlotte. It was too late now for second guessing. They were on their way to the restaurant where the negotiation table was set.

"Why haven't you told Pete?" Megan asked, as she got into the car with her parents. "Shouldn't he be coming along to this meeting?"

"Not at this stage," Louise said. She had her mind made up, and was directing this little drama with precision.

"But won't he want to make the decision?" Megan persisted. "Doesn't he care what she looks like, or anything?"

"The girl is not even going to be there. We're going to meet up with her sister and father."

"This sounds so weird," Megan said. "Where do you get all these ideas from?"

"That Indian couple across the road." Russell joined the conversation.

"Yes, they told us all about how their families worked out every detail of their marriage. How they went through the process of choosing the right partner, and negotiating a bride price etc."

"You're not going to buy the girl, I hope," Megan said, alarmed.

"No, we're only going to choose her. If she's right for Pete, then we'll arrange a wedding, and it will all work out," Louise said.

"Dad!" Megan turned towards Russell. "Do you honestly think this is a good idea?"

"Not sure, love. But you know your mother. Once she gets an idea in her head …"

"Usually, once she gets an idea in her head, she writes a novel. We're talking about real people here. Do you think it will work?"

"Pete and Carrie are not going to stand at the altar and exchange vows if they don't feel right about it themselves," Louise insisted. "Once we've done our part, it will be up to them to see it through."

"Carrie?"

"Carrie Davis. Thirty-two-year-old teacher. Never married."

"And she's sent her family to meet us?"

"Not sure about that. I've been liaising with her sister, Ellen. I guess we'll find out when we get there."

***

Mrs Brooker had arranged that the two families would meet at a Chinese restaurant halfway between their two homes. As the Davis's lived right across the other side of the city from the Brookers, it meant they both had a forty-minute drive to reach the restaurant.

When Ellen arrived to pick up her father, Mum was dressed and waiting to come too.

"I thought you objected," Ellen said.

"I can't let you and your father go into this alone. You might need someone with a sensible head on their shoulders."

"You couldn't resist it, could you?" Ellen teased.

Dad laughed. "She won't admit it, but the idea of romantic intervention is something she'd like to have done with all of you."

"I hate to remind you, but she did offer plenty of advice with me and Brad, and I daresay it won't be long before she's handing out nuggets of wisdom to Mark and his girlfriend."

"I just give little pieces of sound advice here and there. I'm glad you think they're nuggets of wisdom."

"I do. Thank you Mum." Ellen smiled. "I've applied your advice and we're together and happy. Now, let's see what we can do with Carrie."

"You're as bad as your mother," Dad laughed.

"Speaking of Carrie…" Ellen paused. "She called tonight and when she found out I was going out to dinner with you, she wanted to come too."

"You told her?"

"I told her we were going out to dinner on a father/daughter date."

"She would never buy that," Mum said. "When have you and Dad ever done anything together, just the two of you?"

"Not the point. Carrie wanted to come, and I said no."

"Did you tell her what you and your father were scheming?"

"Of course not! She doesn't need to know about that until we're sure it's something safe to pursue."

"Do you think I should give her a call?" Dad asked.

"In a couple of days. I told her you'd probably take her out for dinner next week or sometime."

Mum laughed.

"What?" Dad cast his wife a hurt look.

"All these years I've said you need to get more involved with your girls."

"I was involved. I bought them their cars and made sure they were always serviced."

"Yeah, thanks, Dad. I know you meant well."

"Well I did."

"Anyway, you taking an interest in this project means a lot to me," Ellen said.

"I hope Carrie sees it the same way you two do." Mum raised her eyebrows and gave her husband a pointed look.

"If this young man turns out to be a good find and Carrie falls in love with him, I can say I was behind it from the start." Dad raised his eyebrows and glared back at his wife.

"And if it all goes pear shaped?" Mum asked.

"Carrie will never know," Ellen said.

***

When Louise saw the family actually standing before her, she had a rush of anxiety.

What am I doing? This isn't a game. These are real people.

If she hadn't been such a confident person she might have turned tail and run, but she had set this particular ball rolling and she had to stay the course for the time being.

"Bill Davis." The older man, obviously Carrie's father shook Russell's hand firmly.

"Russell Brooker, and this is my wife, Louise, and my daughter, Megan."

"I'm Ellen." The attractive young woman who accompanied the group stepped forward. "I'm the one who applied on behalf of my sister."

Russell stepped back and made way for Louise to come forward.

"I'm Louise." She shook Ellen's hand and looked into her eyes. You could tell a lot about people with eye contact. Mmm. No sign of anything disturbing so far.

"I was very excited to read the information you sent," Louise said.

"We're reserving commitment until we know more about your son." The middle-aged woman with the group was obviously the mother, and Louise sensed her reservation with this statement.

"You must be Anne?" Louise held out her hand in greeting. "Of course. This will go no further if we're not all satisfied tonight. That's why I thought it would be good for us to get together and talk about the kids."

Before they could go deeper in discussion a waiter approached their table, and encouraged them to take their seats. It took a while for the business of ordering to be done and during this time Louise assessed the family who sat around the table with them. The daughter, Ellen, was eager. The father, Bill, was an easy-going character, but the mother, Anne, was uncertain. That made a good balance.

On her side of the family, Russell seemed to click with Bill the moment they started talking. They discussed jobs and were moving onto sports. No problems there. Megan seemed to be anxious. She wasn't saying much, just sipping her water.

So far, the discussion had only been surface and she guessed that everyone was sizing each other up, just as she had been. With the waiter dispatched with the meal orders, it was time to begin some serious talk but, surprisingly, she'd lost her nerve when it was needed most. She began to panic wondering if she would find the right way to begin the discussion.

"So your son is searching for a wife?" Bill decided to take the initiative.

"Yeah!" Russell replied. "He's a good kid …"

"Dad, he's thirty-five," Megan said.

"He's a good man," Russell amended. "I think he deserves a good marriage, not like that last piece of work he was engaged to."

"Dad!" Megan objected a second time.

"So he's been engaged before?" Bill seemed to be taking the interview process seriously.

"He's had three serious relationships, but hasn't had much luck in making it to the altar."

"Why not?" Anne sat up, alert. "Whose fault was the break-up? Is he a player?"

"Not at all!" Megan vehemently defended her brother. "The trouble with Pete is he's naïve and idealistic. He always imagines a woman wants what he wants."

"What does he want?" Now the sister, Ellen, entered the conversation. "How demanding is he?"

"Ahem!" It was time for Louise to take control of the situation she had created. "I think, before we all jump to unnecessary conclusions, we should follow the process we decided upon." She paused and waited for the attention to come back to her. "I have a folio about Pete here for you to go through, and I assume you have something similar about Carrie for us to take a look at?"

"Right." Ellen bent to retrieve the folder she had in her shoulder bag.

Louise handed her prepared folio to Ellen and took Carrie's from her. Russell and Megan drew their chairs closer to her, and she noticed the Davis family also huddled closer to read through what was written down.

"She likes Aussie Rules Football," Russell said. He sounded pleased.

"Absolutely!" Bill replied. "I brought my girls up right."

"Which team does she barrack for?" Megan asked.

"The Crows, of course!" Anne said.

Louise exchanged a big smile with Megan.

"You know, Pete is a member of the Crows football club and has season tickets," Russell said.

"You're kidding! Season tickets!" Bill was obviously impressed. "Do you know how hard it is to get a membership with the Crows? I've been on the waiting list for over two years now."

"That's why Pete still has them. He wanted to give it up last season but we talked him out of it."

"Why on earth would he want to give up the membership?" Anne asked.

"His former fiancée hated football, wouldn't go with him to any of the matches, and mostly prevented him from going with any of us. That's why we put the football question in the survey."

"Well you have a match there," Bill said. "If Carrie backs out, I'm available to go to games."

"Dad!" Ellen objected this time. "There's more to a relationship than whether they enjoy football together or not."

"Not much more," he grumbled.

They settled back down and continued going over the files.

"You're people of faith?" Louise said, feeling a flush of warmth as she read the note.

"Yes, we are," Bill replied.

"Carrie too?"

"Carrie especially. She's the one who became a Christian first and encouraged the rest of us to consider faith."

Louise caught Russell's gaze and nodded. This was one of the crucial points. Pete hadn't thought faith would matter when he got engaged to Collette, but his faith and associated values had often brought conflict into their relationship.

"And Pete?" Anne asked. "Is he a man of faith? I think Carrie would find it difficult if she were with a man who didn't care for her commitment to church."

"Pete's a Christian. He's always been active with our church's 'feeding the poor' program. He'd want someone he could pray with and who'd support giving. See, he has that written on the list." Louise leaned over and pointed to the relevant spot. Were Bill and Anne feeling the good vibes she was feeling?

"She's a fine-looking girl, isn't she?" Russell looked to Louise and smiled.

"That she is." Bill sounded proud. "Any man worth his salt would think she's beautiful."

"You might be a bit biased," Ellen said.

"He's not biased," Anne said. "Carrie is a beautiful young woman. I've always said so."

"And your boy is nice looking too," Bill said. "I think they'd look good together."

"There's more to a relationship than looks, Dad," Ellen said.

"Still, so far, things appear fairly promising, don't you think?" Bill directed the question to Louise.

"Well," Louise said, "I think the next step is to take this information back to them both, and have them review it with time to think it through. Perhaps we can be in contact in say … a fortnight?"

"Sounds good to me," Bill said. "I'll be voting yes, anyway. You folks seem real nice."

"Thank you," Louise said. "Anyway, you have my email address. Let me know what Carrie thinks and we'll see what Pete thinks, and go from there, shall we?"

Chapter Six

Carrie sensed something was odd the minute Ellen turned up at her door holding flowers.

"What's this for?"

"I felt bad about turning you down on our dinner date the other night."

Carrie shrugged. "Didn't matter."

"Are you sure? You sounded a bit desperate."

Carrie clenched her teeth. There it was again. The word 'desperate'.

"I'm not desperate." If she said it enough, she would eventually convince herself.

"I know, but I felt mean saying no to you when I was going out with Dad and all."

"Which brings me to my next question: why were you going out to dinner with Dad?"

Ellen walked past her ignoring the question. "Have you got a vase for these flowers?"

Carrie followed her into the kitchen. "You're avoiding the question. What's going on?"

Ellen was opening and closing just about every cupboard in the kitchen.

"Ellen?"

"Vase." Ellen turned and gave Carrie a determined look. "I spent fifteen dollars on these flowers at the servo."

Carrie couldn't help but laugh. Cheap flowers—usually stocked for people who were in the bad books, who had forgotten an anniversary or something. Wait. Why had Ellen bought cheap flowers?

"What's going on?"

"I'm not going to talk to you until these babies are safely deposited in water."

Carrie shook her head and went to the laundry cupboard. She pulled out the one vase she owned—a cut crystal vase she'd been given for her twenty-first, how many years ago? She never used it. No one ever bought her flowers and she didn't ever buy them for herself.

"Here you go. Now, tell me, what's up? It's really unlike Dad wanting to go out to dinner at all, and on a date with you. It's just plain weird."

Ellen set the vase of flowers on the kitchen bench. She had pursed her lips and then she took a deep breath. Carrie waited. Something was coming, she could sense it. But then Ellen let the breath out again and didn't say anything.

"Ellen! You're killing me. What's going on?"

"Do you think we could have a coffee and sit down first?"

"No. You've come here, cheap flowers in hand, which in itself is a sign that you've done something really bad, you haven't brought Lucy—where is she by the way?"

"Mum has her."

"You've come alone and you need to say something, and I'm beginning to worry. Is Dad all right? Is he sick?"

"No." Ellen let out a small laugh. "No, he's fine."

Carrie wouldn't let Ellen go from her raised-eyebrow glare. She tipped her chin to add some weight to her glare.

"Why don't we sit down in the lounge for a little while?" Ellen said.

Carrie took a deep breath. "All right. Let's sit down, and then you will tell me everything, OK?"

Ellen nodded and headed for the lounge sofa. They both sat down. Carrie was sitting forward, anxious about what she was about to hear. Ellen was sitting forward too, fiddling with her fingernails. Carrie didn't say anything and just waited.

"So." Ellen started, but then stopped.

"So?"

"You know you said you'd like to get married?"

"Who told you that? Did Mum tell you?"

"Whatever—you did say it, didn't you?"

"Actually, lately, I've been thinking about marriage and family." Was that safe to confess to Ellen? Didn't matter. Mum had already blabbed apparently.

"You haven't found anyone yet, have you?"

Why did Ellen sound worried? Carrie frowned.

"No. I haven't found anyone."

Ellen let out a sigh that sounded very much like she was relieved.

"Good, because we've found someone for you and by all accounts, he's a perfect match."

"What?"

Ellen's face was a picture of guilt. What had she done? "You haven't set me up for a blind date have you?"

"Not exactly." She stretched the words out and enunciated every syllable.

"What exactly have you done?"

"I replied to an ad to engage in a matchmaking endeavor. I've done all the ground work. We've had an initial meeting with the family. He looks great on paper and his family are really nice."

"On paper?" Carrie's mouth had gone dry. Was she hearing correctly? What on earth?

Ellen bent to retrieve something from her shoulder bag and pulled out a manila folder. "Yes, on paper. We have all his particulars, his photo, likes and dislikes—everything. His mother is in charge of the matchmaking, and all you have to do is go over it to see if he could be the one. If you like what you see, we will go to phase two."

"Phase two?" Why was she even listening to this?

"Phase two, we—our family and his family—will arrange your wedding. All done, no fuss, no fear of rejection."

There was an awkward pause. Ellen held the folder out in front of her but Carrie didn't take it. Now her mouth was hanging open as she just glared at her sister, a flush of dread beginning to roll over her.

"What have you done?" Carrie groaned and flopped back on the couch holding her head in her hands.

"Just take a look at it, Carrie," Ellen pleaded. "They seem like really great people and check out Pete's picture. He's hot, even if I say so myself."

"But you responded to an ad in the paper." Carrie couldn't help that her tone was like a whining child. "How desperate does that make me look?"

"They put the ad in the paper in the first place," Ellen argued.

"Exactly! How bizarre is this whole situation? It's crazy, Ellen. What would I tell my friends?"

"You could tell them you met this really great guy and that you're engaged."

"I'm not engaged!" Carrie cried.

"But it would be a fairly simple step from here to engagement."

"Ellen, you've lost perspective on this. The whole thing is nuts. You know that, don't you?"

"Look, I know it's a big surprise to spring on you and so I'm just going to leave the folder with you. When you've thought about it, take a look through and then let's talk again a bit later."

"Ellen!" Now Carrie was pleading.

"It can't hurt to look. It's not like we've signed a deal or anything."

Carrie took a deep breath for patience, and then released it slowly. "OK. I'll take a look if it will make you happy, and then you can go back to this crazy family and tell them 'thanks, but no thanks.'"

"If that's what you want. But when you do go through the file, take notice of all the details. If his family are a gauge of what he's like, I'd say you'd be crazy not to at least consider the deal."

"Yes, well I think you might have a monopoly on crazy already."

"Gotta get home," Ellen said suddenly. "Lucy will want a feed shortly. I'll call you tomorrow."

Carrie waved her hand in a half-hearted fashion as her sister left.

An arranged marriage! They must think I'm really desperate.

YOU ARE REALLY DESPERATE! Her thoughts shouted at her.

"Oh fine," she said out loud, then flipped the folder open. "Let me take a look at you Mr Peter Brooker. Surely you can't be as bad as Kevin."

***

"She loves football!" That was Dad's opening comment the moment they got back home. "And she follows the Crows! It's a match made in heaven."

Pete almost laughed.

"Dad, seriously. So she likes football. There has to be more to it than that."

"The checks on the list appear fairly convincing, Pete." Mum was sounding pleased with herself. "And take note. She's a Christian, which is a huge step in the right direction."

"I don't believe it. I made that list almost impossible."

"Take a look for yourself." Mum handed a folder to him.

Pete didn't quite know what to think. This had started out as an exercise to pacify his mother and get her off his back. He'd consciously and deliberately made the criteria unreasonable—pretended to be unmovable on certain points. He was sure that anyone silly enough to read the list would write him off without a second thought and yet, now Mum was holding out a prospective wife's folio. He should have put a stop to it when she'd first come up with the idea. He wasn't ready for another relationship, was he?

"The parents and the sister are really nice people," Mum prompted as she pushed the folder closer to him. "And if you look at her photograph, I don't think you'll complain."

Pete took the folder slowly. Did he really want to look? He'd felt sure it would all come to nothing, and yet something in him felt excited that there was a prospect. *But am I ready to open myself up again? This might all be too early.*

"Her father seemed really pleased that you have season's tickets to the Crows' games." Dad seemed intent on promoting the football angle. "I really like them, Pete. Good family. Really good family."

Pete shook his head and muttered under his breath as he went off to his bedroom to muse alone.

My family are nutters. The whole lot of them!

As Pete read Carrie's file his emotions flip-flopped all over the place. The hand written answers might have been his mother's except it wasn't her hand-writing. It was as if the girl knew exactly what he wanted to hear.

And when he looked at the two photos that were paper-clipped to the folder, he couldn't take his eyes away from the attractive face that smiled back at him. She was not the model specifications he usually went for, but her eyes were alive with laughter and her smile lit up her face. He didn't know what to think. Collette, Sonja and Rianne had all been tall, blond and as if they'd walked out of a fashion magazine.

Carrie, according to the paper, was quite short, had dark, unruly hair, her make-up was natural, if she was wearing any at all, and if his previous girlfriends had been judging, her fashion-sense would not have made the cut. He already knew that just by looking. He'd heard enough behind-the-hand criticisms and mockery about what other girls were wearing that he figured he was just about an expert himself. Actually, he didn't have a clue, but he certainly knew what Collette would have said about the two photos he was staring at.

But the fact that Carrie was unschooled in the fashion and make-up department was a plus in Pete's estimation. Both Collette and Rianne had been models. He was honestly tired of trailing after his girlfriend while she harangued shop assistant after shop assistant, never satisfied with the clothes that were on display. Collette was worse than Rianne and she had been the one he'd nearly married. When he'd built the house he'd thought he and Collette would live in, she had made some rather large demands concerning the dimensions of her own walk-in robe. He couldn't imagine someone owning enough clothes to fill it, but Collette was still unhappy with it when he'd finished, complaining about the idea of having to store extra things in a wardrobe in the shed.

I just don't know, Carrie. You seem like the real deal, but, I'm not sure I'm game to risk another heartbreak.

***

"So, what do you think?" Ellen was breathless as she asked the question of her sister over the phone.

"Calm down, Ellen," Carrie said. "I've only just got in from work. I haven't had time to really think about it yet."

"Come on, Carrie," Ellen pleaded. "You read the file last night. I know you did."

Carrie couldn't deny it. Her curiosity was way too active to ignore the temptation.

"I still think the whole idea is strange. I can't imagine what people would say if I went for it."

"So you're considering it?"

Carrie sighed. Time to be truthful. Of course she'd considered it, but she'd also considered how embarrassed she was that her family had put her name forward as someone incapable of finding a relationship for herself.

"Hello? Are you there? Stupid phone has dropped out again!"

"I'm here," Carrie said.

"Well?"

"I'm not sure this is something I should go for. It's kind of … crazy."

"Once you find yourself in a happy relationship, with kids, who cares what people say."

"Did you know he wants five kids?" Carrie asked her sister.

"Yeah. I saw that written there. I always say, one at a time, hey?"

"But what if I have a couple and I can't cope with it?"

"Carrie!" Ellen sounded frustrated. "You are responsible for classrooms full of kids all the time and you manage."

"I know. I like kids. I really do and I want to have my own—I'm quite sure of that since I met Lucy."

"So, what's the problem?"

"Five is a large family in this day and age. We'd have to buy a minivan to cart them all around."

"There you go, you see? You're getting into the idea of things. And just think, I'll be Auntie Ellen, and Lucy will be their cousin. And maybe I might get pregnant again and we can have babies together."

Carrie smiled at her sister's infectious enthusiasm.

"You've really got hold of this, haven't you?" she said. "What if Mr Pete Brooker wants to wait a while?"

"Check the last point. He wants to get started straight away."

Carrie felt the blood rise in her face.

"You make it sound all so practical, Ellen. I'm sure there must be something emotional and intimate that goes on before the babies arrive."

"Well, duh! We don't need a biology lesson."

"This is not biology, it's relationship. I'm a bit dubious about the whole breeding program angle."

"He didn't say breeding program."

"Not in so many words, but the implication is there."

"He's thirty-five. You're thirty-two. What are you waiting for?"

"I don't know—to get to know him perhaps. To see if we really are a match, and perhaps we might like to fall in love or something."

"So you're willing to consider the next step?" Ellen's tone sounded like she was busting with excitement.

"You're so pushy, Ellen," Carrie complained. "I'm thinking about it, but do you think you could hold off for a day or two before printing invitations?"

"I knew you'd go for it." Ellen said. "I can't wait to tell Mum and Dad."

"Ellen!" Carrie almost shouted. "I said in a couple of days, I'll let you know. Do you understand me?"

"Yeah, Yeah! I'll call you then. Oooh. I'm so excited!"

"You're impossible," Carrie said, "and if you don't calm down, the deal's off, OK?"

Ellen calmed slightly but Carrie could tell she was quite dizzy about the prospects of arranging her marriage to this 'handsome' guy. Carrie took a deep breath, shook her head and came away from the phone. Ellen was like a runaway horse now that she'd said she would consider it. Carrie didn't know whether to be angry, amused or excited. In the end she opted for a cup of tea and huge slice of cheesecake, straight from the freezer.

Chapter Seven

Pete was on the roof hammering joists to ceiling beams when his phone pinged. Who was messaging him? He flicked a glance to his watch. Nearly lunch time. He'd just finish this joist then take lunch and he could check the text then. Curiosity would have to wait as he didn't want to climb down and then climb up again.

Once he reached the slab below, he took a long draught of ice water from his water cooler, and even poured a little over his head to cool himself off. It was a hot day and he'd already said to Max he thought they might knock off early so they didn't pass out in the extreme temperatures.

Once he was seated on top of his esky, his sandwich in hand, he retrieved the mobile phone from his work belt pouch and opened the text.

She wants to take the next step! Call me!

Suddenly the half-eaten sandwich sank to the bottom of his stomach like a stone. He knew what his mother meant, and all at once he felt a rush of anxiety. What was the next step? Could he face meeting a new woman, one who was actually considering marriage to him? And if he'd understood correctly, ready to have his children?

"Man!"

"What's up?" Max asked. "Bad news?"

Pete took a few moments weighing the idea of what exactly he should say to this inexperienced teenager.

"Let me give you some advice, Max," Pete said. "If you think you're in love with a girl, think again. Women are nothing but trouble."

"You don't have any luck with women, do you?" Max said before stuffing his bread roll into his mouth.

"Actually, I have a whole group of women working on my love life at the moment."

"A whole group? Lucky man!" Max said around the mouthful.

"Yes, it includes my mother, two sisters, and another couple of well-intentioned matchmakers."

"That doesn't sound good."

"Mmm." Pete wasn't really prepared to go into all of his internal thoughts and feelings on the matter. "I'm thinking we only work till two today," he said instead. "The mercury is tipped to hit thirty-eight, and I don't fancy frying up there on the roof."

"Me either. Thanks boss."

Pete smiled, and then turned his mind to what he was going to say to his mother once he got home in a couple of hours.

***

"I can't do it!" he blurted out.

"What do you mean?" The disappointment in Mum's tone of voice was priceless.

"I'm not up for it, mother. I just can't face another rejection."

"But we're not talking about rejection," she said. "We're talking about confirming an engagement and arranging a wedding."

"How far do you think you can go with this?" he asked, just a little frustrated. "Once she meets me, she'll see I'm a closed book."

"Well, don't be a closed book. Just turn on your usual charm."

"I don't have it to turn on any more. Collette walking out on me did me in. Even if Carrie is the nicest girl in the world, do you really think it's fair to lump an emotional wreck onto her?"

"It's not that bad, Pete. Sure you're a little gun-shy, but once you get to know her, I'm sure you'll learn to trust again."

"Mother, we're not talking about those silly romantic chick-flicks. This is real stuff."

"Listen Pete, what I have in mind is something from another time and another culture. Arranged marriages in the past were never based on the emotional connection or said happiness of the people involved. They were always based on a decision that would determine the wellbeing and preservation of a family. In this instance, the fact that you don't love Carrie, and don't even think you have the capacity to love her, really isn't an issue. What we're really talking about here is securing a family for the future. A companion, children and home."

Pete opened his mouth to argue, but Mum cut him off.

"Every couple I know who marries because they believe they love each other eventually come back to just that. The mad, romantic warm-fuzzies don't last much longer than the honeymoon and then it's real life that's there to face them. All you skip is the heady out-of-control feelings of the honeymoon. You can just get on with life with a woman who is compatible and who shares the same goals and values as you do. Now how hard is that?"

Pete frowned. Not hard at all unless you were the one getting on with life with a woman you've never met. He shook his head.

"Let's just take the next step and see what happens," Mum coaxed.

"Could you let me sleep on it?" Pete asked. "Promise me, you won't rush further without letting me catch up in my own mind."

"I promise." Mum kissed him on the forehead as she got up from the couch to start making dinner.

Pete went to the bathroom to shower before dinner. *She wants to take the next step. Did she read all the criteria?* Pete couldn't imagine what she must be thinking. He'd been in a bad place at the time he'd written the list. He'd written down just about every idea Collette had ever objected to, and made it non-negotiable. He hadn't thought that anybody would actually take it seriously—that it would be a deterrent. He hoped Carrie was OK, that she hadn't come out of some emotionally abusive relationship where her partner had been as demanding as he sounded on paper. Pete took the towel to his wet hair and gave it a thorough drying. On paper, Carrie sounded like a really lovely person. He half wanted to meet her but then was half afraid she must think him an egotistical demanding sort of person. Non-negotiables indeed. What had he been thinking? *That no one would respond.* Well it was up to him now. Would he let his mother take the next step or would he pull the plug on the whole venture? Was he really ready to open his heart up again?

***

Carrie was a pack of nerves as she sat in the back seat of her parents' car. They stopped by to pick up Ellen and the baby, and now they were headed across town to the Chinese restaurant where the Brookers had first met the Davises.

This could be the first time I meet my husband, Carrie thought to herself.

"How do I look?" She asked her sister.

"Like yourself."

"That's so reassuring," Carrie replied.

"When have you ever worried about your appearance? You're famous for your resistance to the pressure of fashion."

"That's all very well, until you're coming face to face with the man you might be going to marry."

"You're taking this seriously now?"

"I thought you wanted me to take it seriously. I'm not going to drag all these good people to this meeting if I'm not serious about it, now am I?"

"I'm glad," Ellen smiled. "I didn't think you'd go for it for a while there."

Carrie sat back and tried to remember she was a highly-paid professional and no longer fifteen-years-old. Pete Brooker was a successful builder, owned his own business and he wasn't an immature teenager who was ruled by his hormones. Pete Brooker was not Kevin Pole. She needed to get that firmly organized in her mind.

But when she walked into the restaurant and met the group of smiling friendly people, she couldn't see one among them who looked like the photograph she'd seen, or who even matched the description.

"He's not here," Ellen whispered in her ear. She sounded more disappointed than even Carrie felt. "Surely he hasn't backed out."

"You must be Carrie?" The older woman in the group approached Carrie with her arms extended. Carrie responded easily and allowed the woman to kiss her cheek.

"We've been so looking forward to meeting you. My name is Louise, and I'm Pete's mother."

"How do you do?" Carrie offered the polite greeting, trying not to scan the room to see if the man himself was present.

"And this is my husband, Russell, and Pete's sisters, Megan and Chloe."

Carrie allowed herself to be greeted, embraced and fussed over. But she was still a little guarded.

Where's Pete?

"I guess you're wondering why Pete isn't here," Megan said.

Carrie didn't want to sound rude so didn't say anything, but thoughts did cross her mind. *Of course I'm wondering why he isn't here. This whole drama is about us meeting to discuss a permanent future with kids!*

"I have something for you," Louise broke into her thoughts. "While you read this, the rest of us will sit down and order some drinks." She held out an envelope for her. "Is that OK? Do you want to go somewhere else to read it?"

"What is it?" Carrie asked. "Has he started out with a 'Dear John' letter before we even start?"

"No, oh no!" Louise said.

"He's explained it in the letter," Megan added. "It's better if you read what he's got to say. I hope that's all right."

Well, it has to be, doesn't it? Carrie couldn't help feeling annoyed. *I never take this amount of trouble on my appearance. You'd think he could have put in a little more effort to attend.*

But instead of saying any of these things, she graciously took the letter and excused herself. She decided to go outside into the little courtyard where there was a water fountain amongst some ferns.

OK, Pete Brooker. This had better be good.

Dear Carrie,

Hi, I'm Pete.

I'm sorry I haven't come to this dinner. I feel like a real coward, but I thought I'd better give you a fair chance before proceeding any further.

I'm sure my family has passed on my recent history—my broken engagement two days before the wedding.

I have to be straight up about it because, in all honesty, that one incident has just about done me in emotionally.

When Mum and the rest of the family began this whole arranged marriage process, at first I didn't think they'd ever find anyone who'd even slightly fit the very tough criteria I put together for them, but by all accounts, you seem to fit the bill perfectly.

However, you need fair warning. I'm emotionally absent at the moment. I've always wanted to get married and have children, and though I was really busted up over my recent breakup, I still really hope for that one day. But I'm only just beginning to recover from the break-up and I don't think I have it in me to engage emotionally. I need you to know this as I get that emotional engagement is a large part of a relationship.

At this stage, I know I can be polite, kind, pleasant, even caring, but I'm not sure about madly in love.

If you tear this letter into pieces and storm out of the restaurant, I wouldn't blame you.

But if you have bought into my mother's far-out theories about arranged marriages—working towards building a stable home and family regardless of emotional feelings—then I can only say, I'm prepared to continue.

If you are still reading, and are still prepared to consider the arrangement, then I ask you to read the last page separately.

Carrie was intrigued. She didn't want to shake Pete or slap his face. She completely understood what he was saying. She had been emotionally disconnected since she broke up with Kevin ten years ago, and she was the one who'd done the breaking-up. And she knew what it was to reserve emotional investment. But she had to give pause for a few moments before reading the last page. If she continued, would she be able to live knowing she had a husband who didn't feel any deep feelings toward her? Would it always be like that? Would they come to love each other eventually? Could she live her whole life knowing her husband didn't love her?

Too many questions. She decided to read the last page.

Carrie Davis, if you can imagine me on bended knee, then you have me in the right posture. Will you marry me? I promise I will look after you and our children carefully, and I will always be faithful to you.

If your answer is yes, then you can show my parents this letter and you can all order some champagne. If it is no, then don't mention it to the others. We'll think of another way to let them down slowly. I'll leave it up to you.

I kind of hope you will accept because you really do sound like a great girl. And you love football (which is really a good selling point with my dad).

"He's serious!" She couldn't help speaking aloud. "He's just proposed, and I haven't even met him yet."

She sat down on the wooden bench amongst the ferns and read the letter through again. She wasn't ready to face the two families yet. She needed to process all of this information carefully because once she went back inside it was either all on or all off.

Chapter Eight

Charlotte let the letter fall in her lap. Benjamin Hart had accepted her father's proposed alliance—the man she'd been in love with since she was a girl in the schoolroom. A wave of giddy happiness rose and made her flush warm, but was quickly followed by a wash of cold terror. Benjamin didn't love her. He hardly acknowledged her the times they attended the same assemblies. Of course, she'd been sitting with her chaperone waiting for a gentleman to ask her to dance and he'd had Kitty Coleborn on his arm, dancing with her as if there were no other woman in the world. Charlotte was not stupid. She knew Benjamin was betrothed to Kitty, and he gave all the signs of a man in love. She also knew Kitty was going through the motions—it had been evident in her indifferent posture and false smile. It was confirmed when word had spread in recent times—Kitty had eloped with some officer, leaving Benjamin humiliated and broken-hearted. And now he'd agreed to marry her. Would the indifference now be all on his side? Would she be the lovelorn partner—always hoping; desperate for a glimpse of affection? Should she accept this offer of marriage?

"What do you think?"

"It's a risk."

"What? Mother!"

Louise snapped back to attention from having drifted to the 19th Century.

"Sorry, what do I think about what?"

"Carrie's been a long time outside reading that letter," Megan said. "I'm worried she might think this whole thing is a ridiculous prank."

"I'm worried she'll think Pete is an emotionally stunted coward." Chloe never minced words, bless her.

"It is a bit cowardly of him not coming to meet her. I doubt she'll go for it since he's proving to be so emotionally absent."

Megan's statement hit home. Louise was also worried. Carrie seemed like just the right sort of woman for Pete, but would she go for this arrangement when Pete was showing so little encouragement? Louise took a sip of her drink and started to drift back to her characters. They were easier to sort out.

"Stay with us, Mother," Chloe said. "You started this thing. You're going to have to direct us through to the finish."

Why did she come up with these hair-brained schemes? The stress was incredible. Louise took another sip of her drink and watched the interaction around the table. Chloe had turned to Carrie's sister and was engaging in baby-talk. Russell was lost in sports talk. Only Carrie's mother, Anne, sat quietly. She was feeling the pressure as well.

"Here she comes." Megan's announcement was loud enough to have the entire gathering sit up and take notice. What would Carrie say? What would Carrie do?

***

Carrie took a deep breath as she returned into the air-conditioned restaurant. Her family were sitting down, her father and Russell were engaged in a deep conversation, and Pete's sisters were fussing over Lucy like she was their own niece. The whole lot of them seemed to have hit it off famously and she was about to make an announcement. She was still in two minds, and it wasn't until she got right up to the table and noticed that everyone's attention was focused toward her that she mentally flipped a coin in her mind. Show them the letter, or evade the questions?

Suddenly, it was as if her hand had a mind of its own and she brought the last page of the letter out and placed it on the table in front of her father and Russell.

"Perhaps you would be so good as to read that out to the rest of the family," she said, and then went to her own seat and sat down demurely.

Russell looked to Bill for permission, and then he took the letter and began to read it out loud.

"*…If your answer is yes, then you can show my parents this letter and you can all order some champagne.*"

Once those words had come out of Russell's mouth, all the women disintegrated into a babble of shrieks, crying and shuffling around to hug and kiss her.

Carrie smiled, quite broadly considering the circumstances, and allowed herself to be congratulated.

It would really have been nice for you to be here, Pete. This is really about us, not just about me.

***

Pete was jerked from his sleep by the sound of his mobile phone ringing. He took a few moments to orientate himself. It was obviously early hours as he'd been in a deep sleep. He picked up the mobile, his hand shaking slightly, and through bleary eyes he saw 'Andy' flash across the screen.

"Andy?" He was conserving words as his brain wasn't in full function yet.

"Sorry to wake you mate," Andy apologized. "I've got a bit of an emergency."

"Are you all right?"

"I've got to take Karen to the hospital. She's gone into premature labor. Her parents live four hours away, and my folks are not well at the moment. Can you come over and sleep here with the kids?"

Pete pulled his shorts and t-shirt on, and fumbled around in the half-light searching for his keys. Andy had assured him Karen was all right, but still, it was alarming being called out in the middle of the night. It was 2.37am and Pete wondered how he was going to manage with the two toddlers if they should wake up.

As he drove the fifteen minutes from his parents' house to Andy and Karen's, his mind woke up. He was surprised at how soundly he'd been asleep. After the bombshell his dad had dropped on him last night he would have thought he'd have tossed and turned for the entire night.

He couldn't believe she'd said 'yes'. She was really prepared to marry him on the say so of his family.

But it obviously sat well with him, as he'd gone out like a light and it took an emergency to rouse him from the depths of a peaceful and dreamless sleep.

"I'm so sorry to pull you out of bed, mate," Andy said the moment he opened the door. "Karen's parents will probably arrive some time mid-afternoon."

"You won't be back before then?" Pete asked.

"She's four weeks early, so if they can they will try to put the labor off, but sometimes these things have a mind of their own. Don't know, mate. I'll give you a call a bit later to see how the kids are."

Pete didn't feel confident, but didn't say anything. He just watched as Andy bundled his wife into the family car and took off into the night. He was fully awake by this time but felt he should try to sleep. Functioning properly at work without the full quota of sleep would be difficult—that was if his good friend managed to organize another babysitter before he was due to go to work.

The only adult bed in the house was Andy and Karen's but Pete didn't feel like trespassing on that sacred ground, so he organized himself on the couch as best he could. Unlike when he'd received the news that his marriage proposal had been accepted and he'd fallen asleep immediately, now he was wide awake and couldn't quiet his thoughts. He tossed and turned, threw pillows, and retrieved them again.

Finally, he decided he would check his Facebook and email. He didn't really expect anything to be there, being the middle of the night, so was surprised to find a lengthy email from his new fiancée.

Hi Pete,

She'd written in a casual fashion.

Thanks for your letter, and for your proposal. I guess by now your folks would have conveyed to you my response. It's all a little odd isn't it? Not quite like we see in the romantic movies on TV. Still, your mother has been quite detailed in her plan, and so far the information and the logic of it seem to be working out OK.

Being as you felt you had to give me fair warning about your emotional state, I figured I'd better be equally forthcoming with a couple of things. I have a feeling my sister has glossed over some points in her enthusiasm to make the plan work.

Your sisters are lovely. We got on really well. However, in conversation with them last night, they were quite open about your previous relationships and the fact that you usually choose tall, leggy model types. Then your mother carefully added that you had insisted that one of your criteria was that I had to be taller than your Nan. I hate to ask, but how tall is your Nan? I haven't got very much in the height department, and I don't want you to feel like you were ripped off. I'm not a great fashion person either. Some of my closer friends say I'm challenged in the fashion department.

Also, I noted with some interest that you are keen to have five children. I'm ready to have kids, and I love the idea that I can actually take motherhood on as my first priority without having to split my time with an employer. However, I wouldn't be honest if I didn't tell you that I don't really know if I could manage five. Ellen tells me I'd manage fine, being as I've been a classroom teacher for years. I might, but I can't promise. Is this a deal-breaker? I'd hate to come into this arrangement under false pretences.

I think I can cope with your emotional state. I've been in a similar state for the last ten years so can hardly demand more of you when your break-up is so recent.

Maybe sometime I'll tell you about the notorious Kevin of my past—the man who managed to put me off men properly. Megan and Chloe have reassured me that you're a treasure, even if they are your sisters.

Anyway, feel free to keep in contact on this email address. Let's think about meeting up sometime soon.

Kind regards,

Carrie

With Carrie's words going over and over in his mind, Pete didn't manage to get back to sleep until half an hour before eighteen-month-old Tyson woke up crying.

When the toddler's crying finally roused him, Pete felt as if his head was full of cotton wool. He dragged himself from the couch and wandered through the house until he found the room where the crying infant stood, clinging to the side of his cot, red-faced and tearful. When Tyson saw it was Uncle Pete, not his father or mother, his crying intensified.

"Hey, Tyson," Pete said in a soothing tone. "Did you have a good sleep?"

Tyson wasn't going to be distracted, and he continued to cry loudly. Very soon, his three-year-old brother, Zac, started to call for his mother. Pete picked the protesting Tyson up from the cot, and moved into the next room to see Zac sitting up in his bed looking alarmed.

"Hello, Zac." Pete tried to sound calm and in control when he felt anything but. He'd played with Andy's kids before when he'd been over visiting but he'd never been left in charge. He didn't have any nieces or nephews yet, so he was inexperienced to say the least.

He wanted to call someone else, but knew Andy's sister lived interstate, and Karen's siblings all lived up country near their parents.

"I'm new to this, boys." He tried using a normal tone, over and above the screaming. "Zac, can you show me where Tyson's bottle is?"

This seemed to appeal to Zac's sense of responsibility and he slid from his bed and toddled out to the kitchen.

An hour later, Pete was frazzled. The boys were sitting in front of *The Wiggles* on TV. Both had their blankets and bottles. There was calm for the moment but it was only just 7am. Pete was sure he should try to get them dressed. He should probably have tried to change Tyson's nappy, but hadn't had the courage to attempt it yet. He took a deep breath, made himself a double-strength coffee, and hoped Andy would call to let him know the cavalry was on its way.

But no phone call eventuated and Pete was faced with the challenge which, by the time he got to it, had risen in stakes from a wet to a dirty nappy. It was not a good start to parenting. Suddenly he knew that Carrie's hesitation about committing to five children was perfectly reasonable. Five had been a number he'd pulled out of the air to make it unreasonable. Yep, it was unreasonable all right.

I hope she realizes I wasn't serious.

Chapter Nine

$\mathcal{P}$ete lost a whole day's work in the finish. Karen's parents had arrived shortly after lunchtime to relieve him of the responsibility. But he'd had such a bad night with disrupted sleep, and keeping Tyson and Zac entertained all morning had thoroughly worn him out. He called Max and gave him the whole day off.

With an afternoon to spare, he thought about going home and trying to catch up on sleep, but instead he decided he'd drop by his Nan's house and answer that question Carrie had asked.

"Pete!" Winnie Brooker smiled broadly when she opened the door. "Your mother tells me you're getting married at last."

"It seems that way," he answered.

"She's arranged it for you like a matchmaker, she tells me." His Nan turned back inside, waving him to follow. "Do you want a cup of tea?"

"That'd be nice, Nan." Pete sat down at the kitchen table.

"So are you happy with your mother's choice?" Winnie was not the sort of woman to beat around the bush.

"I don't know." Pete shrugged his shoulders.

"What do you mean?" Winnie placed a plate of biscuits in front of him and then sat down.

"I haven't met her yet."

Winnie laughed. "Then I'm one up on you." she said.

"What do you mean?"

"Chloe took me out shopping this morning, and we decided to drop by Carrie's school so I could get a look at her."

"Are you allowed to do that? I wouldn't have thought they'd let just any random stranger in to visit during school hours?" Pete was struggling to imagine his diminutive grandmother in a classroom setting.

"As your young lady is acting principal, she was working in her office and when the reception staff rang through, she was pleased to welcome us for a half hour."

"What's she like?" Pete couldn't help asking.

"A whole lot better than those other bimbos you insisted on bringing home."

"Nan!"

"Well, I always told you if you want a wife, you're going to have to choose someone suitable, and those other girls, especially Collette—"

"OK." Pete held up his hand. "I don't want to talk about Collette."

"Quite right, when we can talk about Carrie instead. What a lovely respectful young woman she is."

"You liked her, then?"

"I did at that, Pete. I liked her right off."

"So can you tell me what she looks like?"

"Probably like her photographs," Nan said, pouring the tea.

"How tall is she?" This was the one unanswered question.

"A shade shorter than I am, I'd say. She could look me right in the eye."

Pete tried not to let his uncertainty show, but was obviously not successful.

"You listen to me, my boy," Nan said. "Her height has nothing to do with whether she will make a good mate or not. Once you're lying next to each other in bed, it won't make one scrap of difference."

"Nan!" Pete laughed.

"Your grandfather was about your height and we got on very well, despite our difference in height. Don't let that small discrepancy give you any pause."

Pete loved his grandmother's direct, no-nonsense approach. And yet he hadn't listened to her the many times she'd warned him about Collette, Sonja or Rianne. She hadn't liked any of them at all. She'd thought similarly of each one: that they were too self-absorbed and spent far too much time admiring themselves in the mirror to be of any use in a real relationship. It had always annoyed Pete that his Nan would never give her approval. He'd wondered if she would ever think anyone good enough. Now she was giving her full endorsement to his new fiancée. He decided it had to be a good sign.

***

When Pete finally got home, he sent a reply email to Carrie.

Thanks for your honesty. Neither your height nor the amount of kids you want are deal-breakers. I get your reservations on the kids issue. I just babysat my mate's two toddlers for the morning and am now in possession of actual experience. By the way, my Nan tells me you are just the right height. She's a fan.

Mum and the girls have organized a meeting tonight. I'll let you know what's being planned from then on.

Do you find this whole thing weird? I have a feeling I should be finding it unsettling, and yet I haven't slept better than I did last night.

Hear from you soon

Pete

***

It was a good thing Carrie was the acting principal and didn't have to explain her spontaneous visitors to anyone. She was able to usher them into her office, serve them coffee and have a lovely chat before seeing them off. They'd only stayed for half an hour and Carrie couldn't help but smile. Chloe was unrepentant about dropping in unannounced and uninvited. And her Nan was priceless. She was opinionated and forthright. And her position as Pete's number one supporter was well and truly established before she'd left Carrie's office.

"I like you," Winnie had said to Carrie, pinching her cheek as she departed. "At last, he's found someone who is intelligent and not vain. You'll do for my boy."

Carrie couldn't help but smile at the memory. She really liked Winnie, and Chloe too. As far as in-laws went, she felt as if she was falling in love already.

But what about Pete? She'd already as good as said yes, even though she'd never spoken to him. A moment of doubt flashed in her mind, stirring up a ripple of panic. Loving the family was one thing, but what if she and Pete never experienced love together?

This troubling thought was arrested when her mobile phone rang.

"Hi Amanda," she said, having read the caller ID before answering.

"Carrie!" Amanda sounded breathless with enthusiasm, but that was normal. "What are you doing Friday night? I've got this double date I need you to go on with me."

Carrie hated when Amanda dragged her into her wild schemes of blind dates.

"I can't." Carrie said.

"Oh, come on, Carrie. I know full well your usual Friday night routine consists of sitting on the couch with a block of chocolate and watching a movie."

"Not this week," Carrie said. "I already have a date."

"Ooh! Can't you break it? What lame family function do you have to go to this time?"

Carrie paused for a moment, not sure that she wanted to tell Amanda all about the arrangements so far. But Amanda was her best friend and had stuck with her through thick and thin since they were at university together.

"I'm meeting my fiancé." There. It was out.

For a few seconds, which seemed momentously long when one knew Amanda, there was silence.

"What are you saying?" Amanda sounded worried.

"I'm engaged to be married." Carrie used her matter-of-fact voice, with no embellishments to her tone. Still her friend's response was wild and loud.

"Engaged? Engaged! Carrie, when have you been dating? You haven't said a word to me … me … your best friend … about any man in your life. What's been going on?"

"It's a long story, Amanda," Carrie said, trying to stay calm in the face of her friend's emotional outburst.

"I should say it probably is. When can I meet him? When can I catch up with you and hear all the gory details?"

"What about you come around for dinner tonight and I'll fill you in," Carrie offered. "I have a lot of explaining to do, and I'd prefer to do it face to face."

"I'll say you have a lot of explaining. How could you do that? Go out with a man for who knows how long, and you haven't breathed a word of it to me. I'm not sure I shouldn't be offended."

"Well if you do decide to be offended, I'll have your favorite Boysenberry Ice-cream on hand. That usually smooths your ruffled feathers."

Now that the date was made Carrie was suddenly nervous. Amanda was a whirlwind at the best of times, and Carrie often felt as if she just glided with her gusts because it was easier that way. Now she knew she had to sit down with an objective outside party and explain that her family had arranged a marriage for her. She wished there had been another person to try the speech out on first, as there was no predicting how Amanda would react.

On the way home, Carrie stopped at the supermarket, picked up the Boysenberry Ice-cream and some other bits and pieces she was going to use in a stir-fry. As she was chopping up the meat and vegetables ready for the wok, she talked non-stop to her two dogs, testing out wording.

"You know, I have a really funny story …" She started out. "No! That won't work. Guess what?" She tried the second phrase with an exaggerated tone of excitement that actually made her Labrador raise his head and perk his ears up.

"Bottom line, I'm such a desperate loser, my family have arranged a marriage for me." Those were the words that eventually popped out when Amanda had pushed for all the details.

The stunned expression and lengthy moments of silence were so funny to see that Carrie started laughing.

"What are you laughing at?" Amanda demanded.

"The look on your face—it's priceless. I've never seen you so lost for words."

Amanda opened and closed her mouth several times, but couldn't seem to formulate a sensible sentence.

"Come on." Carrie got up from the couch and went into her kitchen. "This calls for some serious dessert."

Amanda got up from the couch and followed her. Eventually her thoughts and mouth began to re-attach and she began to talk.

"Are you completely serious?" Amanda asked.

"Totally. My sister answered an advertisement for a family involved arrangement. She did all the ground work and didn't tell me until after."

"Did you totally slap her face?"

"I was mortified when I first found out but they were all so enthusiastic about it, I decided to play along for a while just to see how it turned out. And … ta dah! I'm engaged!"

"Carrie! Have you lost your mind?"

"I know it seems like the craziest thing in the world, Mand, but honestly, his family are really, really nice. They and my folks get on like a house on fire. It all seems to work."

"And how do you get on with … what's his name?"

"Pete."

"How do you get along with Pete?"

"Well …"

"Stop right there!" Amanda held up her hand. "If there is any hesitation, you should pull out of this straight away. It's not the family you'll be marrying. It's him!"

"There isn't any hesitation. It's just I haven't actually met him yet."

Amanda threw her head back and gave a high-pitched scream. "Are you mad?" she asked for the second time. "Why haven't you met him yet?"

"Because this is an arranged marriage, like they do in other countries."

"We are not from another country!"

"I realize that."

"Well, what are you thinking?"

"I heard it was only in the modern era that people married for love. Before that it was always arranged by family for financial benefit and convenience."

"Yeah, in the time right before women had the right to vote, or own land, or be independent. Get a grip, Carrie."

"Oh, Amanda, this is not about that. Pete's family and my family have taken on the principle and have been really sensitive and caring about finding us someone who we will fit with. It's not like it's not done these days. Sometimes that's how it happens."

"We are not from one of those countries, Carrie. We are Australian and this is not the way we do it."

"But that doesn't mean it couldn't work."

"Aren't you interested in falling in love?"

"To be perfectly honest— I'm not sure—"

Amanda opened her mouth ready to relaunch her objection, but Carrie held her hand up. "Let me finish, Mand. I know a lot of young couples who were madly in love when they first got together, and many of them are either struggling badly now or have split completely. So much for love. We've been working on the principle of compatibility and commitment."

"You keep telling yourself that."

"Amanda, please."

"Is this about Kevin?"

That old chestnut out for examination yet again.

"No, Amanda. This is about me and Pete. It has been coming along very well so far. I'm happy with the arrangements, and I expect, once I meet Pete on Friday night, we'll begin a very satisfying relationship."

"Well if you think he's a dork at least you can pull out before the wedding."

"Yes, there's always that fail-safe. Of course, he might take one look at me and see something he doesn't really like, and he might pull out."

"What's not to like, Carrie? You're gorgeous—you know you are."

"I do not know I am, at all," Carrie said. "It's not like I've had men running after me the last ten years."

"There was—"

"Don't you say Kevin! Don't you dare say Kevin."

"I was going to say Josh Hargraves, actually. And he was a really great guy, as I kept telling you at the time."

"Mmm." Carrie conceded the point.

The pair of them returned to the couch and began to eat their Boysenberry Ice-cream.

"You know," Amanda said, after some minute's thoughtful silence, "I guess it really is kind of … romantic … in a way."

Carrie laughed. "If he doesn't turn out to be a dork."

Chapter Ten

Pete hadn't mowed the lawns for his father in years, but now he was back living with his parents he figured he should pull his weight with household chores. Taking hold of the mower and pushing it back and forth was just the thing he needed on this Thursday evening. It was daylight savings and still light. The weather was warm and he needed to be alone with his thoughts. The loud roar of the mower engine meant no one was likely to approach him for conversation.

His mother had arranged a first meeting for him and Carrie tomorrow night. When she'd first told him, Pete had wanted to run and hide under his bed. *I don't know if I'm ready.* This thought had persisted.

He hadn't said anything to his mother. He'd been the one who'd agreed with all the proceedings so far, and he'd been the one who had written the proposal. He'd encouraged Carrie in the few emails that had gone back and forth. But meeting her face to face suddenly seemed like a huge terror and he wondered why he was so lacking in confidence when it came to meeting women—or more specifically, the woman he was going to marry.

He could hear his Nan's advice ringing in his ears. "You need to get back on the horse, my boy," she'd said to him. "Don't you let the likes of that Collette woman rob you of your chance at having a happy family."

Pete smiled at the memory. He wondered what Carrie would think of Nan's horse metaphor. Then he began to think about the

Carrie he was beginning to know. She was a caricature that had been pieced together from the reports of various family members and from the few emails they'd shared. What he knew of her seemed to be good—excellent even, if Nan's opinion counted for anything. But Pete had to admit he was still feeling gun-shy.

As he emptied the grass clippings from the catcher beneath the rose bushes, he looked up to see their neighbor watering the plants in his front yard. Pete decided it was time to get the message straight from the horse's mouth, since they were using horse metaphors. Ramesh and Meera had been living across the road from the Brookers for over five years, having emigrated from India. Pete already knew they'd walked this road of having had their marriage arranged by family and he wanted to talk to Ramesh about the experience.

"Nice evening," Pete said.

"Very nice," Ramesh answered with his pronounced Indian accent.

"Would you mind if I talked to you for a few minutes?" Pete asked.

"I would be very pleased to," Ramesh said. "You have questions about your marriage?" He was obviously more aware of the situation than Pete would have guessed, but then, that would be like his mother to have interviewed them first. She'd probably put them through the third degree shortly after they'd moved in, garnering all sorts of information to be used in her next project. Only this time, *he* was her next project.

Pete neatly jumped his front fence, walked across the road and leaned against Ramesh's gatepost.

"I guess it's a usual practice in your culture," Pete said.

"Most often," Ramesh replied.

"Did it bother you? I mean, did you ever think to yourself you would've preferred to have found your wife yourself?"

"I never expected that I would. I always knew that my parents would find the daughter of a family they felt was worthy of us."

Pete found this concept hard to grasp.

"Did you know your wife before your families made the arrangement?"

"No. I had never met her before."

"Wow!" Pete could hardly relate. "When did you meet her for the first time?"

"We met with our families to formalize the engagement." Ramesh made it sound so straight forward.

"Did you never socialize with her alone before the actual wedding?"

"I had seen her once in passing and at the formal engagement meeting. But I was not concerned with this. The union was settled and there would have been no benefit in meeting her again before the wedding. This is what our parents wished for us, and we, as dutiful children, followed our parents' wishes."

Pete couldn't reply for a few moments.

"The customs here in Australia are much different, I am thinking." Ramesh smiled at him.

"Much different." Pete said. "Are you happy?"

"We have a good home, a good business here in Australia, three wonderful children. There is no reason not to be happy."

This didn't really answer the question Pete was asking. But then, what was he really asking? Western culture had a funny sort of gauge to measure happiness, and often that gauge could change in a moment, depending on the way a partner acted or felt at the time. Gratitude and contentment were not much part of the western culture, and relationship breakdown seemed to be as commonly heard of as stable relationships. Ramesh and Meera never complained—at least not that he'd ever heard. What was the secret to contentment in marriage and family?

Pete allowed a stray thought about Collette and he cringed. He was finally at that place where he was grateful he hadn't married her. She was beautiful and he'd been physically attracted to her, but with eight months hind-sight he could now admit she had been demanding, demeaning and emotionally destructive. He had a brief glimpse of what it would be like to be trapped in a marriage to her. The physical attraction would not have made up for the emotional torment he knew he would've suffered. She simply would not have been happy with him, and he now doubted he would have been happy with her either. Dodged that bullet.

But his question to Ramesh—was he happy in his arranged marriage? Ramesh didn't seem to think happiness was an issue.

"Your father seems to be very pleased with his choice of bride," Ramesh said. "Your mother too, I think, seems very happy."

"Yes, they are." Pete smiled. "I haven't met her yet. I'm supposed to meet her tomorrow night, but I feel anxious about it."

"Why?" Ramesh asked.

"I was involved in a very nasty relationship breakup a number of months ago. Frankly, I'm afraid of rejection."

"But there is no danger of this," Ramesh replied. "Your parents and her parents have agreed. The arrangements have been made."

Pete smiled. His father had had very little to do with it. His mother and Carrie's sister had done most of the arranging.

"Do not go to this meeting if you feel anxious," Ramesh said. "It makes no difference. You will still marry and you will have a very satisfying life. The woman your family has chosen is the right one for you."

Pete wished he had Ramesh's simplistic confidence. But they'd been brought up in completely different cultures with different ideals and expectations. He thanked Ramesh and finished mowing the lawn.

***

"What do you mean?" Mum asked him when he told her how he was feeling.

"I mean I'm not ready to meet her and have decided I'll leave it until the wedding day."

His mother went quiet. He studied her face and could see the cogs were turning.

"So, you're happy to do this like that reality TV show?"

"Which reality TV show?"

"You know, the one where they marry strangers. The psychologists pick the partners for them, and then they don't see each other until the wedding day."

"This is nothing like that. You and Dad have been fully involved with the process. I trust you."

"There's another reality TV show where the mother does the choosing."

"This is not reality TV, mother. This is an arranged marriage, which was your idea, by the way."

"Yes, but I thought you'd meet her before the wedding, just to make sure."

"I trust you."

"Really?" She looked surprised. "Then it is like that reality TV show."

"If you insist, except, there won't be a TV viewing audience of millions of people watching to see if I'll make an ass of myself."

"No."

"And I won't appear on that other TV reality show where they show people watching TV reality shows and making ridiculous comments."

Mum laughed. "No. I think I can promise you we'll be safe from all that."

"So you're OK with it then, that I won't meet Carrie until the wedding?"

"Are you sure?"

"At the moment, I think it's best. I think Ramesh is right. It won't make any difference if I meet her before or after. We will still have a satisfying relationship."

***

Carrie was disappointed when she received Pete's email. She had been anticipating the Friday meeting, hoping Pete would be everything Ellen had said he was.

This whole arrangement is not how we would usually get together, Pete had written. *At this point in time, I'm happy to wait until the wedding to meet. I hope you understand, but then I know you might not, but it's all part of that emotional disconnection I mentioned to you earlier. I'm not ready emotionally, though I am prepared in every other aspect. I trust my family's judgement and recommendations. They all think very highly of you. I'm sure we will get on well together. I just don't want to get involved in a lot of emotional pre-wedding drama. When I meet you, I want to stay with you and not have the fear of whether you will want to see me again or not.*

It's a fairly big ask, I know. If you find it's too much, I'll understand, but I hope you will be OK and still want to go through with it.

Carrie was not sure what to feel. On the one hand she was annoyed. On the other, she was relieved. She had been anxious about measuring up to his inspection with the risk of him backing out. He was happy to sign on the dotted line without having the trial relationship period. No 'try before you buy'. He was trusting his agents. So if it was all right for him, it would be all right for her. *The family want to organize this wedding, so let them organize. All I have to do is turn up and say 'I do'.*

***

"And live with him afterwards!" Amanda shrieked when Carrie cited her reasoning.

"It will be OK," Carrie said. "I'm not worried about it."

"Well, I am," Amanda said. "I'm not at all happy about all this secrecy."

"There's no secrecy. He's very open and above board." Carrie found it easy to defend Pete.

"It's not normal, and I don't like it."

"Well, thankfully, it's not you who has to like it," Carrie said. "This is my life and I'm confident it has as much chance of working out well as if I was madly in love with him and blind to all his faults."

"Are you? Are you really?"

Amanda held her in a glare. Was she? Carrie swallowed a lump of anxiety that had crept up in her throat. The only other option was to throw a hissy fit and call the whole thing off. Hysterical manipulation was not her style, to start with, and besides, she was already invested in Pete Brooker and a future with him. No—she was confident. Amanda had said her piece and Carrie had maintained her position. She thought her friend had accepted the decision, if somewhat reluctantly.

***

Pete knocked on the door of the modest brick home. He'd already cast an educated eye over the façade and begun to calculate how difficult this particular renovation would be, if the home owner accepted his quote.

"You must be Pete." An attractive young woman opened the door and shared a friendly smile. "I'm Amanda Keenan. Come inside."

Pete followed the woman indoors. Ms Keenan had said a friend had recommended him as a builder. Pete wondered which previous client had given his number to her.

"Can I get you a drink?" Amanda asked. "It's fairly hot out."

"Thanks," Pete replied. "Cold water, if that's OK."

Pete carefully took in all the structural aspects of the house, looked at the current décor and began a mental list of questions to ask.

"So you're looking to extend your living area?" He accepted the tall glass of ice water.

"Yes." Amanda smiled sweetly at him.

Pete hid the frown he felt building. Why was she looking at him like that? It's like she expected him to go all weak at the knees just because she has big eyes, and big … cut that out. He'd seen low cut tops on women before. Collette was famous for them.

"As you can see, there is only this one small living area doubled as a dining room, and I'd like a larger entertaining space that extends out from the sliding door." Amanda walked through her lounge space and waved toward the glass doors that faced the back yard.

Pete's eyes followed her. He put his professional demeanor on, but that didn't mean he hadn't noticed her short skirt, her long legs, and the way her hips swayed as she walked. Was she doing this on purpose? He swallowed his water and got up from the table. With his notebook in hand he began to ask questions. He did not need to look at Ms Keenan again. He knew what she looked like. What he needed to do was run the tape measure around the perimeter she'd indicated and write numbers down.

When he'd finished, he turned back to the prospective client and spoke.

"I'll need to take all this back to my computer and do up a proper quote. I can get it back to you in say—a week?"

"That would be great," Amanda said. "Would you like to come over for dinner?"

Pete was not surprised by the direct invitation. He was shaken by it, however.

"Ah … I … that is, I can either email you the quote or post it."

"Oh, yes, that would be fine, either way. I just thought perhaps you might like to get together socially."

"Oh … ah … no! Sorry. I'm engaged."

"Engaged?" Amanda smiled and batted her eyelashes at him. "Like, off limits engaged? Not allowed to have any fun engaged?"

"I'm sorry." Pete didn't feel sorry. He felt upset by her flirting, and uncomfortable. "I'm definitely well and truly engaged. Wedding on the horizon."

"That's a shame." Amanda put a well-manicured hand on his upper bicep. "Nice looking guy like you."

"Um, I better get going. I'll get this quote back to you as soon as I can."

Pete picked up his things and walked to the front door.

"What's her name?" Amanda called after him.

She couldn't have misinterpreted his brush off. He was obviously leaving.

"Her name?" Pete wanted to cut her off. He didn't care if he was rude.

"Your fiancée?"

"Carrie."

"You must love her very much."

"Yes. Ah, this is a little awkward. Like I said, I'll get that quote back ASAP."

Pete fled out the door. How could she think that sort of blatant flirting was attractive? He didn't look back as he got in his ute and drove away.

That will be one quote you will not be able to afford, Ms Keenan.

***

"Where does this builder live?" Carrie asked. "We've been driving for over an hour."

"He came very highly recommended," Amanda said. "Besides, what else have you got to do tonight?"

Carrie shrugged. It was Friday evening and unless her family or Amanda had something planned, she usually sat at home and did schoolwork.

"We'll just stop by, pick up the quote, then we'll go out for coffee or pizza if you're hungry."

"Sounds good," Carrie replied. "I guess I've had my head down with end-of-semester school stress, a long drive with my best friend won't kill me."

"Um … Carrie?"

There was a change in Amanda's tone. She was almost always upbeat, and now she sounded anxious. Carrie was immediately alert.

"What? What's the matter?"

"I have a confession to make."

Carrie turned in her seat and adjusted the seatbelt so she could look at her friend. Amanda's eyes were on the road, where they should be, but Carrie could see there was guilt written on her face, even from the side angle.

"What have you done?"

"I met Pete the other day."

"Really? Where? How?"

"I just did."

"What aren't you telling me?"

"I came on to him, to see how he would respond."

"Amanda! Why would you do such a thing?"

"You aren't going to take the opportunity to test him, so I decided to do it for you."

"But he'll think I set him up!"

"I didn't tell him I knew you."

"When you say came on to him, do you mean you threw yourself at him?"

"I did my best …"

Carrie groaned.

"… but he wasn't having any of it. He's well and truly engaged."

Carrie put her face in her hands and groaned again.

"I gave him plenty of opportunity to be unfaithful to you, and no one would have known if he'd—how should I say—indulged."

"Oh, Manda. Did you come on real strong?"

"I tried."

"Manda!"

"He didn't bite, I tell you. In fact, he couldn't get out of there fast enough."

"Manda, that is … you shouldn't have … why do you do these things?"

Amanda shrugged her shoulders. "I needed to know my best friend wasn't getting herself entangled with a man who was a player or a sleaze."

Carrie just shook her head. She hardly noticed that Amanda had pulled the car up outside a house until she spoke.

"Well, we're here."

Carrie just shook her head and let out a sigh. She hoped Amanda was picking up how cross she was with her.

"Hey, Carrie?"

Carrie screwed up her lips and turned toward her friend. "What?"

"Would you run in and pick up the papers for me?"

"Why can't you go in and get them?"

"I've got to send off a really important text. I just remembered it has to be done now, or I'll miss an opportunity."

"Bully for you."

"Carrie … please?"

Carrie rolled her eyes and unlatched her seatbelt.

"What is it you're supposed to be picking up?"

"Just tell them you need to pick up the papers for Amanda Keenan."

Carrie got out of the car, mumbling under her breath. Sometimes Amanda made her so mad.

Just as she got to the front door and rang the doorbell, her mobile phone pinged. She had it in her hand so flipped it over to see who the text was from.

I'll explain later.

It was from Amanda. All at once the front door of the house opened, and she turned back to see Amanda's car pulling away from the curb.

"Carrie!"

Louise Brooker stood at the door. Realization clicked in, and then chagrin. She should have connected the dots, especially since it was Amanda she was dealing with.

"Come in, come in." Louise stood to one side and waved Carrie into the house. Could this be any more awkward? If Amanda had not just driven away, Carrie would have run back to the car and throttled her, figuratively speaking.

"It's so lovely to see you," Louise was saying. "Are you all right? You look a little flushed."

"My good friend, Amanda Keenan has …" Has what? How was she supposed to explain this?

Chapter Eleven

*P*ete was working on a quote when he was alerted to a text on his phone. He finished the figures he was entering, pressed save, then looked at the message. It was that woman, Ms Keenan. He had thought his quote was suitably expensive that he wouldn't hear back from her again, but she was nothing if not persistent. What other deterrent could he throw her way?

Hi Pete.

Well that was too informal for a start with. Who did she think he was?

I have a confession to make.

Uh oh, this didn't sound good.

I'm Carrie Davis' best friend, and I set you up to test you. Before you get all hopping mad, Carrie didn't know anything about it. It was my idea. She is way too trusting and I needed to reassure myself that you weren't that sort of man. Obviously you're not. Anyway, sorry to have troubled you, and by the way, your quote for renovations is ridiculous. Oh, and also, I just dropped Carrie outside your house. She thinks she is picking up the quote. She doesn't know any of this. Be kind to her.

Your soon-to-be-best-friend by association,

Amanda.

There was no time to process the text before there was a knock on his door.

"Pete." It was his mother. He got up and went to the door. "There's someone here to see you."

"Carrie?"

She nodded. "She's a bit upset. Apparently her friend …"

"I know. She just texted me."

"Carrie didn't know."

"I know. Give me a minute. I'll just clean up a bit."

Pete went into the bathroom and looked in the mirror. He'd taken a shower when he'd gotten home from work, but that was the extent of it. He was dressed in board shorts and a tank top. It was hot weather, so why not? But his soon-to-be bride was sitting in the kitchen, and whether they were ready for it or not, they were about to meet face-to-face for the first time.

He ran a brush through his unruly hair. It didn't make much difference. He sniffed his armpits. He smelled all right, but deodorant wouldn't hurt. He decided a t-shirt and jeans would be less imposing than a tank top that showed half his torso. Whatever his reservations had been, Amanda Keenan, his soon-to-be-friend, had dropped him and Carrie right in it. He took a deep breath and decided to face his life.

"Pete." His mother stood up from the kitchen table where they were sitting and waved him over. "This is Carrie."

She was there, in front of him, like a rabbit in the headlights of an oncoming car.

"Well, I might just leave you two to catch up. I'll be with your father in the lounge room, if you need me."

He hardly noticed his mother leave the room. All he could see was the woman in front of him.

"I'm really sorry," Carrie eventually spoke. She stood up to face him. Just as Nan had said, she was quite short.

"Your friend just sent me this text." Pete unlocked his phone and held it out to Carrie. She took it from him and began to read, shaking her head as she did so.

"I am so sorry."

"You already said that."

"She just has moments of crazy, and there's no controlling her."

Pete smiled. He knew that Ms Keenan had been coming on strong, and she *had* been attractive—just the sort of woman he would have responded to in the past. His ego had been stroked, no doubt about it, but something had made him clam up and flee, and now, as he faced Carrie, he was grateful. If he had responded to the flirtation in any way at all, Ms Keenan would have gone back and told Carrie and he would have undermined her confidence—damaged their relationship before they'd had a chance to begin.

"Can I get you something to drink?" Pete asked, suddenly aware how awkward it was, the two of them just standing there.

"Your mum got me a glass of water." She pointed to the empty glass on the table. "I was supposed to pick up some papers for Amanda—at least that's what she told me."

"I emailed her the quote a few days ago."

"She's set me up."

"She's set both of us up."

Carrie dropped her head, and Pete felt sorry for her. "Listen, I know it's not your fault, and hey, we were going to meet eventually, so at least now Amanda can rest easy."

Carrie gave a weak smile. "She might not rest so easy once I've got hold of her and given her a piece of my mind."

"I assume she's not still outside waiting for you."

"I doubt it. She pulled away the moment I rang the doorbell."

"Do you think she's coming back?"

Carrie shook her head. "I'll call her, but my guess is her phone will suddenly be switched off."

Carrie went through the motions and shook her head.

"I can drive you back home, if you don't mind," Pete said.

"It's over an hour away, that's a two-hour round trip for you."

"What else would I do on a Friday night?"

Carrie smiled. "You sound like me. If she hadn't dragged me on this trip, I would have been at home doing schoolwork."

"Come on." Pete grabbed his keys from the kitchen bench and indicated they go. "This is probably a good opportunity. We may even end up thanking Amanda later."

"After I've choked her," Carrie said.

***

This certainly hadn't been planned, and Carrie had not had any time to emotionally prepare herself for it but sitting beside Pete in his work ute as they drove across the suburbs, was nice—more than nice. They chatted easily about Carrie's work, Pete's Nan, other members of the family who'd been driving the whole scheme.

"Yesterday, Amanda announced she was going to be my chief bridesmaid," Carrie said. "Before that she'd been preaching caution. Now I know why she's suddenly taken a notion to jump on board."

"Announced? You weren't going to ask her?"

"I wasn't sure how much of the traditional wedding we were going to have."

"My team have been scheming. I probably need to ask them the details soon, or they might get carried away."

"I thought it would just be something simple. I wasn't sure you'd want a big show."

"What do you want, Carrie?"

"I'm not sure yet. What do you want?"

Pete shrugged. "I want to get married, but you heard about my break-up last year."

Carrie nodded.

"We had everything ordered and half paid for. We were going to have every possible wedding fangle just short of pink swans."

Carrie laughed. "You don't like pink swans?"

Pete turned his head and smiled at her. "Couldn't track any down."

Carrie felt a rush of warmth as she met his gaze for that brief second. She turned her focus back onto the road ahead.

"Let's keep it simple," she said. "I don't want stress and monster-bride syndrome."

"Me either."

It had seemed like forever on the drive to Pete's house. The return trip took only a few minutes—or at least, that was how it felt.

"This is my house," Carrie said.

"You don't live with your folks?"

"No, I bought this place about seven years ago and have been steadily paying it off ever since."

"Does Amanda live with you?"

"Amanda?" Carrie laughed. "No! Can you imagine? I have enough trouble with her as a friend. Imagine if we were house mates."

"So just you then?"

"Me and my two dogs. I read in your mother's report that you like animals. Is that true?"

"Love them. I haven't had one for a few years because … well, I'm going to leave the past in the past. But yes, I love dogs."

"Would you like to come in and meet them?"

There was an awkward pause, and Carrie suddenly felt as if she'd been too forward.

"I'd love to, Carrie, but … I don't want you to think …"

"It's OK. You can meet them later. After the wedding."

"I'm kind of glad we've had this opportunity to meet and talk. Are you still keen to get married?"

"Very." That slipped out too quickly, and Carrie felt the blood rise in her face.

"OK then." Pete grinned at her. He undid his seatbelt and got out of the car. Before she'd got herself together, he opened the passenger side door for her.

"Thanks." She suddenly felt shy and didn't look at him until she was standing up. "Thanks again for bringing me all the way home."

"It was my pleasure."

Carrie couldn't avoid looking at him—looking *up* at him. Their eyes met and he smiled. Despite nerves, she smiled too. He really was very good looking.

"I best be off then," he said.

Carrie nodded. He held out his hand and she took it. It happened naturally, as he leaned down and gave her a warm kiss on the cheek, but he didn't let go of her hand.

"I think we might forgive Amanda this once," he said. "What do you think?"

Carrie nodded. She would forgive Amanda but wanted to make her squirm a bit first.

***

As Carrie had told Pete, Amanda was now putting her full effort into getting the wedding organized. Carrie had found it difficult to be mad at her for long.

"Did you enjoy meeting him?" Amanda asked at their first wedding planning meeting.

"Yes, but …"

"But what? I tested him out, and he's good value. Isn't that right, Ellen?"

"I wouldn't have even told Carrie about it if he hadn't been good value," Ellen said.

"Not to mention he's hot as." Amanda's grin showed she was unrepentant.

"Manda!"

"Don't pretend you didn't notice. And now you can get all that angst out of your system. You clicked, I take it?"

Carrie nodded. They'd clicked—to a degree. As far as you could on a first meeting.

"Now we need to get you into the shops and find your wedding dress," her mother said.

Carrie shook her head. "No."

"What do you mean, no?" Ellen closed the wedding magazine she'd been reading and pinned Carrie with her stare. "The wedding's set for January. That's not long away, and you need to get organized."

"Yes, but I'm not going to buy a wedding dress."

"Don't be ridiculous!" Amanda said. "You're going to have a proper wedding dress, and I am going to have a proper bridesmaid dress."

"But this isn't a real wedding," Carrie objected.

"What?" Carrie could tell by Ellen's tone that she was preparing to argue.

"Well, it's not normal," Carrie said.

Ellen blew out a lung-full of air, and Amanda shook her head.

"Just ignore her, Ellen," Amanda said.

"This is the only wedding you'll ever have," Ellen pointed out. "You'll want to have photographs to show your children, and what will they say if you're not in a proper wedding dress?"

"If it's a matter of cost," Mum said, "then let me set your mind at ease—your father and I intend to pay for it."

"But Mum, it's so much money."

"They spent a heap on my wedding," Ellen said.

"Yeah, but you and Brad were—"

"Were what?" Amanda asked mercilessly.

"Well they were in love." Carrie felt as if it had been dragged out of her.

"Are you having second thoughts?" Mum asked.

"No. I want to get married, and I haven't got any reason not to like Pete—from what I know—it's just that we're not madly in love, or anything."

Carrie didn't miss the exaggerated sighs and eye-rolling that the other three exchanged. But it was true. She'd clicked with him when they'd met, but they'd also discussed their individual emotional states. Pete was not ready to let himself be knocked over by the heady 'in love' feelings. And she was OK with that.

"Well, I don't care," Amanda broke the silence. "I want to wear a proper brides-maid's dress, and I'll look silly if you don't have a proper wedding dress, so that's settled. All in favor?"

Ellen shot her hand up, and her mother nodded. Carrie was out-voted, even if she wanted to insist. They were not having a bar of toning down the wedding. Was she secretly pleased? Perhaps just a little.

***

"No, Mum!" Pete said.

"But you have to have a reception," Chloe complained.

"We'll have a small family dinner, and that's all."

"But what about Carrie?" You could always count on Mum to be logical. "Won't she be disappointed not having a full lavish affair with all her friends?"

"If she wants something lavish with a large guest list, we'll have a first anniversary party. I don't want a whole heap of people I don't know, and even ones I do know, watching us closely when we've only just met for the second time. In fact, I'm thinking, the family dinner might only be for the family, and Carrie and I might leave you to it."

"Have you asked Carrie about this?" Megan asked, raising her eyebrows.

"I'll check with her. But I don't want a huge reception—not then, anyway."

It was one thing to be firm with his family, but now he was incredibly nervous about broaching the subject with Carrie. He had flashbacks of the wedding arrangements with Collette and the fights they'd had. Pete suddenly wondered if he was about to find out that Carrie had feet of clay after all. He could have called her, now he had her number, but he elected to send an email and give her time to consider it before being expected to answer.

You might feel differently, he wrote, *but I'd really like for us to get away from public view, sit down and just talk, and get to know one another. Perhaps we can have a welcome home party or something once we return from our time away.*

'Time away?' He'd thought about writing honeymoon but had decided not to. The word honeymoon usually implied all sorts of intimate and passionate experiences. Pete wasn't sure their time away would be anything more than a holiday together, getting to know one another as friends. He didn't want to take anything for granted.

Once he'd pressed send on the email, he became anxious waiting for her response. He couldn't help imagining what sort of things Collette would say. Even now, the memory of her words still cut him.

I couldn't agree more, Carrie eventually wrote. *My family want all the pomp and ceremony, and I don't want to disappoint them, but if we could just have a nice little afternoon tea, a toast, and kiss them all goodbye, that would be more than enough. If you've put your foot down with your family, then I can use that as an excuse to calm my family down. I'm afraid I've been talked into a proper wedding dress though, and hope you don't mind, but I'm glad, as I do want to have a formal photograph to remember the day by.*

I'm glad we've set the date for next month as if it were any longer, these wedding-planners would get right out of control and it would be hard to wind them back—given that you've met Amanda, I know you'll know what I mean.

I'm looking forward to seeing you again, and getting to know you more.

***

"I can't say that I'm happy about this travesty you call a wedding reception," Amanda said, as she read over the notes.

"It's not really a reception," Carrie replied. "Just a small celebration for immediate family …"

"And friends." Amanda looked stern.

"Just you and Pete's best man, Andy."

"It's hardly adequate," Amanda complained.

"It's what we both want, and it's perfectly adequate."

"So you've sat down and talked it all through with him then?"

"We've emailed."

"But you talk on the phone, right?"

Carrie shook her head. "It will all happen, Manda. Give it some time."

"You've already spent the evening with him, thanks to me. That should have broken the ice."

"It did, and it settled all our worries."

"You should call him and see how he is."

"What excuse would I use?"

"That you're just checking to see if he's OK."

"I don't want to be an annoying, needy girlfriend."

"Hardly. You're going to marry him in a few weeks. Call him."

Carrie bit her bottom lip.

"Honestly, you're behaving like a fifteen-year-old schoolgirl. Here." Amanda took out her phone and scrolled through.

"You have his number?" Carrie asked.

"He might be my building contractor one day, if he sorts out his quote." Amanda handed the phone to Carrie.

Carrie felt panic as she held the phone. What was she supposed to say?

"Just say hello," Amanda apparently could read her thoughts.

The call connected and Carrie heard Pete's voice. It was deeper than she remembered, and she forgot to answer.

"Speak to him," Amanda said in a stage whisper.

"Hello, this is Carrie." She used her professional acting principal voice. Amanda rolled her eyes.

"Hi, Carrie. How are you?"

"Good. Busy."

"Me too. Trying to get a whole lot of work sorted before the wedding."

Now what should she say?

"You still there?" Pete asked.

Carrie nodded and then laughed at Amanda's stern frown.

"Sorry, yes. I'm still here. I just called to say hello."

"Great. I'm glad to hear from you."

"I have Amanda here coaching me along. I'm trying to keep her from doing something new and crazy."

Pete laughed, and Carrie felt her shoulders relax.

"Well, she's part of the organizing committee, so I hear," Pete said, "so I guess we'd better be prepared for moments of crazy."

"I'll try to keep her under control," Carrie said. "By the way, I think your idea of something very simple and very short by way of reception is great. My crew are not too pleased, but I'm with you on this one."

"Thanks, Carrie. I really appreciate that."

There were a couple moments of awkward pause.

"When do you finish for the school year?" Pete asked.

"Our summer holidays start next week, then there's Christmas, New Year, and the wedding first thing next year."

"I'm looking forward to it," Pete said. Carrie could easily imagine he was smiling.

"I have to go, but it was nice talking to you again," Carrie said.

"Perhaps we could catch up for coffee if there's time before Christmas," Pete suggested.

"I think that would be nice."

Carrie finished off the conversation, and Amanda frowned at her.

"Why do you have to go?" she asked. "You looked all soft and dreamy talking to him. You should have talked some more."

"It feels funny talking to someone I hardly know while you're standing over me, monitoring every word and response. Give me a break, Amanda."

Amanda laughed. "Well, at least you've taken another step. Did you like the sound of his voice?"

"I heard him good and well when he drove me home the other night," Carrie said, "And yes, of course I love the sound of his voice."

"Good. Job well done on my part, don't you think?"

"You just concentrate on your part of the arrangements, and no more making phone calls to him, OK? He knows who you are now."

Chapter Twelve

It was done, and now all Benjamin had left to do was wait for the appointment before the Vicar where he would be wed to Lady Charlotte Featherstone. He wracked his brain trying to remember when he'd seen the girl in person. He must have seen her any number of times at balls and assemblies. Her father, Lord Edward Featherstone, was often in attendance. The daughter was of age to be out, so she must have been there. But Benjamin had only had eyes for Kitty these past years—the woman he'd had his heart set on marrying. Blast it all. Why must he continue to think of her. She was gone—wed to an officer of dubious rank. Benjamin should be congratulating himself on having secured Lady Charlotte's hand. After all, it did come with thirty thousand pounds. I am such a cad. Fancy thinking only of the financial benefits in marriage, and nothing of the poor woman who was to become his wife.

"Your guests have arrived, Mi-lord." Jenkins held the door open for Benjamin.

"Is there any way I can get out of hosting this party, Jenkins?"

"It is Christmas, Mi-lord. Your mother and aunt will expect you at the head of the table to toast good health to the family."

Benjamin checked his image in the glass. This would be his last family celebration as a single man. Next year, Lady Charlotte would preside over all the arrangements for Christmas dinner. If only he could remember what she looked like.

"He is a cad. I could shake him." Louise snapped her computer shut. But it was her own subconscious worry that plagued her. What if Pete was like her Regency hero? What if he gave no thought to Carrie, and just married her for … for what? Carrie was hardly an heiress to a great fortune.

"I should have asked Carrie over for Christmas dinner," Louise said to Russell as she met him in the kitchen.

"Well, why didn't you?"

"Pete hasn't been keen to socialize with her before the wedding."

"He's a strange boy," Russell said. "Remember how you and I were before we got married?"

"Don't remember." Louise grinned.

"Young and full of passion, if memory serves."

"Yes, well, we were young. A good deal younger than Pete, at any rate."

"He's not an old man yet," Russell said.

"But he's not got much enthusiasm for life, love and relationships, has he?"

"He's been torpedoed by three different women—especially the last one. He'll be all right."

"Do you think?"

"He's not a kid anymore, Louise. He'll find some passion when the time is right."

"I hope so. I wouldn't like to think he's a cad."

***

Pete loved Christmas pudding. It was the highlight of Christmas in his mind.

"Next year, Christmas won't be so easy," Mum said, as she placed a serve of pudding and ice-cream in front of him.

"Why?" Dad asked. His spoon was already dividing off his first mouthful of the traditional dessert.

"Because all the children will be married, and they'll have other families to consider when planning Christmas visits."

Pete thought about Carrie. The woman he would wed in a fortnight and who would become part of the family. How did he feel about her—about marriage to her? Nothing. Not excited particularly, but not anxious or reluctant either. It was a strange state to be in.

"Well next year will definitely be different." Megan's comment drew Pete's attention back to those present at the table. "Umm…"

She hesitated, which made Pete sense she had something important to say. Chloe also picked up on her sister's hesitation.

"What will be so different, apart from the fact we'll include Carrie in everything?" Chloe asked.

"Next year, there will be your first grandchild." Megan was beaming, and so was Cam as he put his arm around his wife.

"Heck!" Dad said. "Congratulations!"

"Oh, that's so exciting." Chloe gushed. "I can't wait to be an auntie."

"Darling, that is the best news we could hope to have," Mum said. "What a wonderful Christmas present."

"Yeah, congratulations." Seeing his parents' animated response, Pete followed suit and gave the expected response. But the announcement had hit him hard and rocked him out of his emotional complacency. Now he had an emotional response, and it wasn't positive. Why couldn't he forget Collette and the plans he'd made? It was all so stupid. Now, on this side of the break-up, he knew the plans had all been in his own head—that Collette had never, and would never have, agreed to them. But they had been stupid, sentimental plans, and he'd been looking forward to having a child. The first Brooker grandchild. He hadn't realized his melancholy must have shown on his face until his mother placed her hand on his arm. She gave him an encouraging smile.

"There's good reason to hope there might be two babies," she said.

"Twins! Heavens, I hope not!" Megan laughed.

"I had a job convincing her to have one," Cam said with a grin.

"And even now, I'm not confident I'll know what I'm doing." Megan leaned into Cam's embrace.

"You'll know," Chloe said. "Besides, Mum will be there to coach you along, won't you 'Grandma'?"

Far from being cowed by Chloe's teasing, 'Grandma' took it in her stride as she continued. "Pete and Carrie might have a baby by next year, too. It's all quite possible."

The dinner table conversation stalled. His mother had no concept of tact.

"Perhaps we shouldn't rush them." Chloe was the one to break the awkward moment.

"Rush?" Mum said. "Good heavens! I'd hardly call early thirties as rushing."

"Mum." Megan said. "Do you realize the time schedule they'd have to set to get a baby by Christmas?"

"Is this really good conversation for the dinner table?" Pete asked. "Seriously?"

Sure, he'd been feeling sorry for himself that he'd lost the dream of having kids with Collette. He'd indulged in self-pity and completely forgotten Carrie. But a baby-making schedule? He felt uncomfortable and was thankful Carrie wasn't present to hear it. "If you eager beavers could calm down," he said, "perhaps we should allow Carrie some time to adjust to this crazy family before we inform her she's on a tight schedule to produce."

"That sounds sensible." Dad said. "I think it must be time for a nap."

"Dad!" Chloe complained. "Why should it always be the women who get to cook *and* clean up after?"

Pete just rolled his eyes. "What am I, chopped liver? I always help clean up."

"Yeah, but Dad is so old school—women don't wear frilly aprons and run to fetch his slippers anymore."

"I heard your lecture last year, Chloe," Dad said, unrepentant.

Mum laughed. "I don't wear frilly aprons, and he doesn't wear slippers."

"You know what I mean."

"Let him sleep," Pete said. "Old dogs and new tricks. You know how the saying goes."

"You can go and sleep too, if you like, Hun," Michael said. "I'll help Pete with clean up."

"You guys are killing me," Megan said.

"I was going to offer to help as well," Cam looked at her. "You're pregnant and need a nap."

"Well that is lovely." Mum pushed up from her chair. "I'll enjoy spending the clean-up time with you boys."

"No, Mum. You did most of the cooking," Chloe said. "You go and read your new novel, and I'll help the boys."

Working with Chloe, it didn't take long to get all the dishes in the dishwasher. Michael and Cam left the kitchen but Pete stayed with Chloe to help wash up some saucepans. It wasn't long before Mum had come in to help anyway. She began to wipe down the benches.

"You know Carrie is expecting to have children straight away."

Pete nearly dropped the saucepan he was wiping when his mother spoke. She didn't know the word subtle.

"How do you know?" Chloe asked.

"It was on the list of non-negotiable criteria."

"Mum!" Pete said.

"It was probably the second thing you had written down."

"I know that. I did it on purpose, but I didn't actually think anybody would accept the list. I didn't really mean it."

"Gee, Pete, what else did you have written down?" Chloe asked.

"Honestly, I can't remember, and really, I had no notion anybody would ever take it seriously."

"None-the-less, that was one of the points high up on the list, and when we talked with Bill, Anne and Ellen, they confirmed that Carrie was of the same mind."

"Are you sure?" Pete asked. "Did you hear it from her mouth, or was it her enthusiastic sister?"

"Ellen was the one who told me … but …"

"She probably thinks I'm a Cretan."

"You are a Cretan," Chloe said, "but I love you anyway."

As Pete left the kitchen, he couldn't stop thinking about what Carrie must think of him. *Must want children straight away.* He knew he'd written it. Carrie had apparently read and accepted it. But being reminded of it did make him nervous. Now that he was going to marry her, he didn't really want her to think he was an alpha male. He had hopes they might come to love each other eventually. Love usually started with respect.

"You guys OK if I go out for a while?" Pete asked, as he walked back into the family room.

"Where're you going?" his mother asked.

"I thought I might try to catch up with Carrie and wish her Merry Christmas."

"So you've met up with her then?" Megan asked.

"Just the once and spoken to her on the phone a couple of times."

"She's nice, isn't she?" Chloe said.

"She seems to be. I'm going on your recommendations."

"Then go and meet up with her, and make sure and certain," Mum said.

***

Carrie was a pack of nerves. She hadn't expected to see Pete again before the wedding, but when he'd called to ask if they could meet up for coffee, she responded immediately.

"There's not much open on Christmas Day," she said.

"Would it be OK if I drop by your place then?" he asked.

She'd left Ellen's place and gone straight home, set up the espresso machine ready to go, and now sat waiting nervously. She knew when he arrived by the way her two labs stood alert at the door.

"Be good." She patted each one on the head before opening the door.

"Hi, Pete," she said when she saw him standing on her doorstep. He sure was tall.

"Hi, Carrie. Merry Christmas."

"Merry Christmas. Come inside." She stepped back and waved him in, but he only took two steps and was prevented from going further by her two faithful dogs. Her heart warmed as Pete stopped and patted each one.

"Hello, and what are your names?"

He really did like dogs. Louise's folio was proving to be accurate.

"The golden one is Flo, and the black one is Lucky."

They eventually got past the dogs and Carrie settled him on a stool at the kitchen bench while she went about making coffee.

"Are you still set for the wedding?" he asked.

"Yes." Suddenly Carrie was worried. Why would he ask such a thing? Surely he wasn't going to back out of the arrangement at the last minute.

"It's just that my mother reminded me of the things I'd written as my criteria, and I can't stop thinking about it. I felt … like …"

"I can't even remember seeing the list," Carrie said. "In fact, I think Ellen reviewed the list and did all of the negotiating."

There was a long silence, and Carrie turned around to see what was wrong.

"Are you all right?" she asked.

"You must have seen the list, surely?" Carrie could hear panic in Pete's tone.

"I can't honestly remember, but what was on it that has you worried?"

"We talked about kids, remember?"

"Yeah. After your friend's baby was born."

Pete's sigh of relief was accompanied by his shoulder's relaxing.

"What are you worried about?" Carrie asked, feeling pleased she could sense his angst. "Pete?" she prodded when he didn't answer immediately.

"I'd written down that I want kids straight way, and that it was a non-negotiable."

Carrie laughed and it seemed to lighten the atmosphere. "Yeah, I remember. So?"

"I'd forgotten I wrote that, and at the time, I never dreamed Mum would actually successfully find someone who would fit the criteria, so I didn't ever imagine it would be a problem."

"Is it a problem?"

"When Chloe recited it back to me it sounded a bit … man-drags-woman-to-cave."

Carrie laughed again. "Yeah. It does sound a bit chauvinistic, but hey … You've got to have some faults, surely."

He stiffened up again.

"I'm joking, Pete. It's going to be OK."

"Are you sure?"

Was she? "I better be," Carrie said, pushing down the sudden surge of doubt. "Are you?"

"Yes. Of course. I've been counting the days."

"Well, that's a relief!" Carrie set a frothy coffee down on the counter in front of him. "For a moment there I'd begun to think you'd had second thoughts."

"I wouldn't do that to you," Pete said. "I've been on the receiving end of a jilting, and believe me, it's not nice."

"But you've thought about it?"

"No! Not at all. I considered what I'm doing—long and hard—before I wrote you that proposal. I'm not backing out, so long as you're OK with … you know."

"I'm fine with it, Pete. Honestly. Besides, we're not really on a schedule, are we?"

"I'm just looking forward to the wedding, and then having plenty of time to really get to know you. Why don't we just let the children thing happen naturally, OK?"

"That sounds like the best idea."

As Carrie waved Pete goodbye, her cheek was buzzing from the kiss he'd planted there, and she couldn't help the wave of warmth that shot through her when she considered what he'd said. *Let's just let the children thing happen naturally.* Phew! She made a conscious effort to calm her racing heart down. One thing at a time. Wedding first.

***

Carrie was feeling something, but wasn't satisfied that she could accurately categorize what it was: excitement, anxiety, plain weirdness, all of the above. Amanda had taken her maid of honor duties seriously and was in complete charge. Carrie didn't mind as things like fashion and frippery were not on her list of strengths, but sometimes she also had a slight feeling of panic not knowing completely what sorts of things Amanda had organized. Considering she and Pete had both been adamant that following the church ceremony there would be light refreshments and toasts for family and wedding party only, she didn't think Amanda could get too far out of control.

Tomorrow she would meet her husband for only the third time face-to-face, and without delay they would exchange vows and rings. It verged on the romantic at one moment, the pragmatic the next, and the plain ridiculous the moment after that. Carrie decided she would just stop trying to analyze and try to enjoy the evening meal that Amanda and Ellen had planned for her, before getting a good night's sleep.

"Pizza?" Carrie complained when she saw Ellen opening the take-away boxes.

"You love pizza." Ellen gave her a brief glance, showing just the smallest sign of a frown. "What did you want on your last night as a free woman?"

"Steady," Amanda chimed in. "What she meant was, your last night before you celebrate your special marriage to a wonderful guy."

"I hope he's wonderful," Carrie said without thinking.

"So do I," Ellen said, "otherwise I'll never hear the end of it."

"Stop it! He's wonderful, you both know it. Stop getting all antsy and come eat this pizza."

Carrie didn't argue further. She sat down on the couch and yielded to the girls' choice of entertainment. Ellen and Amanda had widely differing taste in romantic movies, but finally Ellen won. It was decided they would watch the full five hours of the *BBC's Pride and Prejudice.* The argument over the movie had gone on for so long Carrie didn't have the heart to admit she didn't really want to think about *Mr Darcy* tonight. She wanted to think about Mr Brooker. Mr Peter Brooker.

Halfway through the second episode, the drama was interrupted by Carrie's phone ringing. She wasn't aware of her reaction when she saw the caller ID, but it must have been quite clear on her face.

"Pete." Both Ellen and Amanda said together, just a hint of teasing in their tone.

"Look at her," Ellen continued. "She's gone all dreamy."

Carrie was annoyed by their unnecessary close analysis, and waved her hand at them, fixing a stern frown that was designed to quiet them down.

"Hi Carrie." Pete's voice came over the phone, and Carrie could feel she was beaming. And why not?

"Hi," she returned.

"All set for tomorrow?"

"If Amanda and Ellen have anything to do with it. You?"

"My mother is in her element. It's quite amusing really, seeing her run around with full license to meddle."

"You don't mind?"

"I don't usually let them have quite this much control over my life, but since it was her idea of rescuing me from the depths of despair, I've let her have her head. But come tomorrow, that's it."

"No more meddling?" Carrie asked.

"Not from my mother and sisters at least. I imagine we'll have some talking to do and sorting out how we'll live together."

"I've been on my own for a while," Carrie said. "I hope I'm not too set in my ways."

"Even if you are, from what your sister says, you seem to be more like me than … well, I get the impression you're easy going."

"Sometimes."

"Sometimes?"

"You should see how I sort out troublesome middle-school students who are sent to my office. Not much easy-going nature then."

Pete laughed.

"I'll keep that in mind and try to keep my troublesome persona in check."

"Are you nervous?" Carrie asked.

"A little, but truly, the team have taken all the pressure organizing. The only thing I'm worried about is you."

"Why?"

"I'm worried if you're really happy to go through with this. You don't think it's too weird?"

"Oh, it's weird—who let's their family arrange their marriage? But, you're right, the team have really absorbed the stress. I haven't had one wedding worry. No bridal meltdown."

"So you're OK?"

"With you?"

"Yeah."

"I'm pretty sure we'll be OK."

"I'm glad to hear you say so. I don't want you to have any regrets."

"I'm going into this with my eyes open, Pete. I don't think your family have hidden anything from me."

"Well, I guess all we have to do is wait for the morrow."

"I have to watch a romantic drama with the girls first, but …"

"But?" Pete's question hung in the air for a split second.

Should she say it? Were they at a place in their relationship where she could say what bordered on a confession of love? Time to take a risk. This was how she felt. "I'd rather be with you."

Chapter Thirteen

Everyone from the village crowded around the churchyard, even some standing outside the stone fence, waiting as the carriage pulled up. Charlotte saw the floral archway held by two village boys in readiness for her entrance. It was a surprisingly beautiful winter's day, the sun shining through the fluffy clouds, with no threat of rain. The general atmosphere in the crowd as Charlotte began her journey up the churchyard path to the arched doorway, was one of excitement and joy. It was infectious. Charlotte allowed herself to indulge. Benjamin Hart was standing before the robed vicar, his back toward her. He was there and waiting for her. But she could not see his face. He did not turn. Suddenly, anxiety crept in to steal her joy away. Was he here to go through the motions in securing her dowry? Was this a business transaction for him? Heaven only knew if he had any feeling towards her—his soon-to-be wife. Had Kitty Coleborn ruined his heart forever?

"He is a good man," Charlotte's father said in her ear. "This will be a good and safe marriage for you."

"But what if he never grows to love her?" Louise said out loud.

"Stop worrying," Russell said. "You were the one who decided this was a good idea, and you were the one who decided Carrie Davis was the girl for our Pete."

Pete and Carrie. Earth to Louise. Today was about Pete. He'd been so emotionally disconnected ever since that disastrous engagement to Collette. Would he open up again and learn to love?

"It looks like you've swallowed a lemon, woman," Russell said. "This is your son's wedding day. You need to inspire some confidence here."

"Do you think I've done the right thing?"

"Too late now. Come on. It's time to get Pete to the church."

Andy came into the living room, miming the cut it signal across his throat. Pete followed on his heels looking dashing in his formal suit, but wearing a frown on his face.

"Mum?"

They'd overheard her second-guessing herself.

"You look wonderful, Pete."

"Do you know something you need to share?"

"Not at all. Carrie Davis is the right girl for you, and *she'll* be waiting for *you* if we don't get going."

"Come on," Russell said. "I'll drive."

Louise picked up her clutch purse, checked her hair in the hall mirror and followed the men from the house. Lord, please make this thing work out. Charlotte and Benjamin's story she could edit. Carrie and Pete were real life, with a real possibility it could fail—and it would be all her fault.

***

Carrie had refused to let Amanda and Ellen hire wedding cars. It was a ridiculous expense for such a small wedding and she couldn't justify it. So she arrived in her brother-in-law's two-year-old sedan, white ribbons attached, Brad at the wheel, and her father by her side. Amanda, Ellen and Mum were driven to the church by Carrie's brother, Mark.

"Are you nervous?" Amanda asked as she fussed about, holding flowers and straightening Carrie's train.

"Of course she's nervous," Ellen chimed in. "It's her wedding day. All brides are nervous on their wedding day."

"That, and the fact I've only met him twice before," Carrie said. "It's rather a momentous occasion, don't you think?"

"You'll love him," Ellen said. Carrie sensed only calm and confidence in her sister's tone.

"You haven't met him at all," Carrie felt bound to point out.

"I've met the family. I've read the paperwork. It's going to be fine."

I hope she's right.

Carrie stood facing the church steps ready to go inside. There was no more time to ponder the wisdom of her decision. She'd had the facts before her for several months; she'd heard the anecdotes of Ramesh and Meera from across the road, and how their marriage was a mutually satisfying family arrangement; she could have married Kevin Pole whom she'd at one time thought she loved. But it was Pete Brooker who stood at the front of the church with his mate, Andy, waiting for her to come to him. She inhaled a deep breath for courage and took her father's arm. It was time to wed her lifetime partner.

***

Pete had experienced all levels of emotion as he'd dressed for his wedding. When he'd heard Mum questioning herself, it had undermined his shaky confidence. Thankfully, Andy could read him like a book. He'd all but kicked his backside once they were waiting in the vestibule in preparation.

"What if she 'pulls a Collette' and does a runner?" Pete had been unable to stop the question.

"Shut up, Brooker!" Andy had said. "I can't wait to get you to that altar and out the door. You're becoming a pain in the neck."

Pete had felt chagrined and feigned a look of hurt.

"Honestly. Today is about you and Carrie. That other person, whose name will not be mentioned again, has no part of the day. Is that understood?"

Thank goodness for a mate who knew him so well, and who didn't let him become overwhelmed with anxiety. The threat of Andy giving him what-for made him focus his thoughts in the right place—Carrie.

Pete moved to the front of the church and Andy took his place next to him.

He glanced out over the small congregation. Mum and Dad. Was Mum looking worried? Dad gave him the thumbs up sign. Megan and Cam. They appeared to be happy, and so did Chloe and Michael, standing next to them in the same row. Nan, bless her, was there. Carrie's number one supporter. Karen was sitting next to Nan. Her kids were being babysat. There were a couple of people on Carrie's side of the church. Pete wasn't sure, but guessed probably her brother's girl-friend and her mum. All, without exception, smiled his way as if to encourage him that he was doing the right thing. He felt his mouth go dry and worried when his watch ticked past the designated time. Every minute that passed felt like an eternity. The anxiety threatened again.

"Would you relax, mate," Andy said to him, not even bothering to lower his voice to a whisper. "She'll be here. I just got a text from her Dad to say there was a bit of a traffic delay."

Pete forced his breathing to slow and gave a weak smile.

"Don't worry, Pete," Mum said from the front row. "She's the right one for you."

That's what she said now. What was she saying before they left the house? Pete breathed a sigh of relief when the minister came up the aisle from the door.

"They're here," he said. "Are you ready?"

"Yes," Andy answered on his behalf. "More than ready."

Pete turned around to watch for her. He could feel his heart hammering madly. This was the moment his life would change. Then she was there, in the doorway, and suddenly he couldn't breathe. Her curly dark hair was piled on top of her head, with bits escaping and adding fun to her face. Her bridesmaids had obviously prevailed as she was dressed in white and holding a bunch of flowers. He searched her unveiled face for a sign of reassurance, and saw a nervous glance come his way. They held the gaze for a few moments as she began the walk down the aisle, and then she gave a tentative smile. Pete smiled back.

"She's beautiful," Andy said in his ear.

"I can see that," Pete responded quietly.

"Then for goodness sake, would you relax. You look like you've swallowed a roll of barbed wire."

The comment was so ridiculous, Pete couldn't help but laugh.

***

"What's he laughing at?" Carrie asked her father in a quiet tone.

"Just keep walking, Carrie. You can ask him in about five seconds."

Carrie's heart rate was so accelerated, she struggled to slow her breathing. Finally, she had finished the long walk and was at the front of the church. All she could see was Pete. He was here and looking a million bucks.

"Who gives this woman to be married to this man?" The minister seemed keen to get on with the ceremony.

"We do." Carrie's parents both answered the question, then Dad took her hand and held it out for Pete to take. Carrie worried he wouldn't respond, but eventually he took it, and smiled.

"Hi," Pete said. "I'm glad you came."

Carrie smiled. "How are you feeling?"

"Nervous," he replied. "You?"

"Same."

"Good, now that we're all caught up," the minister interrupted, "let's begin, shall we?"

Carrie heard everyone shuffle to take their seats, but that was about all. She hardly heard what the minister said. All she could think of was the tall man who stood next to her, and who held her hand within his. This was real. From this position she now totally understood why he'd wanted her to be taller than his Nan.

Then suddenly, she was aware that the minister had directed a question to her.

"Yes," she said. She wasn't sure what the question was but hoped that 'yes' was the right answer.

"I do," Amanda whispered to her.

"I mean, I do." He must have asked if she would keep all those promises. *I do so promise*, she thought to herself, and then determined she would pay closer attention to the words being spoken.

The minister didn't dwell long on his short sermon. He spoke of covenant—how it was different to contract. He talked of love as the Bible described in Corinthians. But Carrie struggled to focus and absorb. Pete had hold of her hand and she wished she could step back and look up at him. She would put her neck out if she tried to see his face from this proximity.

"You may kiss your bride."

Kiss! Carrie's emotions went to war. She loved the idea, but how awkward. This time she did step back a little and searched Pete's face to see what he was feeling. He responded, leaning down to her with a quick friendly kiss on the cheek.

"You can do better than that," Amanda said, loud enough for everyone to hear. Everyone laughed.

"I can," Pete replied, "but I'm sure Carrie would agree with me, that we'd prefer to rehearse it privately first."

"I do," Carrie said quickly. "I completely agree."

"I thought you would have had a rehearsal already." Typical Amanda. She had no tact. Carrie felt warmth flush her cheek. Pete squeezed her hands and gave her a smile. She smiled back.

"Then all that's left is for me to pronounce you to be husband and wife." The minister was obviously satisfied with the cheek kiss.

There was a clamour of applause, and Carrie checked back with Pete. She was still smiling and he squeezed her hand again.

"Are we good?" he asked.

"So far, so good," Carrie replied.

"Come on, you two," Amanda pushed into their conversation. "It's time to let your family kiss you, and then take photos. Time for talking later."

"Sorry." Pete smiled at Carrie. "It seems we're on a schedule."

"I tried to rein her in," Carrie replied, "but she's like a runaway train. We're going to have to go with it."

"Hurry up," Amanda said.

Pete took Carrie's arm and turned to walk down the aisle.

"Wait for the music," Amanda said.

There was a pause of a few seconds while one of the church ushers hit play on their phone, and some very emotive music began to play over the sound system.

"Amanda and Ellen organized all this," Carrie whispered to Pete. He had to lean down closer to her to catch what she was saying.

"It's nice," he said.

"Now you can go," Amanda said from behind.

"Let's do this," Pete said.

***

Carrie felt like she was in a whirlwind—a bridesmaid controlled whirlwind. They had insisted she have a proper wedding, but she wasn't quite connected with it. She was going through the motions, but she just wanted to stop and look at Pete. *Look* up *at Pete,* she amended. She wanted to take him in, to talk to him, and try to establish that connection she believed was there to be made. But Amanda, Ellen and Pete's sisters were directing them like actors in a play as the photographer took photographs to memorialize the day.

"Can we have the bride and groom on the steps of the church?" the photographer asked. "I'd like to take some intimate shots of just the two of you."

Carrie opened her mouth to object but was cut off.

"That would be great," Pete said.

Carrie looked up to him. "Are you OK with that?" Pete asked.

Carrie nodded and he used that dynamic smile again.

What is that? Carrie felt a shot of electricity through her stomach as she was momentarily lost in his dark eyes. The haze of confusion prevailed and Carrie allowed herself to be ushered outside and to be put into various poses. Mostly the photographer had Carrie stand two steps higher than Pete so she appeared on an even level with him.

"Now let me have you kiss," the photographer called to them.

Carrie's heart thudded.

"He doesn't know about the arrangement," Carrie apologized.

"Do you want to skip it?" Pete asked.

"Do you?"

Pete gave a grin. "No." He laughed. "You look beautiful, and you are my wife."

Carrie felt a wave of color flood her face.

"Stop fussing, Carrie," Amanda called from behind the photographer. "You'll be sorry later if you don't get this shot now."

"I'll skip it if you want," Pete said. Already Carrie could hear his offer was half-hearted. He wanted to kiss her.

"OK."

"OK, we'll skip it?" he asked.

"OK, let's kiss."

She turned her face toward her new husband, and they gazed at each other for a few moments. She didn't know how to proceed. She needed him to lead. He leaned in toward her and quickly kissed her on the lips. It was not enough. Carrie wanted more but didn't have the courage to act.

"Could you take a little more time about it?" the photographer called from behind his camera.

Carrie saw her bridesmaids all smiling smugly, and so were Pete's best-men.

"We need some practice, obviously," Pete said to her.

"Sorry."

"No need to be sorry," he said.

"Hurry up," Amanda called.

Carrie turned her face back to Pete. This time he put his arms around her and pulled her close. They were caught in each other's gaze for a few moments, and then he caught her mouth with his lips, soft, gentle and warm. Carrie responded and it was a few seconds before she was aware that their attendants were clapping enthusiastically. Pete ended the intimate contact but kept his forehead rested against hers, and he grinned at her.

"That was a fairly good effort, I reckon," he said.

Good effort! Good heavens! Carrie was in a dither. She hadn't expected this on her wedding day. Actually, she hadn't known what to expect, but it sure as houses wasn't this surge of passion that came flooding in. They weren't supposed to be all overcome with heady passion. This was supposed to be a pragmatic, logical choice to unite in marriage. So much for the best laid plans.

Chapter Fourteen

Their wedding reception was over and quite suddenly Carrie was overcome with shyness. Pete's sister, Megan, and her husband, Cam, had offered to drive them to the city hotel where they would begin their marriage. Carrie was glad her wedding dress was not too glamorous. Amanda had unfixed the flowers from her hair before she'd got in the back of Cam's car, and now her dress looked like any other nice formal dress. Pete had his suit on and just like she'd thought earlier, it made him look suave and handsome. Not that he hadn't been handsome in his jeans and t-shirt, but she just wanted to sit and stare at him—to really take in who he was, but she felt awkward. He must have sensed something, as he reached across and took her hand in his. She gave him a quick smile, which he returned warmly.

"Not much talking going on back there," Megan said from the front passenger seat. "What's going on?"

"Leave them alone," Cam said. "They're hardly going to start making out in the back seat when we're all of ten minutes away from the hotel."

Megan laughed. Carrie's face heated.

"Thanks Megan," Pete said. "You have a real charm about you sometimes."

"Well, I thought you'd be keen to get to know each other, now that you're alone."

"We're not alone," Pete said. "You're still here."

Carrie was somewhat mortified by the sibling banter.

"Sorry." Pete leaned over toward her and whispered. "We Brookers get carried away sometimes."

"She's a Brooker too, now, don't forget," Megan announced from the front.

"Thank you, Megan. You've got supersonic hearing."

"Leave them alone," Cam said again.

Carrie was glad when they pulled into the set-down area outside the five-star hotel. She began to open the door.

"Hold on a tick," Pete said and hurried out of his own door and around to help her out of the car.

"This chivalry thing probably won't last forever," Megan said, smiling at them through her wound-down front window. "Make the most of it while you can."

Cam got the two suitcases from the boot of his car and set them on the footpath.

"Have a great time, both of you," he said. He shook Pete's hand and then gave her a kiss on the cheek.

"Mum is going to be impossible to live with after this," Megan said. "Three for three. We'll never hear the end of it."

Pete leaned over toward his sister and gave her a kiss on the cheek, through the car window. "You put your fair share into the meddling too, Megs."

"And I'm proud of it," she smiled at her brother. "You two will be perfect together." She gave Carrie a wink, smiled at her and waved as Cam pulled the car away from the curb.

Pete turned back to Carrie.

"Three for three?" she asked.

"Long story. This wasn't Mum's first rodeo."

"She arranged your sister's marriages too?"

"No. But she set them up. They managed to do romance and proposal on their own. I'm so sorry about that."

Carrie laughed. "I'm sorry about Ellen and Amanda. Between the lot of them they've been having the time of their life, meddling and plotting and planning."

"Are you unhappy?"

"No." Carrie replied. "A little anxious maybe, but not unhappy."

"Don't forget, as of today, the meddling stops."

"You have more confidence in them than I do," Carrie said.

Pete picked up the two suitcases. "Let's check into our room, have a drink, and take some time to catch our breath."

"Yes, lets."

***

Talk about an assault on her emotions. Stressed, excited, awkward, happy, scared, worried, eager, impatient, shy, anxious, overwhelmed. Yup. She felt it all, every single emotion, all at once. And she, an education professional, responsible for the learning of some four hundred individuals. Yet here she was with no clue as to what she should do next.

"You OK?" Pete turned to her after checking in and receiving their room key. All Carrie could do was nod.

She was like a deer in the headlights. Say something. But it was no use scolding herself. Her words had dried up. If Amanda could have seen her now she would pull her aside and give her a good talking to.

Pete took hold of his suitcase and was going to reach for hers as well.

"It's OK. I can manage." Finally. Words. But did she sound too harsh? Perhaps he thought she was one of those independent women who resents a man who opens doors and carries bags. "I'm sorry," she said. "I should say thank you, but it will be easier for you to open doors if you have a hand free."

Pete gave a short laugh and shrugged his shoulders. It was obvious he was nervous too. Should she say something to put him at ease?

Carrie worried over this all the way to the lifts, while they rode to the tenth floor, and until he'd opened the door to their room with the key card.

"Pete." She had followed him into the room and let the door shut behind her. He stopped in the small cramped entryway, turned and looked at her. "This is incredibly awkward."

"It is a bit," he said.

"Do you want me to get another room?"

Pete frowned. "I mean, I don't want to force you into something you don't want to do."

"What, like marriage?"

"Are you worried you've made a mistake?" Pete said. Carrie could hear the anxiety in his tone.

"No."

Pete held her eyes in a stare for several long moments.

"No, honestly," Carrie said. "I'm happy I made this decision, it's just ..."

"You know I was jilted the day before my wedding—my last planned wedding."

"Yes, I know."

"I've been an emotional head case this last week—scared you'd back out."

"I'm not going to back out." Carrie watched his face closely again. Was that a shade of relief? "I guess I'm just not sure what should happen next."

"Well, while I'm sure you must have heard from my sisters that they have a breeding schedule set up, I'd be just as happy if we settled into our room, changed into something a little less formal, and had a drink together. Once we've accomplished that, perhaps we can plan what happens next."

The shock must have registered on her face, as Pete backtracked.

"I'm sorry, I shouldn't have said breeding schedule."

There it was. He'd said it again. "What do you Brookers talk about at the dinner table?" She hoped to lighten the atmosphere.

"Do you honestly want to know?"

Carrie took a deep breath. "I just said 'I do'. I guess I'd better find out the worst up front."

Pete smiled. "Let's get changed first, and then I'll let you in on the inner workings of my mother and sisters' minds."

Pete had lifted his suitcase onto the luggage rack and then reached over to take hers. There wasn't a second rack, so he put it on top of the small sofa that was in the room.

"Do you want to take a shower, or just get changed? I can order some room service."

"Believe me, my zealous bridesmaids made sure I was well and truly showered this morning. I'll just get changed."

"Do you want me to order up some food?"

"Honestly, I think I'm too nervous to eat."

"Wine? Champagne?"

"Champagne would have me under the table in about ten minutes. I wouldn't mind a nice red though."

Pete nodded and went over to the phone to make the call.

Carrie unzipped her suitcase to retrieve something to get changed into but was stunned by what she found. She quickly lifted a few bits and pieces, desperately hoping to find what she was looking for, but it wasn't there. No jeans, no t-shirts, no casual skirt or top. She swallowed back a lump of nerves in her throat and slammed the lid of the case shut again. She turned around and looked at Pete. He'd just put the phone down and saw her.

"What's wrong? You look like you've seen a ghost."

Carrie shook her head and bit her lip.

"Is everything all right?" Pete asked.

Carrie felt her eyes fill with tears and was chagrined to find all the emotion of the day had got the better of her. She stared at Pete. He was her husband but he was close to a stranger. Amanda had pulled an outrageous prank, and she had no idea what to do next. She did the only thing she could think of in the circumstances. Fled to the bathroom.

***

Pete was stunned when Carrie ran from the room and closed the bathroom door behind her. What had he done? Well other than the obvious. Married her on the strength of a matchmaking program. That was fairly outrageous. But they all assured him they'd worked out the details. It was all agreed. Pete was stumped. His entire family had said Carrie was an emotionally stable, sensible woman. Reliable, responsible, pragmatic. What was this? Bursting into tears and running to hide in the bathroom. Was it just him? Perhaps he had this effect on women. Collette had run, so had others in the past. He took a deep breath and decided that jumping to conclusions was not the best course on his wedding day.

He loosened his tie, shrugged out of his jacket, and unzipped his case. He had some casual clothes there and thought it best he change quickly before Carrie re-emerged. They were too uncertain of each other to be completely natural in each other's company just yet.

Once he was in his jeans and t-shirt, he went to the bathroom door and knocked lightly.

"Carrie, are you OK? Is there anything I can do to help?"

Carrie opened the door and stood looking up at him, her eyes wide and an unidentifiable emotion shining there. He thought it looked like terror.

"I'm not going to hurt you," he said. "Let's just have a drink and talk together for a while. Get to know one another."

Carrie nodded and emerged. She was still in her beautiful formal gown.

"Did you want to get changed? I can go into the bathroom if you're shy about it."

"Pete, I'm not really a silly emotional woman but Amanda has pulled the most ridiculous stunt. I feel so embarrassed."

"What do you mean?"

Carrie went over to her case and lifted the lid. She took a moment to look and then slammed it shut again.

"Has she filled your case with confetti or something?"

"Worse."

"What could be worse than confetti?"

"I had sensible, modest, casual clothes packed for this entire week …"

"And?"

"I feel really embarrassed."

"Can I see?"

Carrie shook her head.

"What's in the bag?"

She sighed heavily and turned around, opened the lid and began to pull several things out. Pete felt his mouth go dry. She held up about three outfits, none of which would be useful outside the bedroom. See-through, low cut, revealing and provocative lingerie.

"She left my toiletries bag, hair dryer, and towel, but she's taken out anything sensible to wear. It's like she thinks …"

"She's re-packed your bag to suit the activity."

"I'm sorry, Pete. I told you she has some crazy ideas."

"Don't worry about it. We'll stop in at a shopping mall tomorrow and grab some sensible clothes before we fly out."

"What about tonight?"

Pete went to his case and pulled out a t-shirt.

"Given our difference in size, I'd say this should probably serve as a safe night dress."

Carrie came across the room and took it from him. "Thanks," she said. She went into the bathroom. Pete wanted to offer to help undo the dress, being as it had pearl buttons right from top to waist, but he didn't have the confidence. Right now he had a job trying to erase the sight of the lingerie from his mind. He wasn't sure if he wanted to thank Amanda or not.

A few moments passed and the bathroom door cracked open again.

"Would you mind helping me with my buttons?"

Pete nodded. It was sensible. She was his wife. Then why did he feel like an awkward schoolboy as his large fingers fumbled with the pearl buttons. The dress opened at the back and he could see her nicely shaped shoulders tapering down to her waist. She held the dress up at the front and he backed up to the bathroom door.

"Is that all you need?" he asked.

"For the moment."

Pete went out just as room service knocked on the door. Thank goodness. His mind had taken off and was about to launch into orbit.

He needed the activity of signing the docket for the delivery, just to drag him back to earth.

He took the wine bottle and glasses and set them up on the table. He'd also ordered some fruit and cheese. He didn't want to get all lightheaded with only alcohol and no food in his stomach. Then he laughed. Who needed alcohol to get lightheaded?

Carrie crept back into the room. She was gorgeous. His t-shirt reached to just above her knees. It was loose and gave no indication of her shape, but he knew. Her finely toned legs were evidence enough. But he didn't stare. She was obviously anxious enough without him sexualising the occasion. Who was he kidding? Amanda had done that for him already. Still, that was not what he'd planned on his schedule, not for tonight anyway.

"Do you feel better now?"

"I'd feel a lot better if I had proper clothes."

"There's the hotel robe in the wardrobe if you want." He walked across and fetched the terry-towelling robe from the hanger.

"Thanks." Carrie allowed him to hold it while she shrugged into it. It was way too big for her, and her body was completely hidden now. He still knew.

"I got some fruit and cheese as well as wine. Better to have something in your stomach if you're going to drink."

Carrie nodded.

"So do you want to hear about my family and their dinner table conversations?"

"I think I better."

Carrie took the glass of red Pete held out to her and began to sip.

***

Carrie knew the wine would make her relax. It was nearly two o'clock in the morning before she realized they'd been sitting and talking easily for nearly four hours. The fruit was gone, and half the cheese as well.

"I guess we should …" She stopped short. We should go to sleep. That should be easy enough to say. No need for this awkwardness.

Pete stood up from the small table and suddenly Carrie was very aware of him, not just as a friend laughing and chatting together, but as a man. Her husband. On their wedding night.

"It's a bit awkward, isn't it?" Pete said.

"A bit."

"Good job we have a king-sized bed."

Carrie nodded.

"Do you mind if I give you a hug goodnight?"

Carrie also stood up. She wanted to hug him, but it still felt strange, especially considering her face only came up to his pectoral muscles. He stepped closer and took her in his arms. She turned her face sideways and could hear his heart thumping in his chest. He was very tall—or was it that she was very short? Probably a bit of both. Whatever, there was no danger of her face being anywhere near his— no looking directly into his eyes, or seeing him look at her lips. She felt warm and safe with her arms about his waist. Then she felt a kiss pressed on the top of her head.

"Goodnight, Carrie. Thank you for today."

Carrie leaned back and looked up. The distance could be closed between them if he craned his neck down and she stood on tip toes and reached her face up. But she didn't. Too soon.

"Goodnight, Pete."

He let go and went into the bathroom. This was her cue to dispense with the robe and jump into bed, quickly before he returned.

Chapter Fifteen

Pete checked the clock when he woke up. True to his usual form, it was 6am. He woke this time every morning with or without an alarm. But he'd only got to sleep at 3am and he'd expected to sleep longer. He carefully rolled over to observe his bride. She was carefully placed on the other side of the king-sized bed—no danger of touching accidentally. He would like to touch her on purpose, but that wasn't within the rules at present, so he just watched her in the dim light coming in from behind the curtains. Her curly hair was barely restrained by a hair tie. She appeared happy in her sleep—a natural beauty. It was her look, apparently. Make-up was a hastily applied necessity for work, so she'd told him. The glamour look Amanda had insisted on for the wedding was not her usual style.

Thinking of Amanda, Pete remembered the prank she'd played on her best friend. Fancy leaving her with only naughty lingerie to wear on her honeymoon. Poor Carrie had been so embarrassed, and now all she had to wear was his t-shirt. It was a good job they weren't ensconced on some luxury resort on a deserted island—on the other hand …

Pete rolled carefully out of bed. He didn't want to wake Carrie so early. He grabbed his jeans from the chair where he'd tossed them and went into the bathroom.

***

Carrie heard the shower as she woke up. She rolled over to glance at her watch on the bedside table. 6.30am. Why was he awake so early? They didn't need to be at the airport until eleven. She decided to close her eyes and try to catch up on some lost sleep. But she was still awake when Pete emerged from the bathroom. She opened her eyes to observe him. His hair was wet and ruffled, and he only had his jeans on. He was cut with abs and pecs to die for. For a moment Carrie felt guilty, but then decided she had no need to be. He was her husband.

"Hey, you're awake." Pete spoke to her, once he'd pulled his t-shirt over his head.

Carrie felt the blood rise to her face as he caught her ogling him.

"Sorry, I didn't mean to wake you."

"That's OK," she said.

"I'm always up at six. I couldn't go back to sleep, so I thought I'd get an early start and see if I could get into the mall as soon as the shops open."

"Don't you want me to come with you?"

"You want to go shopping wearing my t-shirt?"

Carrie flushed again.

"I'll just grab you something to wear on the flight, and we can go shopping together once we get to the Gold Coast."

"I could send a demanding text to Amanda and have her drop my things to the hotel before we check out."

"If you like. Do you think she will?"

Carrie thought about it for a moment. Amanda had some kinky ideas and probably thought she was helping her relationship with Pete along.

"I'll text her."

"I'll get you something just in case."

Carrie began to pull herself up on her elbow.

"Don't get up," Pete said. "Try and make up for the late night. I'll go out and see what shops are around and go into the first one that opens."

"I'm sorry to put you to that trouble."

"No trouble. I just need your size, if you don't mind sharing."

"I'd have thought Ellen would have included that in my file."

Pete grinned at her. "No, I think she was trying to camouflage the height difference."

Carrie did sit up now and carefully dropped her legs over the side of the bed. "Do you mind the height difference?" she asked.

Pete came over to her, held out his hand and got her to stand up. "Let me see." He stared down at her and she tilted her head up towards him. "You are a little short, but I think we could make it work. Do you want to try?"

"Try what?"

"Kissing."

Carrie couldn't help the rush of feelings that went through her. Did he have any idea what he was doing to her?

"Well?"

Carrie stood on tip toes and reached her arms as far as she could and only just reached the back of his neck. He leaned down and met her lips with a warm kiss. They lingered for a few delicious moments, and then he stood up straight again. Carrie still had to crane her neck to watch for his reaction.

"Well?" she mimicked him.

"I think it will work out fine."

"Especially if I get some clothes to wear."

Pete smiled at her and raised his eyebrows. Carrie felt the heat again.

"You blush very prettily," Pete said.

"You tease mercilessly."

"I'm sorry." He leaned down and kissed her again, quickly this time. "What size should I shop for?"

***

Amanda didn't answer the text so Carrie decided to call her.

"Why are you calling me? It's only seven, and you are supposed to be on your honeymoon."

"Amanda Keenan, you are the giddy limit!"

"Did you have fun?"

"You better have my clothes here at the hotel before checkout time. I've never been so embarrassed in my whole life."

"Oh, come on Carrie. Don't tell me you didn't …"

"Stop! I am not going to discuss this with you. Just bring me my clothes."

Amanda went quiet. Carrie knew she had used her acting-principal tone. She let out a sigh.

"I know you meant well," Carrie said. "But you could have left me my other stuff. At least then I would not have had to wear his t-shirt to bed."

"T-shirt? What about the other outfits?"

"Amanda, this is really awkward. Pete and I are just getting to know each other. I don't have any plans to seduce him at this stage."

"Maybe later?"

"I won't be discussing it with you in either case."

"Carrie …"

"Amanda."

Silence.

"Thank you for your thoughts," Carrie said. "Pete and I will get to know each other, and I'll give you a report when we get back, but first, please bring me my clothes."

***

Pete was aware he appeared out of place in the mall dress shop, but he had shopped with Collette and Rianne in the past. He knew how it worked. He chose a pretty print sundress and picked up a pair of slip on sandals. It was forecast for hot weather, and he didn't think Carrie would need anything else. Hopefully Amanda would return her other things before they flew out.

He knocked at the hotel room door, even though he had a keycard. He didn't want to burst in on her if she wasn't ready for him.

"I thought you had a keycard," Carrie said when she opened the door.

"Didn't want to catch you unawares." He held out the shopping bag for her. "I hope it fits."

Carrie smiled at him as she took the bag. "I can't believe we've been married five minutes and already you're out shopping for me."

"Desperate times call for desperate measures."

He followed her into the room and watched as she took the dress from the bag.

"I hope you like dresses." He had a few moments of uncertainty as she held it up to examine it. "Do you like it?"

She held it up against herself and turned to look at him.

"I'm not a great fashion person. How do you think it looks?"

"So far—great. Try it on." He noticed she hesitated. Still not familiar enough. "I've got to … Um, I can go …"

"I'll go into the bathroom," she said. "We'll sort this out soon."

Pete watched her go into the bathroom and waited. It only took a few minutes and she emerged with the floral patterned, 1950s style dress on.

"What do you think?" she asked.

"Fantastic. Good choice, if I do say so myself." He was pleased to see a huge smile on her face. "Do you want to go down for breakfast?"

"Just give me a few minutes to sort out my hair—and I guess I should do my makeup."

He let her go back into the bathroom. He wasn't an expert in fashion either, and would not normally have thought about it. Now that he was thinking about it, he supposed he should see if his hair was up to standard. He usually went to work with the rolled-out-of-bed appearance. Max didn't care. No-one ever said anything about it. He checked in the mirror on the wall and ran his fingers through his hair. Chloe and Megan had insisted on putting product in his hair yesterday. They'd fussed over him beyond what he thought was necessary, but it was his wedding day. There would be photographs.

The bathroom door opened and Carrie emerged. She looked wonderful.

"OK, I'm ready," she said.

Pete held out his hand. "Let's eat."

With her hand firmly held in his, they walked out into the hallway and set off to eat their first breakfast together.

Chapter Sixteen

Carrie's clothes arrived at the hotel before they checked out. Amanda had left them at reception and fled the scene, apparently avoiding any danger of meeting her outraged friend. When Carrie got the phone call to say a package had arrived for her, Pete laughed with her about the prank and that was the end of it.

They took a taxi to the airport, got the flight to Coolangatta without any drama, and arrived at the resort on the Gold Coast. By the time they'd booked in to this room, Carrie was feeling a lot more confident. Pete was easy to talk to and, just as Ellen had said, they shared a lot in common. It was nearing dinner time by the time they'd settled in, so they found a restaurant and sat down to eat together.

"Are you feeling better?" Pete asked Carrie, as she sipped her water.

She nodded and smiled.

"Do you think we should let the family know?"

"Know what?" Carrie asked. "That we've decided to make a go of it?"

"I thought that was settled before the wedding?"

Carrie sensed Pete was worried by the comment. "Sorry, I was only kidding. Yes, it was settled, and yes, I'm feeling good about it now. I think the family did a good job of matchmaking. What do you think?"

Pete nodded, finishing his mouthful of entrée. Swallowing, he eventually answered. "I think they did a cracking job, but I'm not sure I want to tell my family that just yet."

"Why not? They're probably anxious about how we're getting on together."

"Yes, but if I tell them we fit like hand in a glove, they will gloat, and I'll never hear the end of it."

"Did you doubt their judgement?"

"Didn't you? Weren't you worried about leaving a decision like this to your family?"

"Actually, Ellen had got all the groundwork done before she even told me. I was blissfully unaware of all the clandestine meetings. Did you know what your mother was up to?"

Pete nodded. Carrie held his gaze. She wanted more information.

"I was at rock bottom—felt like such a loser after … you know, the failed engagement."

"So whose idea was it to arrange a marriage?"

"My mother came up with the crazy idea. She writes romance novels and is used to manipulating characters to do whatever she wants."

"Did she ask you if you were OK with her using you as a character in her romance story?"

"She asked, but I didn't give it any serious thought at first. Then I figured it would amuse her and it would get her off my back. I didn't think she would ever find anyone who'd be silly enough to answer her ad. I made the criteria almost impossible to meet."

"And yet, my sister thought it was just the plot to enter me into. And apparently, I met the impossible criteria."

"Except the height detail."

Carrie frowned at him. "Is it still a big deal to you?"

Pete nearly choked on his water. He reached across the table and took her hand. "Sorry, I shouldn't have said that. I don't care about height. Especially not now that I've met you. I couldn't imagine you being any taller than you are, and really, you're perfect."

"I think it would be kinder if we let the folks know we're OK, and so far so good. I'm guessing they won't rest easy wondering how it's going between us, knowing they're responsible for setting us up."

"You're probably right. But that's all I want to tell them."

"What?"

"So far so good."

"Not that we're perfect for each other."

Pete shook his head.

"Or that we're having a fabulous time."

"Not that either."

"Even though I think it's true—well for me, anyway."

"I've done it again, haven't I?" Pete looked worried. "Sorry. Yes, I think we're perfect for each other, and I'm having a fabulous time, I just want to let them stew for a bit."

Carrie laughed. "I guess so. Especially Amanda. She wants all sorts of intimate details."

Pete raised his eyebrows.

"I'm not going to tell her, don't worry."

"There isn't anything to tell—"

"Yet." Carrie smiled at him. "This is only our first day."

Pete stood up from the table and reached out for her hand.

"Mrs Brooker, you're killing me. Let's go for a walk along the beach."

***

Pete loved having Carrie's hand in his, their fingers laced together, as they walked along the water's edge. The sun had gone down, but the light from the moon and the cityscape behind them was enough for them to see where they were going. It was a warm night and the cool water lapping at their feet was refreshing.

"I guess we should head back," Carrie said.

"You don't want to go for a swim?" Pete asked.

"Too dark for swimming. No lifeguards, can't see what's in the water."

"It's not too dark for getting wet."

"Don't you dare." Carrie pulled away from him and began to back up towards the dry sand, but Pete lunged after her and caught her hand. He pulled her towards the water. Carrie screamed like a young girl, but Pete wasn't alarmed. She was laughing as well and pulling against him in a tug of war. It wasn't long and she had changed tack and charged toward instead of away from him. He was caught off balance and fell back into the shallow surf. But he wasn't going to go down alone. He still had hold of her hand and pulled her in after him.

Together, they emerged from the water. Carrie was laughing and wiping wet hair from her face.

"So you want to play?" she said.

Pete looked at her in the dim light. They were still standing knee deep in the water.

"If it were daylight, I'd take you out and throw you in some deep water."

"You think?"

Pete rushed at her and grabbed her around the waist. She screamed again and started to slap at him. He had picked her up and was dangling her above the water as if to drop her in completely.

"Now what do you think?" he asked.

"I think you are taking advantage, using your superior height and strength against me."

If it wasn't that he could see her smiling face and hear the laughter in her voice, he might have taken her seriously and apologized, but he could tell she was enjoying the game. He faked and pretended to drop her in the water. She screamed again.

"Easily scared, aren't you?" he said, as he settled her in his arms. She threw her arms around his neck like a frightened cat avoiding water.

"You'd better be careful, Mr Brooker. I might be shorter than you, but I will attack when you least expect it."

This time Pete laughed. "I look forward to it."

"So you say now. Just you wait."

Pete hefted her again to balance her in his arms as he waded back to dry land. Unlike when they walked side by side, now her face was close to his. Her arms around his neck, her breath on his cheek. This proximity was nice, but it was also tempting. He didn't know if she was ready for that sort of physical interaction yet. As much as he would like to have pursued the urge to kiss her, he dumped her on the sand instead.

"I guess we'd best get back and into some dry clothes," he said.

***

Carrie missed his closeness the moment he set her down. She had wanted him to kiss her, but he hadn't. Now, as they headed back in the direction of their resort, she longed for him to take her hand again, but he didn't do that either. She felt insecure. One moment they were laughing, the next there was a surge of emotion between them, and the next they were apart and walking in silence towards their room. She wanted to ask but didn't have the confidence, so she didn't.

Once they were inside, Carrie went to the bathroom first. "I'll need to wash the salt out of my hair. Are you sure you don't want to use the bathroom before me?"

"No, you go first. I'll flick through the sports channel for a bit."

Carrie hurried the shampoo and conditioner. She didn't want to make him wait too long as he would be uncomfortable in his wet clothes. After having wrapped her wet hair in a towel, she shrugged into the robe and cinched it tight around her waist.

"Bathroom's free. I'll get dressed out here while you shower."

Pete stood up from the couch. He'd shed his wet t-shirt and Carrie couldn't help looking at his bare chest. With a great effort, she tore her eyes away from him as he went to the bathroom.

Once she could hear the water running, she felt free to find something dry to wear. She went through her clothes, returned by Amanda, but wasn't satisfied with any of them. It was getting late and she was tired, so she decided to get into her pajamas. The water had stopped running already. She was frazzled trying to find the pajamas she'd originally packed, but they weren't there.

Amanda Keenan. You are the giddy limit. She could almost hear her friend say, "You said clothes. You didn't say anything about pajamas."

Carrie didn't have time to figure out what else to do. She grabbed Pete's t-shirt that she'd worn to bed last night and pulled it over her head. There was no time to put the robe back over the top before he re-entered the room.

"I hope you don't mind me using your t-shirt again," she said.

Pete looked her up and down. "I don't mind. Did Amanda hi-jack your pjs?"

Carrie felt her face flush. She nodded. "I can't control her once she gets an idea in her mind."

"I quoted for an extension on her house, remember?"

Carrie laughed. "I forgot. So you know what I'm dealing with here."

Pete smiled. "I like the way it looks on you anyway."

Carrie felt self-conscious, but didn't say anything. She simply picked up her hair-brush and dryer and went back into the bathroom to dry her hair.

***

Pete propped himself up against the headboard of the bed and was flicking through the TV channels, but he didn't land on any one program. He wasn't interested in TV. All he could think of was Carrie. How it had felt when she was in his arms with her arms about his neck. How she looked in his t-shirt. How easy she was to be with. And even if Amanda's special gift to them never made it from the bottom of the suitcase, it had done its job. He was physically stirred—not that he'd needed the lingerie to do that, but it had helped his thinking along that path. He heard the sound of the hairdryer coming from the bathroom and wondered how long he had to pull himself together. Was it too early to become intimate? Then he reproached himself. I told her I was emotionally absent; that I didn't have the capacity to love at the moment, and yet here I am thinking about sex. He was a man of the world—well not really, but he figured that a man of the world wouldn't much care if there was no real love involved. But this wasn't a one-night stand. This was marriage and he had plans to make this marriage last a lifetime. Yes, it was too early. It wasn't fair to Carrie to just use her because he was physically stirred. He needed to give her time to know him, to trust him, to want to be intimate with him. He threw the remote control on the bed and leaned forward, pushing his fingers into his hair and gripping hold with frustration. This was going to be harder than he'd imagined.

"Are you OK?"

He hadn't noticed that the hairdryer had stopped, and was surprised by her coming back into the room.

"Yeah. Sorry. I was just thinking about some things."

"Were you thinking about us, you know, being married?"

"Yeah."

Carrie didn't move, and it took a moment for Pete to realize she had stalled and was just staring at him. She was worried.

"It's OK. All good things." He hurried to reassure her.

"Then why were you looking so ..."

"So ...?"

"So troubled?"

Pete got up from the bed and came around to stand in front of her.

"I'm not troubled—well maybe a little troubled."

"Is it me?"

"No! Well, yes, but not really."

"You're not making any sense."

"I know. Don't worry about it. It's just me in my emotionally disconnected state."

Carrie didn't appear to be reassured and she walked past him and pulled back the sheets on her side of the bed.

"Carrie, I'm sorry. I'm just trying to figure out how fast is too fast, or what pace we should take things."

Carrie had gotten in the bed and pulled the sheets over her knees.

"I thought we decided just to let things happen naturally."

Naturally! If you knew what was on my mind ... But he didn't say that. He just nodded and returned to the bed, getting in his side.

"Do you want to watch TV?" he asked.

"Not really."

"OK." Pete switched off the set, and lay back against the pillows that were stacked up behind him.

"Are you tired?"

Carrie nodded.

Pete was disappointed.

He turned the light out and lay down fully. Carrie also turned her light out and lay down.

***

Just say it, Carrie.

She could almost hear Ellen and Amanda giving her advice. She wanted to talk. No, she didn't want to talk, she wanted to move into his embrace—to cuddle and kiss and whatever else happened naturally. But he seemed disconnected. Was that the problem, or was there something else? They should talk about it. But he'd turned the light out and now he was lying down under the sheets. She could see he was lying on his back staring at the ceiling. The dim light coming from various standby lights gave her enough vision to see him in the dark. She gritted her teeth for a bit, tossing ideas around in her mind. She knew what she wanted but didn't know if she had the confidence to bring it up. And he had stopped leading. Why? *That's it! I'm going to ask.*

"Pete?"

She saw him turn towards her. "Yeah. You all right?"

"Not really."

"I'm sorry." Carrie could hear the insecurity in his tone.

"No, I'm all right. I just want to talk ..."

She stalled. How to say it?

"About ...?"

"I don't know exactly what. I just think ..."

She stalled again.

"Just think what?"

Why can't he read my mind? This is too hard to say out loud.

"Carrie?"

"I just think we should, you know, get closer together in the bed."

Closer together in the bed? Did that sound lame? But apparently not so lame that Pete didn't understand. Before she knew it, he was right next to her having crossed the great divide that exists in a king-sized bed. Then it happened, naturally. She moved so she allowed his arms to go around her and she was leaning against his chest. She could hear his heart beating strongly in his chest.

"Is that better?" he asked.

"A little."

"You have any other plans?"

"I think it would be better if you would kiss me a little bit." Where did this boldness come from? It didn't matter, he responded. More manoeuvring so she could find his lips and he hers. The kiss was warm and soft. Then as if someone had changed gears, it became more passionate and demanding. Then hands began to move. His and hers. Wow, that was fast.

"Are you OK with this?" Pete asked.

Carrie nodded. "There's just one thing."

"Your wish is my command."

"I'm thinking we should dispense with these t-shirts."

Chapter Seventeen

So that was how things worked naturally. Sometimes there was too much discussion and one just needed to get on with it. Carrie couldn't stop the well of feeling that kept overflowing. She didn't know if Pete loved her, or even if she loved him—in that long term, deep way that lasted a lifetime of ups and downs—but she knew they were enjoying each other. Still the text message sent home said 'so far, so good'. She didn't want to include any detail of what that actually meant, but there was no doubt about it. For the last few days, even in an emotionally uncertain state, passion could be fun, and they were having fun.

"How do you want to spend our last day away together?" Pete asked her over breakfast.

In bed. Carrie smiled as the thought crossed her mind, but she didn't say it out loud.

"What?" Pete asked.

"Never mind."

"I want to know."

"I'm sure you do, but I don't know that it's the right answer."

Pete held her gaze and placed his hand over her hand that was resting beside her plate.

"Have you had a good time?"

"You can't tell?"

Pete smiled. "I just wondered if we've been a bit remiss not having gone out to see the sights, or gone to the theme parks or something."

"You're more exciting than a theme park, Pete Brooker, and I don't mind saying so."

He grinned.

"So what do you want to do today?"

Carrie gave a seductive smile that would have made Amanda blush.

"OK. That's settled then."

Pete stood up and held out his hand to her. She took it and together they went to pay the bill. Then they walked back to their room, his arm about her shoulders, her arm about his waist.

"What are you going to tell your mother and sisters when we get back?" Carrie asked.

"What are you going to tell yours?"

"Good job!"

Pete laughed. "Yes, I have to admit they did a good job and I'm a pretty satisfied test case."

"We have to get back to the real world tomorrow and they say that's when the rubber hits the road."

"You're sure you're happy to have me move into your house?"

"Unless you want me to move into your parents' house with you."

Pete laughed. "No. Mum has had her fun. I think it's time for me to finally move on."

"I'm happy for you to look at us moving closer to your work, if you want," Carrie said.

"But that would mean a really long commute for you to your school every day."

"My contract as acting-principal is finished. They've given me a classroom position, but I'm not that tied to it. I'm happy to let it go."

Pete raised his eyebrows. "Did you want to try to find another school on our side of the city?"

"I might just move into the next phase of life, and leave teaching alone for a while."

"Next phase? As in ...?"

"Parenting."

"Wow!"

"That was on your list of non-negotiables, remember?"

"I remember. But hearing you say it ... it's almost too difficult to believe."

"Why?"

"I've wanted a family for so long now, I'd almost given up hope of it ever happening."

"But you knew I wanted the same thing?"

"Yeah, but in the past, something always occurred to stop it from happening."

"Not much stopping it now, is there?"

Pete grinned. "No. Not much."

"So you're OK with it still?"

"Sure. Of course."

"Good, because, well ..."

Pete looked at her with a fixed stare. "You couldn't be, already?"

"According to my calculations, and if my internet research informs me correctly, I could be."

"So you weren't on the pill, or anything?"

"Now I'm beginning to feel as if this is something we should have discussed, but I thought ... I mean, you said ..."

"Yeah, I said that was what I wanted. Well, at least I had written it on the list. But I wasn't really serious when I wrote it. I'd thought it would be a deterrent, actually."

Carrie felt a rush of panic. "I thought you were serious. I'm sorry, I didn't—"

"No need to be sorry. I knew it was on the list. It is something I want—we both want—so sooner better than later, right?"

"I just suddenly thought that it might not be OK with you, like I should have taken precautions."

"That responsibility lies with both of us. Don't worry about it. Now that I think about it, I'm kind of stoked with the idea."

"Well, I can't say that I am pregnant at the moment, but all the conditions are right."

"This will have my mother and sisters in a fit. A honeymoon pregnancy. They'll go on about it forever."

"Are you sure you don't mind?"

"About you? No, it's really cool. About my family—well. Let's just see how it turns out."

***

"So, looks like the honeymoon went well." This was Max's comment when Pete sat down to smoko the first morning back at work.

"What makes you say that?" Pete asked.

"You look happy and you keep whistling."

Pete grinned. "Well, if you must know, I had a great time."

Max smiled. "Do I want details?"

"No, you do not, and I wouldn't give them to you anyway. You're too young."

Max laughed and got up to return to the tools. "I could probably give *you* tips and pointers," he said.

I daresay. Pete didn't bother to reply. Now that Max had bought it to his attention, he took stock of how he was feeling. He caught himself smiling and realized the smile was coming from deep within. He wasn't as emotionally disconnected as he'd maintained. There were definite signs of being madly in love, and no danger of her backing out. They were well and truly moved in together and he was yet to have an argument. Even with his having to get up at 5.30am to be able to drive the hour and a half to his work each morning hadn't dulled his sense of happiness.

"I'm worried about you," Carrie said, after they'd finished eating dinner, two nights later.

"Why? I'm great."

"But you go to bed so early and have to leave so early each morning."

He looked at the clock on the wall. It was 7.30pm and he was already fixing to get ready for bed.

"I don't mind too much, so long as I get enough sleep at night."

"But I miss your company."

Pete grinned at her, but she performed a sad face. It wasn't like the evil-eye Collette used to give him. There wasn't anything malicious behind it. He was fairly sure, but confirmed it by taking her in an embrace and kissing the top of her head. "I miss your company too. What shall we do on Saturday?"

Carrie moved back a little so she could look up at him. "I have lesson planning for most of the day. I hate coming into new classes with skeleton curriculum. It always means hours and hours of writing unit plans and lessons."

Pete didn't really know what she was talking about, but hugged her anyway.

"How have you been feeling?" he asked. "Any signs I should be aware of?"

He felt Carrie shake her head.

"No?" He held her back and searched her face.

"It didn't work this time."

"Oh." He couldn't believe how disappointed he felt. "I'm sorry. We can always try again."

Carrie smiled at him. "We haven't stopped trying," she said. "Perhaps we should slow it up a little."

"I have to admit, I've been feeling a bit tired." He leaned down and kissed her forehead.

"So do you think we should consider moving to your house?"

Pete cringed inside. He owned the house, having bought Collette out, but he hated it and all it represented from his past.

"It's so much closer to where you work," Carrie said.

"No." Pete shook his head. "I can't go back and live there."

"But you can't keep up this long commute."

"Tell you what. What say you sketch up a plan of your dream house, let's sell both our houses, and I'll build you one in a place that will work for both of us."

He watched Carrie process the idea, a thoughtful look on her face.

"Could you do that?" she asked.

"I'm a builder, I own my own company. I can do what I like."

"But could we afford it?"

"I don't have much of a mortgage on my house, what about this one?"

"I haven't had much to spend money on over the years so have been pouring all my savings into it. There's not a lot left to pay."

"Then, if we sell both, we should be able to afford a good-sized family home in the suburb of our choice."

Carrie smiled. "That sounds doable."

"It is. You think about it—what you think you need for a family home—let's talk about it and get the ball rolling. By the time family comes, we should be well on the way with the build."

Chapter Eighteen

"*I* want to hear all the details." This from Chloe, the moment Carrie stepped in the door of her parents-in-law's home.

"Do you think we could have a moment to say hello?" Pete asked his sister.

"You've been back for nearly two weeks, and this is the first time I've seen you. I'm dying for details." Chloe stepped past her brother and took Carrie by the arm, tugging her close as they walked the short distance from the front door to the family room. Carrie got the feeling that Chloe wanted to haul her into one of the bedrooms to begin the interrogation, but the rest of the family soon swamped them.

"So?" Louise faced her son, with hands on hips and eyebrows raised.

"So?" Pete echoed her, playing dumb. Carrie knew full well his mother wanted confirmation, or affirmation or something of the sort.

"How did it go?"

Carrie decided to put Louise out of her misery. "It went very well," Carrie said, stepping forward to kiss her mother-in-law on the cheek. "You did a brilliant job of matchmaking and we are both very appreciative of your efforts, aren't we Pete?"

She looked up at her husband and saw him roll his eyes. "We'll never hear the end of it now," he complained.

"Don't be silly," Carrie said. "If it weren't for your mother, where would you be?"

"In the spare room down the hall, feeling sorry for himself," Chloe said.

"You needn't sound so smug," Pete objected. "If I recall, you and Megan were both trying to head Mum off before she even got started."

"True." Megan jumped into the conversation. "I'm actually relieved to know that it's turned out OK."

"OK?" Louise sounded disappointed.

"Do not fear, Mother," Pete kissed her on the cheek. "It has turned out far better than I ever expected, and a much better job than I ever managed to achieve on my own. We're indebted to you."

Louise seemed pleased, and Carrie thought she even saw tears shining in her eyes.

"Yes, well, I still want details," Chloe said. "Come on Carrie. You come with me into the kitchen and tell me everything."

Everything? Carried doubted she would be so bold, but she would indulge her new sister-in-law a bit.

As Carrie helped Chloe put the finishing touches to the meal, Louise and Megan joined them in the kitchen.

"Carrie's just been telling me that her and Pete are going to be moving closer to our side of the city," Chloe said.

"That will be nice," Louise said.

"Better for Pete's work," Megan said.

"But what about the commute to your school?" Louise asked. "It will be very tiring having to travel all that distance every day."

"By the time the house is built, I'll probably finish up at my school." Carrie could feel the heat rise in her face, even as she introduced the subject.

"Will you apply for a school down this side of town?" Megan asked.

Carrie pursed her lips, trying not to smile. She couldn't bring herself to say out loud what their plans were. Suddenly, her three in-laws were looking at her as if expecting an answer that she couldn't seem to formulate. It should be a simple response, but Carrie couldn't find the words.

"What?" Chloe asked.

The blood was now heating her face so much, she felt they must notice.

"Are you ...?" Megan put her hand on her own pregnant stomach and cast her eyes towards Carrie's.

"No!" Chloe dragged the word out in a low tone that suggested disbelief. "You couldn't be pregnant already."

Carrie started to laugh and held up her hand.

"Looks like you guys had a better time than I thought," Megan said.

"Cut it out, girls," Louise said. "Let Carrie speak."

"Not pregnant yet," Carrie said, "but open to it happening, if it does."

"No contraception?" Chloe asked.

Carrie shook her head.

"Did Pete pressure you into this?"

"No. Your mother and my sister sorted this detail out before they ever introduced us."

"Yes but, for real ...?"

"It's what we both want, and we're happy to pursue it."

"So obviously, you guys got on together all right?" Megan waggled her eyebrows.

Carrie felt herself blush again.

"Oh, I'm so pleased," Louise said. "I was so worried it might not work out."

"Mother!" Chloe turned on her. "You told us you had full confidence in this plan."

"Well, I did ... do. But you know, there was always the chance that, even despite how it appeared on paper, the two of them would not ... you know ..."

"Well they did. And now they're talking about a baby, so lucky for you, it worked out."

"So far so good." Carrie smiled at them. "And even with baby aside, Pete and I got on really well. We had a lot of fun together."

"A lot of fun." Chloe raised her eyebrows again. "Perhaps I don't want details."

"I wouldn't give them to you even if you did."

The family dinner at the Brooker's proved to be an eye-opener. Pete's sisters were full on. Cam and Michael talked, but they weren't as loud as their wives. Both Megan and Chloe spoke whatever was on their mind, and the word taboo didn't seem to be in their vocabulary. Carrie watched the banter between the siblings. She had a similar relationship with Ellen. They weren't half-way through the meal before Carrie knew she felt at home here in this family.

"How have you been feeling?" Carrie asked Megan, when there was a moment to speak to her without everyone listening.

"Second trimester now. Thank goodness the morning sickness has stopped."

"Did you have it bad? I know Ellen spent most of her pregnancy fighting nausea."

"It was awful, but I realize it's normal, and not so bad that I had to stop work or anything. I can't wait until you get pregnant. Hopefully our babies will only be a few months apart, and then my little man will have a cousin to play with."

"You already know it's a boy?"

"Yes. Last scan."

Carrie felt Pete grab her hand under the table. She looked up at him, sitting next to her.

"You all right?" she asked.

He leaned down and whispered in her ear. "Did you tell them about the baby?"

She whispered back. "Nothing to tell yet, but the subject came up, and they're excited about the possibility." Carrie studied his face. He looked tense. "Are you worried about it?"

"No. It's OK. Let's talk about it after."

Carrie continued on with the discussion over the family dinner table, but something about the way Pete had asked the question worried her. She became guarded in what she said.

***

The thing was, Collette had never got on with his family. She'd thought they were too loud, had no fashion sense and were too clingy. By clingy, she meant, she couldn't see why they insisted on having a family dinner at least twice a month. She was happy to not see them at all. Christmas was enough for her. As Pete watched Carrie interact, it seemed foreign. She disappeared with his sisters and mother, and when they emerged they were talking and laughing. Carrie wasn't as loud as Chloe and Megan, but she added her fifty-cents-worth when the occasion called for it. And then he heard her discussing babies and pregnancy with Megan. He didn't know what to think. This was what he wanted—a wife who not only accepted his family, but who got on well with them. He wanted to get to know her family as well.

Then why did he feel so insecure? He was mature enough to recognize insecurity as it bit as his heels, but he didn't know why it had emerged. He felt unsettled that Carrie would be discussing babies with his sister. That was stupid. Carrie had sensed his reserve and he sensed her pulling back a bit from the conversation.

"I'm sorry if I spoke out of turn back there." Carrie was the first to speak once they got in the car to go home.

"You didn't speak out of turn," Pete replied.

"Then why ... I mean, you seemed upset."

Pete sighed.

"You were upset, weren't you?"

Pete nodded. "But I can't figure out why. It's like I'm insecure or something. Maybe I am insecure."

"Is that how you would have described yourself?"

"After my string of failed relationships, I guess there must be something wrong with me. It can't all have been the fault of someone else."

Carrie reached across and put her hand on his leg.

"There must be something. You don't seem to be the sort to be all possessive and controlling."

"That's what it seemed like, didn't it?"

Carrie shrugged.

"I'm sorry," he said. "When I heard you talking about babies with Megan, I just felt ... like you said ... possessive."

"Well, there isn't a baby, with us at least. Not yet anyway."

"I guess I'd like to be the first to know, that's all. I want to be a part of the whole process, not just someone who's there at conception and then not required anymore."

"Is that how you think I am?" Now Carrie sounded upset.

"No. Of course not ..."

"But you don't know me very well yet, do you. For all you know ..."

"Stop it, Carrie. We're getting each other upset for no reason."

"You started it."

Pete went silent. Yes, he had started it. He did feel possessive, and insecure.

They rode in silence for about twenty minutes before he spoke again.

"I'm sorry that came up and turned to custard so quickly."

He saw Carrie nod in his peripheral vision.

"Will you forgive me?"

She nodded again.

"Do you mind if I ask that you share any exciting news with me first, before my enthusiastic sisters and mother?"

Carrie turned her face towards him. "We've only known each other a few weeks, Pete, and obviously we're going to have to get to know each other better. I guess it's inevitable we will have disagreements every now and then. But I need to assure you, if anything important or exciting comes up, I will tell you first, unless ..."

"Unless what?"

"Unless you cannot be reached, and I happen to be with another family member at the time. In which case, I will ask advice, or get help, or whatever is needed, until I can get hold of you on your phone. Do you think you can manage with that?"

Pete felt that surge of possessiveness again, but pushed it down. It was reasonable. He didn't want to become controlling because of his insecurity. That would be an ugly path to go down.

"I'll try to be in phone range at all times, but if you need advice or help, and I can't be reached, then your family or mine are the next best thing."

Carrie smiled. She squeezed his knee, leaned across and kissed his cheek as he drove.

"Steady," he said. "You don't want me running off the road."

Chapter Nineteen

Carrie opened her eyes and looked up at the ceiling. The ceiling of her classroom. She was flat on her back, and she became aware that there were worried students bending over her.

"Are you all right, Ms Brooker?"

"She's fainted."

"Should someone call the school nurse?"

"Yes, of course."

"Ms Brooker?" Carrie recognised Alicia, one of her year twelve English students, patting her face softly.

"Perhaps we should roll her into the emergency position." This helpful suggestion came from another student who looked on. Carrie blinked her eyes and tried to clear her thoughts. It was time for her to take charge.

"It's all right, Alicia. I'm all right."

But she didn't move. She felt dizzy and nauseous.

"Are you sure?" Alicia sounded doubtful. "Ryan, go up to the office and bring the nurse."

Carrie wanted to object, but she heard the classroom door open and she heard the conversation of a couple of students as they left. She couldn't have gotten off the floor, even if she wanted to. Not quite yet.

How embarrassing. Carrie had never fainted in her life and to find herself in this position was not even slightly amusing. Eventually, Alicia and Ellie helped her sit up. Alicia was a born leader.

"You others go outside for a while. She doesn't need you all here gawking at her."

"Thanks, Alicia," Carrie said. "I don't know what's come over me."

"My cousin used to faint a lot just before they discovered she had a brain tumour," Ellie said.

Carrie sensed more than saw Alicia's frown of disapproval.

"I'm sorry," Ellie stammered. "I shouldn't have said that."

"It's all right," Carrie said. "I'm sure it's nothing serious."

The classroom door opened and the school nurse entered. "I've called an ambulance," she announced.

"I don't think that's necessary," Carrie said. "I'm just a bit dizzy."

"Ryan said you fell like a sack of potatoes and hit your head."

Carrie could neither confirm nor deny this piece of information. She put a hand to her head and felt it was a bit sore in one spot.

The nurse chased all the students out of the classroom and squatted down next to Carrie. "Do you have a history of epilepsy?"

"No."

"Diabetes?"

Carrie shook her head.

"Any other medical conditions we should be aware of."

"I'm hoping to get pregnant. Perhaps this might be something in that line."

The nurse pursed her lips. "Could be. Let's see what the doctor says."

"Are you sure calling an ambulance is necessary? Perhaps I should just call my husband and he can take me to the doctor's."

"Too late." As the nurse spoke the classroom door opened and Alicia showed two paramedics inside. Two young male paramedics. The embarrassment just kept rolling on.

"She may be pregnant," the nurse offered the information. "No other known medical conditions."

Carrie felt the blood rise in her face. The paramedics didn't seem too worried about her sensibilities. They were more concerned she may have suffered a concussion.

"There are no obvious signs of concussion," the first paramedic said to her, "but I think you should probably take the rest of the day off and go to the doctor to talk about any other possible causes, including pregnancy."

"No ambulance ride necessary?" the nurse asked.

"We can take you if you like," the other ambo said. "Do you have medical insurance?"

"I do, but I'd just as soon have my husband take me in."

"Do you want me to have the office call him?" the nurse asked.

"Oh, no. He'll be at work now, the other side of the city. I don't want to drag him all the way over here for nothing."

"Well, I wouldn't advise you drive until we know what caused your faint," the paramedic said. "If it was a sudden drop in blood pressure, it may happen again and I think you should see the doctor. If you don't want to call your husband, we can just as easily drop you into emergency and you can have him come pick you up."

Carrie tried to stand up and found she was still dizzy and nauseous. The paramedics helped her.

"I feel terribly embarrassed," she said.

"Don't worry about it. Given what's happened, I think it best we take you to the hospital and your husband can meet you there."

***

Pete packed up his tools and locked them into the secure toolbox on the back of his work ute. He pulled out his phone to check the time and saw there were four missed calls, two from Carrie and two from an unknown number. He checked voicemail first. The first recording had been three hours ago.

"Hi, Mr Brooker. This is Felicity Sargent from North Campus state school. Could you please call us back on this number as soon as possible?"

He saw the number recorded on missed calls. He pressed to return the call, but it went through to the answering machine. It was past five and the office was closed.

He listened to the second message from the same person.

"Hi again. Mr Brooker, you need to call as soon as you can. Your wife has been taken to hospital in an ambulance." This message was two and a half hours ago. A wave of panic ran cold through his blood. Why hadn't his phone rung?

There was no message left by Carrie, but she had called later than the woman from the school office. Surely that meant she was OK.

He threw his lunch esky into the front of the ute, got in and started the engine. He hadn't managed to pull into traffic before his phone rang again. He pressed the receive button on his steering wheel and the call went through the Bluetooth connection.

"Pete Brooker." He knew he sounded short, but he was anxious and he didn't know who was calling, as there was no caller ID on his car screen.

"Pete! Where the blazes have you been?"

It was his father.

"At work. Look, Dad, I've just had a message to say Carrie's been taken to hospital, but I'm not sure which hospital."

"That was hours ago."

"Do you know where she is?"

"City Central Private."

"Did she call you?"

"No, her sister, Ellen, called me asking me if I could try to find you."

"Is she all right? What happened?"

"Apparently she passed out in the middle of class, hit her head and was in all sorts."

"What about now? What did the doctor say?"

"You sure you want to know?"

Pete felt an icy grip in his stomach. "Tell me what the doctor said."

"She's pregnant."

Pete began to feel dizzy himself. So much so he pulled over to the side of the road.

"What? What are you saying?"

"It's fairly simple, son. Your wife, whom you've been married to all of six weeks, is pregnant. Good going."

The panic merged to shock, merged to wonder, then to panic again. And then the insecurity emerged. Why hadn't she told him? How come everyone else knew?

"I think you should call her and let her know you're on your way in."

"Of course I'm going to call her."

"There's no need to be shirty."

Pete clamped his teeth. He was being short. She had promised him she would tell him first. But his phone had not rung. Stupid phone server. He decided he would change to another carrier. Or was it that his most recent build was up in the hills, and phone reception was dicey at the best of times. Carrie had tried to call, but obviously couldn't get through to him.

"Listen, thanks Dad. I'm on my way in and I'll call her the moment I've hung up from you. The only thing is, do you mind keeping this news to yourself for a while? Until Carrie and I have had time to process and then announce it at the right time?"

"Too late. Your mother has already rung the girls. I believe they were set to go to the hospital and she had to warn them to stop at home."

Pete groaned inwardly. His family were out of control. If ever you needed something spread about the entire country, one phone call would be all it would take. His family would take care of the rest.

***

"What if Pete comes and I'm not here?" Carrie didn't want to move until she'd heard from her husband.

"We can't just sit around the emergency department forever," Ellen replied. "Let's get you home. Pete will catch up eventually."

Carrie hated that she'd been unable to talk to her husband. She'd promised him he would be the first to know. But he hadn't answered any calls. She knew it was likely the phone reception was bad.

"Come on. I need to get home to feed Lucy. You can call him again from the car."

Carrie got up and followed her sister. The doctor had given her something to help settle her stomach, and given her instructions as to what sorts of things she needed to do to avoid succumbing to a sudden drop in blood pressure again.

As soon as she was buckled in, she fished her phone out of her bag. She was just about to press call on his number when the screen lit up with his handsome smiling face. But his tone wasn't so handsome and smiling.

"Where are you?" He sounded frustrated.

"I'm with Ellen. She's driving me home."

Pete swore. He actually swore, and Carrie was shocked.

"What's that for?" she asked.

"I've just walked into Accident and Emergency, and you're not here."

"I've been there for nearly four hours this afternoon. Ellen needed to get home to feed Lucy. You haven't been reachable, so she's taking me home."

"Well, do you think you could go to our home so I might finally catch up with you? And do you think you could possibly keep any more announcements to yourself until we've had a chance to talk?"

"Pete Brooker! You know very well I would have told you everything if you'd only bothered to pick up your phone."

"You know the reception is dicey up in the hills."

"So, what did you want me to do? Sit in A and E all on my own until you finally got the message? You didn't think I should call anyone to come and help me out?"

Pete went quiet.

"Pete?" Carrie was upset with him.

"I'll meet you when you get home," he said, and then disconnected the call.

Carrie couldn't believe they'd really had such a stupid argument. He was upset with *her*. Stupid man.

"You all right?" Ellen asked.

"Yes." But despite her answer, her face crumpled and she broke down in tears.

Ellen patted her knee. "Don't worry, Hun. Men can be incredibly thick at times. It's quite normal."

Carrie nodded.

"Other than this little bluster, he's been OK, hasn't he?"

Carrie nodded again.

"Better than Kevin?"

Carrie smiled. "Pete and Kevin don't even begin to compare. I love Pete, for one thing."

Carrie saw Ellen's smile from the corner of her eye. "Do you? Do you really think you love him, even after such a short time?"

"This is nothing," Carrie said. "He's just feeling insecure – residual effects from the last relationship. He's been the best thing that's ever happened to me."

"Phew!" Ellen said. "For a minute there I was beginning to feel guilty for having answered that ad in the paper."

"Don't. It was meant to be."

"So I can take the credit then?"

Carrie grinned at her. "Yeah. You can take the credit."

Chapter Twenty

When Carrie turned the key in the front door, she was fighting all sorts of feelings. She had done research and knew her sudden fragile emotions were common when pregnant, but it wasn't like her. And Pete was upset with her. Their first major disagreement. Was it major or was he just tired and panicky?

She saw him the moment she set foot in the door. He was standing by the kitchen bench.

"How did you get here so fast?" she asked.

"What took you so long?" he asked in return.

"Ellen had to stop and pick up nappies for Lucy."

"I've been going out of my mind with worry, Carrie. Why didn't you call me?"

"I did call you, and so did the school office, apparently."

"Why didn't you keep trying?"

"Because I felt unwell, so Ellen called your dad and asked him to find you. Didn't he call?"

"Yes, but now the whole family know."

"Know what?"

"About you."

"Well, they're family. There isn't any shame in being sick and having to go to the hospital."

"But you're pregnant!"

"Yes, I know, and everyone else seems to be excited and happy about it." She glared at him. Why was he behaving this way? "I thought perhaps you might have given me a hug or a kiss, or said something to indicate that you're happy as well."

Pete didn't answer. She could see thoughts were churning in his brain.

"Well, while you take your time deciding how you'd like to respond, I think I'll go and lie down. I still don't feel very well."

She walked past Pete and into their bedroom. He still didn't say anything, and now she was angry with him. Closing the door—perhaps a little too firmly—she lay on the bed and curled up. And began to cry again. Stupid emotions.

✶✶✶

What is the matter with me?

Pete went to the cupboard and got a glass, filled it up at the tap and skulled the water in three gulps.

He felt waves of regret knowing he'd gone all territorial and aggressive. *Why did I do that? This is something I've wanted forever. Is it Carrie?*

He thought about it for a few moments and decided this had nothing to do with Carrie. He knew he was not only happy with her as a life partner, but admitted he was feeling love towards her. That emotional connection was there. Apparently, now that he was feeling again, he was also feeling other things—like worry and frustration and jealousy.

Was he jealous? Was this some innate fear that Carrie would connect with her family, her friends, his family, the baby—and just forget about him? It was such stupid thinking and Pete didn't know where it had come from. He couldn't keep blaming Collette and Rianne and Sonja. He had to take his own bad behavior on board.

But now he felt like a heel. He had given entirely the wrong response to everyone this afternoon. And he'd got a speeding ticket to add to his misdemeanors. The traffic cop hadn't been interested in his excuses. One hundred and sixty dollars later.

He took a deep breath and turned toward the closed bedroom door. He'd messed it up and he had to fix it. *You wanted to be married, man. Grow up and take responsibility.*

He took another deep breath before he got the courage to knock gently on the door. There was no answer. He knocked again.

"Carrie? Can I come in?"

Still no answer. How ticked off was she?

He opened the door and poked his head in. She was curled up on the bed, facing away from him.

"Carrie?" Perhaps she was asleep. He tiptoed across the room and sat down on the side of the bed she was facing. She was asleep. Pete felt a jolt of remorse. The happiest news he'd ever heard, and he'd acted like an idiot. He touched her face, pushing hair out of her eyes.

"I'm sorry, Carrie. Please forgive me."

He watched and saw a smile form on her lips. "Are you awake?"

Carrie didn't open her eyes. "It depends. Has that other grumpy man gone away yet?"

Pete laughed. He bent down and kissed her, albeit a crooked kiss.

"He's gone. I shoved him out the door with a good talking to."

Carrie's eyes opened. "Are you sure?"

Pete lay down on the bed next to her, placing his face just inches away facing her.

"Tell me what happened," he said. "I've missed all the drama and excitement, and I'd like to catch up."

***

There was no living with them now. His mother and sisters had swooped on Carrie the moment they'd walked in the front door, literally clucking like a bunch of mother hens. Pete rolled his eyes and went out to the back yard to find his father and brothers-in-law. Typical Aussie barbecue. Men standing around poking at chops and sausages, women in the kitchen making salads.

"So, you've joined the family-wagon, baby-seat, pram-in-the-boot club." Chloe's husband, Michael slapped Pete on the back.

Pete just glowered back.

"What's got you so grumpy?" his father asked. "I thought this was on the top of your criteria for a good wife?"

"Do you have any idea what it's like in there?" Pete waved his hand back toward the house.

"Women clucking over baby plans?" Cam said. "They've been like that ever since Megan announced she was pregnant.

"It's worse for me," Pete said.

"How could it be worse?" Cam asked.

"Mum is like she's just landed in the middle of one of her romance novels. She's got her happy ever after, and now she's having a party."

"Settle down," Dad said. "It's not that bad. Besides, I thought you got on all right with Carrie? And you were the one who's always wanted children."

Pete pulled himself up. Yes, he was being a grump for no reason.

"I guess you're right. It's just I didn't imagine I would become quite the center of attention with all that gushing and clucking."

"Here, mate. Have a beer." Cam handed him a long-necked bottle. "We don't have to talk about a family car just yet."

"Let's talk about the cricket," Michael said. "That'll take your mind off your troubles."

Pete laughed. "That is a whole new set of trouble. I can't believe how our batsmen have just collapsed."

"It's a great spin-wicket," Michael said.

"And if you're lucky, you'll have a boy and can teach him how to bat properly."

Pete looked across at his father and saw the teasing glint in his eye. He smiled. He hadn't quite been ready for all this family focus, but he guessed he should just enjoy it. If he didn't lighten up it was going to be a long nine months, because now that his mother had the bit between her teeth there would be no slowing this horse down.

Chapter Twenty-One

*C*arrie needed to take the morning off work. The hospital staff were not flexible when it came to appointments, and she had to go at the time they gave her. She couldn't wait to have this scan for two reasons. One, she would be able to empty her bladder. The whole idea that she had to drink a bucket of water, and keep her bladder full for the scan, was rather uncomfortable. But more importantly, she couldn't wait to find out the sex of her baby. She was nineteen weeks and had been feeling the little one move around inside for quite some time. Even Pete had caught movement once or twice, but not nearly as often as she felt it.

"Hey." Carrie looked up to see Pete approaching her from the main entrance of the hospital. They'd agreed to meet here, giving Pete time to set Max up on the day's tasks at the work site before slipping away. There was no way he was going to miss this appointment and Carrie was glad. She wanted to be together for this. "Are you feeling OK?" he asked.

"Can't wait to go to the loo, but otherwise, all good."

They took the lift to the second floor where radiology was situated. Pete held her hand as they went up to the reception counter.

"I'm here for a scan," Carrie said.

The nurse gave her paperwork to fill in, and they sat down in the waiting area to complete it.

"So, you think they'll be able to tell the sex in today's scan?" Pete asked.

"They should be able to," Carrie replied, as she filled in her Medicare number.

"Are you nervous?"

Carrie stopped and looked at him. "Why would I be nervous?"

"I don't know. It's a little like meeting our baby for the first time."

"I guess so, but being as this little one is with me every day, I kind of feel as if they are always there."

"Do you think it'll be a boy or a girl?"

"I don't want to guess," Carrie said. "Whatever, I already love them."

"Are you happy to name it today, once we know?"

"I think so, but I'd like to keep the name to ourselves. I'd like to have something new to announce to the family when the baby's born."

Pete nodded. "I think it will be a boy."

"Do you? Why?"

"I don't know, I guess I've always imagined having a son."

"What if it's a girl?"

Pete shrugged. "I'll be just as happy, I guess."

"So you're all set on the boy's name then?"

"Nathan Peter?" He looked uncertain, as if he was waiting for her approval.

Carrie laughed. "If it's a boy then we'll call him Nathan Peter."

Pete leaned across and kissed her.

"If you're finished filling in the forms you can go into the cubicle and change into a hospital gown." One of the nurses had approached them and now pointed the way for Carrie to go. "I'll send your partner in once you're set up for the scan."

Carrie handed the clipboard with the forms to the nurse, turned and kissed Pete again, then went to get changed.

Someone had told Carrie that having a baby helped you learn to get over your embarrassment. Medical staff were not particularly interested in your dignity, and hospital gowns were not designed for either glamour or modesty. Still, once she was set in place and the radiologist had put the squishy gel all over her abdomen, she forgot about how she was exposed, and focussed her attention on the monitor. The door of the room opened, and Pete was ushered in.

"Just in time, Dad," the radiologist said. "Are you ready to see your baby?"

"Can't wait," Pete said. He grinned at Carrie and took her hand.

Carrie was aware he was watching the screen as closely as she was.

"Here's your baby's heart." The radiologist pointed to a spot on the screen that showed the rhythmic pulse. "It's beating nice and strongly."

Carrie felt Pete squeeze her hand.

"Oh, look. She's performing for you today."

"She?" Pete asked.

"Yes, this is definitely a little girl."

Carrie looked at Pete, but there was no sign of disappointment. He smiled and kissed her cheek.

"It's a girl," he whispered near her ear.

"I know, I heard."

"It looks like she's waving to you," the radiologist said. "Hello Mummy and Daddy."

"Hello, darling," Pete said.

Carrie smiled.

After the radiologist had wiped the gel from Carrie's abdomen, Pete placed his hand over the spot where the scanner had been. "My darling girl," he said.

At that moment, the baby gave an exaggerated kick.

"Oops!" he laughed. "Was that a 'hello, Dad' or 'get off me'?"

"Definitely a 'hello, Dad,'" Carrie said.

"Do you want to name her now?" Pete asked.

Carrie nodded. The radiologist was busy writing some notes, so they turned their attention back to the baby bump.

"Hello, Charlotte Grace," Pete said.

"Yes, hello, my darling girl," Carrie added.

***

They had only just come out of the lift into the main foyer of the hospital when Pete saw his brother-in-law, Cam.

"Hey, mate," he said. "Everything all right?"

Cam smiled at him. "Just had an emergency dash to the hospital."

"Is Megan OK?" Carrie sounded worried.

"She is now. We weren't quite expecting the baby to come so soon, or so quickly."

"She's had the baby?" Pete asked.

"Nearly didn't make it in. They hadn't even got to the delivery ward and he just came out."

"Wow!" Pete felt all weak at the knees. He'd only just come from meeting his own little baby, and now was met with the news that his sister had narrowly missed delivering her child in the back of an ambulance.

"Is she up for visitors?" Carrie asked. "I'd love to see her and the baby."

Cam nodded. "She's remarkably well. The nursing staff said it was unusual for a mother to give birth so quickly for their first one, but I've a feeling she may have been in labor for half the night, but just didn't know it."

"How could she not know it?" Pete asked.

"She felt restless and uncomfortable all night. The nurses think she might be one of those who doesn't experience high levels of pain."

"Oh, I hope I'm one of those," Carrie said.

"Lead us to her," Pete said. "So you got a boy?"

Cam grinned. "Number one son for my cricket team."

"I hope he likes cricket," Carrie said.

Pete felt all manner of emotions as he followed his brother-in-law to the maternity ward. He could see how proud Cam was as a new father. He felt the same, but his little girl was still safely in her mother's womb. When he walked into the recovery ward where Megan was, he almost started to cry. His little sister was holding a tiny bundle, cradling him with such gentleness and maternal affection. This was his little sister—the pair of them had fought and teased and played together for years. And here she was, a mother.

"Well, that didn't take long," Megan said. "I sent him out to make phone calls to the family, and you're here already."

"We just had our nineteen-week scan," Carrie said.

"Oh, really? Boy or girl?"

Carrie looked at him. "It's a girl," Pete said. "And I'm very pleased whether she plays cricket or whatever she wants to do. I'm absolutely stoked."

"Congratulations," Megan said. "Come over here and have a look at my little man."

Carrie moved first and Pete followed.

"Oh, Megan, he's gorgeous," Carrie said. "What's his name?"

"Jordan Russell," Cam said.

"Do you want a hold?" Megan asked Carrie.

"Do you mind?" Carrie asked. "He's so new."

Megan held out her precious bundle and Carrie took him in her arms. Pete watched her. It made the perfect picture of maternal grace. She was beautiful, and he couldn't wait for her to hold their own child in the same way.

Chapter Twenty-Two

Charlotte stood at her window and watched as Benjamin got into the coach. His valet had strapped his trunk to the back, and had waited until the horses had drawn the vehicle down the drive and out of sight. Benjamin had gone—again. What was she to think? There were moments when he'd come to her room and she'd willingly given herself to him. But inevitably he'd withdrawn before dawn. And just as often, he left the manor altogether for several days, sometimes weeks. She guessed he'd gone to London, but they didn't usually talk about it. Did he have a mistress there? Someone more beautiful than she, and willing to meet his every carnal need? Why didn't he stay with her? Why didn't he ask her to be his companion? Charlotte felt a tear trickle down her cheek. He didn't love her. He never had and possibly never would.

"What's got you looking so down in the dumps?" Russell stood at Louise's office door.

Louise inhaled a deep breath. "Love."

"What?"

"Nothing. This pair …" she waved her hand towards her computer, "… they're not very exciting."

Russell's expression held except his eyes went from side to side as if he was searching for something intelligent to say.

"I mean, the readers want warm fuzzy feelings and passion."

"Good heavens, woman. I don't think I want to know …"

"Cut that out, Russell Brooker. You know what I mean."

"Yes, but I don't think I want to know the details."

"Stop being so prudish. I'm not talking about sex. I'm talking about love."

"And it's not the same thing?" His eyebrows were raised in her direction.

Louise smiled at him. "You know very well. Stop trying to bait me."

"That passage in Corinthians is my go-to, if I'm trying to define love," Russell said.

"I'm not trying to define love, necessarily. I'm trying to engage my readers, and at this moment—"

Russell held his hand up as he answered his phone.

"What? Yes. Of course!"

"Who is it?" Louise asked. Russell ignored her.

"Yes, we're home. I'll see you in five."

"Who was it?" Louise asked again as he disconnected the call.

"Megan's dropping by"

"Is she bringing the baby?"

"Yes. Quick. Have you got those toys we bought last week?"

Russell left her office in search of the toys. Mention the baby, Jordan, and he went gah gah. Mind you, she was also excited at the prospect of seeing their new grandson.

"Anyone home?" Megan called down the hall as she came through the front door.

Louise swallowed a sarcastic comment. The front door is open, obviously they were home. Instead she hurried to take the baby carry-cot from her.

"How's my little man?" She lifted the cot and kissed the baby on the forehead.

"Don't wake him, Mum. I've only just got him to sleep."

"How's my little man?" Russell met them in the hallway carrying a large, blue stuffed shark.

"Honestly, you two …"

"Can I hold him?" Russell asked.

"No." Megan said. "He's just got to sleep. I was wondering if you would mind him for an hour or so while I went grocery shopping?"

"Yes!"

"Of course!"

Megan laughed. "You're not busy?"

"No!" they said simultaneously.

"No work deadlines?"

"Doesn't matter, we can work later," Russell said.

Megan took the carry cot from her mother and went into the spare room. "You can work now. He will sleep for most of the time."

Megan closed the bedroom door and started back towards the front door. "Don't wake him up."

As if. The moment Megan had gone Russell went to the spare room door and tiptoed in.

"Russell," Louise whispered. "Don't wake him up." But she followed him and joined him as they stood and gazed lovingly at their first grandchild.

This was love.

***

The months had gone by quickly, and Carrie couldn't believe she had less than six weeks to go before she would be a mother. She decided to finish up her work at the school in the mid-year semester break. Pete had got on with the plans for their new house, but he was several months away from being finished. It was likely they wouldn't be able to move in until after the baby was born.

"Are you sure you don't want to move back to the other side of town?" Carrie asked him. "Now that I'm finished work, it would make so much more sense for you to be closer to everything that you have to do."

Pete was sitting on the couch, his feet on the coffee table, the remote in his hand as he was flicking channels.

"It would be sensible, but to go through all the hassle of moving just for four or five months, seems like a lot of work. Especially with you being pregnant."

"I think I'll look for a small place to rent near where our new house is being built. If I find something, I'll get the family to help move. We don't have to unpack everything if it's only temporary. Then I can get this house on the market and put the money against our loan."

Pete nodded. "I guess, if you can find something cheap enough."

Carrie levered herself up from her recliner and waddled over to the sink.

"Do you want a cup of tea?" she asked.

"No. I'd better head off to bed." Pete switched the TV off. Carrie went across to him and put her arms out for a hug.

Pete responded, but didn't hug for long before pulling back. He placed his hand on the protruding baby bump.

"It would be good if I didn't have to do so much traveling each day," he said.

Carrie nodded.

"And I guess if we keep unnecessary stuff in boxes, then it's all ready to move for when the new house is complete."

"Now that I've finished up at work, do you think you could take a couple of days to go baby shopping with me?"

Pete smiled. "You don't want to go with Ellen or your mum?"

"I'll go with them for some things, but I need you to come with me for the big things, like the cot and pram and car seat."

"All right. If you think you need me."

"I do."

Carrie reached up and put her arms around his neck.

"Are you happy?" she asked.

Pete nodded, but Carrie thought he seemed a little distant. She searched his eyes.

"Are you OK?"

"I'm just tired."

Carrie wasn't really satisfied. He had seemed tired and a bit distant lately, but then he worked long hours and it was heavy labor. She watched as he went off to bed.

She decided to get online and look up some baby stores to see what sorts of things she needed, and what they would need to budget.

***

Pete would like to have worked on the new house on Saturday and then spent Sunday afternoon at home after church, but Carrie insisted he needed to go baby shopping with her.

"Do you know exactly what you want?" he asked. He hadn't been shopping for ages. Carrie was not the sort to traipse around shopping centers just for the fun of it. Neither was he.

"I've done my research, and I'm fairly sure we can get all we want at this one major outlet for baby goods."

"So just the one shop?"

Carrie nodded.

"You don't want to go to the shopping mall and go through all the shops, just to make sure?"

Carrie frowned. "What for? That would be a huge waste of your time."

Pete smiled.

"Unless you want to go."

"What? No." Pete looked at her. "No, I hate shopping."

"I know," Carrie said. "That was written in your portfolio."

Pete laughed. "You hate shopping too, don't you?"

Carrie nodded. "I have to psyche myself up to go. Hence the internet research before we leave the house."

Pete reached across and squeezed her hand. "Do you think we can be finished in time to watch the footy?"

"Of course." Carrie looked at him. "Why do you think I suggested we leave now? You haven't had a Saturday at home for ages, and so I'm looking forward to sitting down together and watching the game."

Pete smiled again. "My mother did a good job in finding you."

"Yes, she did."

The purchase of pram, cot and car-seat was incredibly quick and easy. Carrie had done her research, and though the sales assistant tried to interest them in several different, more expensive models, Pete deferred to his wife's opinion. There didn't seem to be any value added by paying more money, so they took the ones Carrie had marked from the internet.

The phone vibrated in Pete's pocket and he took it out to see if it was an important call. It was.

"Can you finish up here?" Pete asked. "This is my supplier. I need to take this call."

"Sure," Carrie said. "I just need to choose a couple other linen pieces. I'll meet you at the cashier after."

Pete mouthed the words 'Thank you' as he held the phone to his ear. "Hey, Jeff. What's the news on that order?"

As Jeff began to talk, Pete moved to the front of the store and stood in the sunshine beaming through the front window. Business was fiddly when strategic building supplies didn't turn up on time, and Pete had quite a bit to say to his supplier.

He'd just finished the conversation when he felt a tap on his shoulder. He expected it would be Carrie, but when he turned, he lifted his gaze to the face he knew so well. Beautiful, blond, vivacious Rianne.

"I thought it was you," Rianne said, leaning in and kissing him.

Pete was flustered. She had kissed him on the mouth and it felt natural. Just like she used to. He'd been madly in love with Rianne, but she'd deferred the idea of marriage and taken a study scholarship to Germany and hadn't returned. Their relationship had disintegrated somewhere between six months to a year's absence. Pete got the message when Rianne emailed and told him about her engagement to a fellow student.

"How long have you been back in Australia?" Pete was genuinely glad to see her again. But then saw her face drop. "You all right?" he asked.

"Sorry, Pete. I'm just getting over … well, you don't want to hear about my troubles."

"Didn't you marry, while you were away?" Pete asked.

Rianne nodded, looking sad. "He passed away several months ago," she said. "Aneurism, so they told me."

"I'm so sorry." Pete didn't even hesitate to take Rianne in his arms. Out of all of his past relationships she was the one he'd been most attached to, and it was just like old times.

"Anyway …" Rianne pulled back and righted herself. "Why are you here in a baby shop?"

Pete felt the blood rise in his face. "Oh, I'm out shopping with my wife. Baby due soon."

"Oh, Pete, that's fantastic!" She reached out and pulled him into another hug, kissing him, on the cheek this time. "I heard you married Collette."

Pete shook his head and gave a short ironic laugh. "Nah. That didn't work out."

"Well, I can't say I'm surprised. I knew Collette at modelling school. I wouldn't have pegged her as the sort to be playing happy families."

"What about you?" Pete changed the subject. "Why are you in the baby store?"

"Oh, no. I was just walking past and I saw you in the window. I had to come in and say hello."

"I'm glad you did," Pete said.

"Have you got a half hour? Perhaps you and your wife could join me for a coffee. There's a lovely little cafe two doors down."

"That would be great," Pete replied. "Let me finish up here, and we'll meet you there in a little while."

Rianne hugged Pete yet again, and kissed him on the mouth, again. "I've missed you, Pete Brooker. I can't wait to catch up."

***

Carrie was pleased with herself. She had all the major items selected and ordered, and was now only looking at some cot blankets. She realized Pete would not be particularly interested in this, though he'd paid close attention to all the structural information for the baby car-seat and pram. It was better she pick the linen while he was at the front of the shop taking a call. Carrie selected a few items she had on her list and put them in the shopping trolley. It took her longer than she'd anticipated. So many choices of color and fabric to choose from. When she was finally satisfied she had everything she needed she headed towards the cashier, but was arrested by the sight of a tall, blond woman who was talking to Pete. Then, the woman threw her arms around him and kissed him—not on the cheek, but on the mouth. Carrie felt her stomach drop. She watched, hoping to see him pull back, or frown, or slap her perfectly made-up face, but he didn't. He was smiling at her. And then he kissed her on the cheek.

Oh, God. What is happening? Was this Collette? Chloe had described Collette to her. Tall, blond, ex-model. This must be her. Why was Pete responding to her like this? He was smiling after her as she left the shop. He didn't even look Carrie's way, though she was standing only a few feet away, right next to the cashier.

"Have you found everything you need?"

Carrie's attention was drawn to the sales assistant. She faked a smile and wheeled the shopping cart up to the counter.

"We've ordered several large items to be delivered." She held out the order form. "I just need to pay for them and add these to the bill."

Carrie was talking. She hoped she was making sense. But all she could think of was how Pete had been happily engaged to that other woman.

"Hey." He was now standing beside her and touched her shoulder. She wanted to shrug and slap his hand away, but she kept her eyes forward and attention on the task at hand.

"Did you find everything you wanted?" he asked.

She nodded. If she opened her mouth, she would break down entirely.

"Are you all right?"

Carrie wanted to scream at him. He sounded as if he cared. Could he sense she was upset? Stupid man. Of course she was upset. He'd just fallen into the arms of his ex-fiancée, and seemed happy about it.

Pete didn't say anything else. She completed the transaction and took the large shopping bags containing the cot linen.

"Here, I'll carry that," Pete said, lifting it out of her hands.

Fine. He could be a gentleman and act all as if nothing had happened.

She followed him out of the shop and to the car. As he flipped the boot open with his remote, Carrie went straight around to the passenger side to get in.

"Hey, Carrie. I've just arranged for us to meet a friend for coffee."

Carrie felt sick. If only she could faint now, it would really help.

"But if you don't feel well, I can tell her we can make it another time."

"I don't feel well." It wasn't really a lie. She felt sick with anxiety.

Pete nodded. He clicked the car doors unlocked. "I'll just go and apologize. I'm really sorry you can't get to meet her. I think you'd really like her."

"When I said to forgive Collette, I didn't mean invite her back into your life."

"Collette?"

"The woman you were hugging and kissing at the front of the shop."

To his credit, Pete blushed. Good. He should feel utterly ashamed of himself.

"Wait in the car. I'll be back in a few minutes."

Pete walked towards the cafe only a few meters further down the street. How was it he managed to make *her* feel guilty? She got in the car and began to cry. Truly, these pregnancy hormones could wreak havoc with emotions. It took her a few minutes to get settled. She looked at her puffed up ankles, her swollen stomach, her small hands, full of fluid, fat and tubby. She didn't have to pull the car mirror down for her to know her face was looking decidedly round. Her hair was quickly pulled back with a hair band, but it was unruly. She didn't have makeup on. Her clothes were not great to start with, and they probably looked awful now with her appearing so large. What did she have to compare to the blond-haired, blue-eyed beauty who could almost look Pete in the eye? Short, dumpy, unruly Carrie. That's who she was at the moment—nothing like that blond bombshell. Why had Louise picked her when she was matchmaking for her son? She was nothing like the woman he'd picked for himself.

The driver's side door opened, and Pete folded himself into the driver's seat. He fastened his seatbelt and started the car.

"You know you completely overreacted back there."

"Overreacted! Are you serious?"

Pete backed the car out and pointed the vehicle towards home. He didn't say anything else.

"Is that all you've got to say?" Carrie was incensed that he wasn't talking.

"What else is there to say?"

"I turn around and find you kissing another woman, your ex-fiancée—"

"That wasn't Collette."

"Well who was it then, that you should be in each other's arms?"

"You're overstating the situation."

"Who was it?"

"Rianne."

"Rianne? Your other ex-fiancée?"

"We were never engaged."

"Is that supposed to make me feel better?"

"She didn't hurt me like Collette did."

"Pete, stop! I can't handle this right now."

Pete stopped talking and kept driving, his eyes fixed on the road. Carrie watched him from the corner of her eye. Why wasn't he apologizing? Didn't he realize what just happened? Apparently not, as he just kept driving and the stony silence sat heavy on them both.

***

Carrie had gone straight inside and by the time Pete had brought the shopping in, she had closed herself in their bedroom. He knew he needed to talk to her, to explain things, but he was also upset that she'd reacted in such a way. He hadn't figured her for a highly emotional, controlling person. But then, even Ellen had said this was not normal for her—that pregnancy hormones were causing all sorts of up and down emotions.

He put the kettle on and made them both a hot drink. He even pulled out a packet of Tim Tams—her favorite chocolate biscuit. Nothing said sorry like a chocolate biscuit.

He didn't bother to knock. They were going to talk whether she wanted to or not.

"Carrie. I've made a cup of tea. Come and sit down with me."

He knew she could hear him. She didn't go to sleep that fast. When she didn't respond, he set the tray with the cups and biscuits on the dressing table and sat next to her on the bed. He placed his hand on her shoulder.

"I brought you some Tim Tams."

"As if I'm not fat enough."

"You're pregnant, Carrie. What do you expect?"

"I wish I was taller."

"Why?"

"So I could look you in the eye, like Rianne did."

"Carrie, Rianne's just come home from overseas because her husband died suddenly."

Carrie rolled over slightly and looked up at him.

"She and I used to be great friends. It was natural to hug her when I saw her and when she told me about her loss."

Carrie bit her lip and Pete could see she was blinking back some tears.

"Did you love her?" she asked.

Pete nodded. It was the truth. It was just that Rianne hadn't loved him in the same way—marriage and family.

"Do you love me?"

"Carrie—"

"I'm sorry, Pete. I know I'm excessively emotional at the moment, and I know I said it was all right if we weren't madly in love, but when I saw you and her together I felt like my whole world had been tipped over."

"I'm not going to have an affair with her, Carrie. I committed to you, and you to me, because we both want the same thing."

"But if you'd waited and not let your mother match-make, would you have picked up with Rianne again?"

"I don't know, but it isn't relevant in any case. My mother did match-make and she picked you."

"But you must be sorry now."

"The only thing I'm sorry about is that the game is into the second quarter and we're sitting here talking about something that doesn't matter when we should be cheering the Crows on."

Carrie closed her eyes and Pete saw a tear slide down the edge of her nose.

"Come on." He took her hand and helped her up.

"I look awful."

"We're going to watch the game, not out to a fashion show."

"I just wish I looked like her."

"I like you the way you look, and that was the best shopping trip I've ever been on. You were so organized and got the job done without any fuss."

Now that she was sitting on the side of the bed, he took her two hands to help her up. She was getting large, but the doctor had said the baby was bigger than usual—that was probably his fault, being the father. Poor little Carrie didn't have loads of room to accommodate an extra-large baby.

By the time he'd settled her on the couch, the TV on, a teacup in her hand and a Tim Tam on a plate right next to her, he felt sure the storm had passed. He sat down next to her with his own cup of tea.

"You all right now?"

Carrie nodded, but she didn't appear happy. "What?"

"Nothing," she said.

***

He still hadn't said he loved her. It was hard to pretend. The image of Rianne, the glamour girl, so animated in Pete's arms, had made her wonder if she had ever looked so happy with him as a married couple. He'd been quite clear that he wasn't getting into this marriage based on love—that companionship and family were all he was expecting. She had agreed, but now she was carrying his baby—his rather large baby—she was craving more. Had she been dishonest in the beginning? Or had she really not anticipated she would fall in love with her husband? Anticipation or not, she knew she loved him and felt bereft wondering if he might never love her in return. She felt miserable and uncomfortable, and wriggled about on the couch trying to find a position where the baby wasn't pressing on her spine, but it was almost impossible.

"Here," Pete said. He got a pillow and put it on his lap. "Lie down here."

Carrie looked up at him, searching his face for a sign, but she couldn't see what she was looking for. Pete patted the pillow again.

"Come on. Lie down."

Carrie forced back the sigh she wanted to release, instead she hefted her large, overweight body into a position whereby she could lie down with her head on the pillow—on his lap. She still felt miserable. Even with her football team blitzing the other side, she couldn't find any joy.

Then she felt Pete's hand on her head. He began to stroke her hair away from her face. That felt good. If only he loved her. She closed her eyes to squeeze back tears that were forming. If only he loved her.

Chapter Twenty-Three

The game was over. It was a huge win and percentage booster, but Pete didn't feel his usual post-game euphoria. Carrie had taken his meeting with Rianne hard. He wasn't stupid. He could see how insecure she felt and once she started comparing herself physically, there was nothing he could do to refute her statements. Rianne had been a fashion model. She hadn't lost any of that style. Carrie was not interested in fashion, but even if she had been, she could not stand face to face with him like Rianne could. Carrie's stature was set and there was nothing she could do about it. He felt sorry that she saw herself as so inadequate. But then he thought it was probably his fault. He had written in his criteria that height was an issue. His nan had given him a good talking to about that, and he got what she'd said. But of course, that wasn't all that Carrie was feeling. She not only felt undesirable, she was craving affirmation and love. Pete knew that, but they were words he found difficult to utter. Did he love her? Pete wasn't sure he even understood what love was. He knew what pain was and he figured that had been because he'd loved too hard. But what was it he felt about Carrie? She could stir him physically. Was that love? And now that she was puffy and carrying excess weight, did she still stir him in the same way? What a stupid thought. A life-long relationship couldn't be based on how a partner could physically perform. There had to be more to it than that. Companionship and shared joy? Well that had been part of why he'd agreed to marry her in the first place. They did get on well together, and she shared so many similar likes and dislikes. Was that love? But what about those warm, deep feelings? Did he feel that? He still wasn't sure.

He used the remote to turn the post-game commentary off. Carrie was asleep on his lap, and he hated to disturb her, but it was getting past time for him to move.

"Carrie." He spoke in almost a whisper. "It's time to move." He thought about using an endearment—honey, darling, baby. It didn't come naturally, and he felt uncertain.

"Carrie. Come on." He put his arms under her and lifted her up. She was dizzy and disorientated.

"The game's finished," he said. "I'll make something for tea. What would you like?"

Carrie frowned at him. Or was it she just frowned. She closed her eyes and put a hand up to her head.

"You all right?" he asked.

"I've got a massive headache," she said.

"Are you allowed to take painkillers?"

"I don't remember."

Pete wriggled out from underneath and let her lie down again. She closed her eyes again, but the frown was still fixed.

"I'll google it and see if it's OK."

"Pete."

He stopped and turned back to look at her. "Yes."

"My head feels like it's spinning at a million miles an hour and I feel sick."

Pete went back over to her and felt her forehead. "You don't seem to be feverish. Perhaps this morning's outing is taking its toll."

Carrie didn't reply.

"I'll look up to see if you can take paracetamol."

He went to his computer and typed in the question, but before the search engine brought up options, he heard noise coming from the couch. He turned back and was immediately alarmed. Carrie's body had stiffened, but was also in spasm, her mouth opened and her eyes rolling back. He had never seen a seizure but that was the word that instantly came to his mind. He flipped open his phone and dialled 000.

"Fire, ambulance or police." It was annoying how calm the emergency operator sounded.

"Ambulance. Quickly!"

"Can you tell me your location, please sir?"

Pete rambled off the address, even as he knelt next to his wife. How he managed to give details and panic at the same time was something he couldn't quite grasp.

"An ambulance has been dispatched, sir. Is the emergency for you or for someone else at this address?"

"It's my wife. I think she's having a seizure."

"Could you please describe the symptoms?"

Pete did so, but he was getting frustrated. "What should I do?"

"Make sure there is nothing in the area that is a danger to either you or the patient."

"It's clear. She's on the couch."

"You should check her airway to make sure she can breathe."

Pete put the phone on speaker. He had done a first aid course a number of years ago, but he'd never thought he'd ever have to use it. He could see Carrie's teeth were clenched. But she was taking in short breaths.

"She's breathing. But still fitting, I think. Teeth are clenched."

"Try to roll her on her side, in case there is any vomiting, so that it doesn't block her airway."

"She's pregnant."

/ "Thank you, sir. Are you able to turn her onto her side?"

Pete stood and lifted her onto her side. He felt awful seeing her so stiff.

"The ambulance should be there in a couple of minutes, sir," the operator said.

Even as she said it, Pete saw the flash of red and blue lights outside the front window.

"They're here," he said.

"Make sure you restrain any animals as you let them in."

Pete left his phone and went to the front door. He unlocked and opened it. Carrie's two dogs were already there barking. Pete took them by the collar and put some effort in leading them back towards the laundry.

"Come on, fellas. Carrie needs help."

"Can we come in?" One of the ambos called at the screen door.

"Please. I've got the dogs. My wife is in the lounge on the couch."

The front screen door opened and the two paramedics walked in, emergency medical kit in hand. Pete watched, still wrestling against the two large labradors who seemed to sense their mistress was in trouble. After dragging the dogs to the laundry and locking them in, Pete returned to the lounge. His heart was racing.

"Are you all right, sir?" One of the paramedics asked.

"Is she all right?" Pete brushed the question off.

"Her blood pressure is way too high. I suspect preeclampsia. She needs to get to hospital immediately."

Even while the paramedic was talking, Pete saw his partner jab an injection needle into Carrie's thigh muscle.

"What's the injection for?" he asked.

"We need to stop the seizure," the attending paramedic said, as he then fitted an oxygen mask over Carrie's face. "We need to move quickly, sir, if you could make sure the dogs are secure we'll bring the stretcher in."

"Whatever needs to be done, just do it," Pete said.

"Can you come in with us?"

"Of course."

Pete watched in shock as the paramedics brought the wheeled ambulance stretcher inside the house and shifted Carrie onto it fixing the safety belt straps to keep her from moving. Carrie had relaxed. Obviously the medication had worked. She opened her eyes.

"Carrie." He walked alongside the stretcher as it was being wheeled outside. "Can you hear me?" His heart hammered with panic as he watched for her to respond, but though he thought she focussed her eyes on him for a moment, she didn't speak.

"It's the post-ictal phase," the paramedic said. "She's still groggy."

"Is she going to be all right?"

Neither ambo answered as they went through the procedure to load the stretcher into the back of the ambulance.

"Is she going to be all right?" Pete asked a second time.

"I think it would be best if you called a family member to help you," the first paramedic said. "You're not looking so great yourself."

"I'll come with you now."

He saw them pass a look between each other, and one gave a slight nod. "You can ride in the front."

"Can't I ride in the back with my wife?"

"Better you're in the front as a precaution."

One ambo got in the back, the other shut and secured the door. "Hop in the front, sir. We need to be quick."

Pete nodded. He could hardly think straight. He needed to call his father, but it took a while to remember where he'd left his phone. "Can I have a second to grab my phone and lock the door?" The paramedic nodded as he walked to the front of the vehicle. Pete turned and ran inside the house. The phone was on the floor next to the couch, still lying open, though the call had been disconnected from the other end. He picked it up and ran out of the house, pulling the door shut behind him. The driver already had the ambulance backed out of the driveway by the time he got to the passenger side and climbed in.

The fact the driver activated the lights and siren didn't do anything to calm him. But they weren't talking to him. He heard the paramedic in the back speaking to Carrie. She must have been responding. He then heard him talking through his radio, obviously letting the hospital know they were heading in. He heard the words high blood-pressure, and numbers that didn't mean anything to him, and the word preeclampsia was also used again. What was it? What did it mean?

"Did you want to call your family?" The voice of the driver broke into Pete's thoughts. He nodded, opened his phone and pressed his father's number.

"Hey, Pete. Great game." Russell's happy tone snapped Pete into action.

"Dad, they're taking Carrie into the hospital in the ambulance."

"What? What's happened?"

"She's unconscious. Had a seizure, or something."

"Is she breathing?"

"Yes. Look Dad, I don't know what to do. I'm going in with the ambulance, but could you come? Can you call Carrie's family?"

"Leave it with me," Russell said.

The call disconnected and left Pete dazed. He didn't know if he could breathe, his stomach was twisted into a knot and his throat was tight. But air kept going in and out on its own, so obviously he could breathe. He had no idea how.

Once the ambulance had pulled into the Accident and Emergency loading bay, the driver jumped out of the vehicle and was around the back, unlocking the door and helping his partner get the stretcher out. Pete felt as if he was moving in slow motion as he watched. They wheeled Carrie towards the sliding doors and saw medical staff run out to meet them. They were running, wheeling Carrie inside. He needed to make his feet follow. What was happening?

"Sir, Mr Brooker." The driver returned, having relinquished his patient to the hospital staff. "You need to go inside and fill in the paperwork."

Pete just stood still and looked blindly at the closed hospital door. Then he felt the paramedic take his arm and lead him inside. He heard him speaking but couldn't seem to register what he was saying. Eventually he found himself sitting down with a cup of cold water shoved in his hands. "Drink this," a voice said. He wanted to throw the cup, but a hand guided it towards his face. He swallowed a mouthful of water instead.

What is happening? Oh God, what just happened?

Chapter Twenty-Four

Pete didn't know how long it was before his thoughts began to clear. He saw his mother and father, Carrie's parents and Ellen rush into the A and E waiting room. His mother came and sat next to him and held his hand, and he began to comprehend what was going on around him.

"She's been taken in for an emergency caesarean delivery." Pete heard one of the medical staff talking to his father and Ellen's parents.

"What happened?" Anne Davis asked.

"High blood pressure brought on the seizure, typical of preeclampsia. They need to deliver the baby straight away."

"Has she been taken into theater?" Russell asked.

"She told us she's thirty-five weeks, is that right?"

Russell looked towards Pete and caught his eye, as if asking for confirmation. Pete nodded.

"How long will it take?" Anne asked.

"Once the general anaesthetic has taken effect, they will have the baby out within ten minutes."

"But she'll be all right?" Anne pushed.

Pete noticed the staff hesitated on answering his mother-in-law's question. Suddenly he took a hold of himself, stood up and went over to where the nurse was talking.

"Will she be all right?" Pete asked. He felt his father's hand on his arm.

"All right, son. We just need to wait."

Pete shrugged his father's hand from his arm. "Why aren't you telling us what's happening?"

"We don't know what's happening, Mr Brooker," the nurse addressed him, using a firm tone. "In about ten to fifteen minutes we'll know more, and by that time we should be able to know about the baby as well."

"The baby will be all right, won't she?" Pete asked. "The seizure won't have affected her?"

"Calm down, Pete." Russell had his arm and was tugging him away from the nurse towards the sitting area.

"Calm down?" Pete turned on his father. "What aren't they telling me?"

"Is there something else we should know?" Bill Davis spoke this time. He had a voice of authority.

The nurse turned to speak to Pete. "They put a foetal heart monitor on when your partner arrived," she said.

"And?" Now Mum entered the conversation.

Still looking at Pete the nurse took a deep breath. Pete could tell she was hesitating.

"What?" Pete asked. He didn't have any presence of mind to monitor his aggression.

"The staff could not find a foetal heartbeat."

Pete's stomach twisted tighter, and a jolt of ice-cold went through his veins.

"What does that mean?" Bill asked.

"It means we will know in about ten to fifteen minutes. I ask that you please be patient. If one of you could come and fill in the paperwork, that would help us."

Dad dragged Pete away from the nurse and forced him to sit down. "Do you have your wallet?" he asked. Pete tugged it from his back pocket and handed it to his father. "Do you have your Medicare and medical insurance card in there?"

"I don't know, Dad, and frankly at the moment, I don't care."

Dad took the wallet and went over to where the registration desk was.

"Excuse me."

Pete looked up to see another stranger. She was wearing a blouse with the hospital insignia embroidered on it.

"Do you know how they are?" Pete stood up immediately.

"I'm sorry, Mr Brooker. I'm one of the hospital social workers. I can take you and your family to a private sitting room while you wait."

Mum stood up. "That would be wonderful, thank you."

Pete let his mother take the lead. It wasn't wonderful. Nothing was wonderful. Carrie and the baby were in danger. He could sense it from everything the nursing staff weren't saying.

Ten minutes. Fifteen minutes. A million years. How long was it? Eventually a staff member wearing scrubs, including a cap to hold hair back, entered the private sitting room. Pete stood up. Everyone else stood up as well.

"Mr Brooker."

Pete hadn't spoken to any of the surgical staff. There hadn't been time. They had literally whipped Carrie into surgery before he'd even got inside.

"Yes." His mouth was dry. His stomach felt like cement.

"I'm afraid your baby was stillborn."

Pete felt tears pricking the backs of his eyes. He felt his father's hand on his arm again. Then he became aware that Anne and Ellen were crying.

"What do you mean?" Pete knew what he meant, but he couldn't accept it.

"Your baby was not born alive."

"And Carrie?"

"There was a placental abruption that has caused a massive maternal bleed."

"Can you just tell us if she will be all right?" Mum had come to stand beside him.

"The team are giving her a blood transfusion as we speak. If there are no further complications, she should recover."

"Can I see her?" Pete was suddenly desperate.

"You'll need to wait until after she's come out of recovery. We'll send her upstairs to ICU to monitor until her condition stabilizes."

"How long will that take?" Mum asked.

"The best part of an hour," the doctor replied. "I'm very sorry for your loss."

Pete couldn't comprehend it. The doctor left. Carrie's family were upset. His father was trying to get him to sit, but he couldn't sit. He wanted to yell and punch something.

"Where's your car, Dad?" he asked.

"Let's just sit down." Dad was tugging on Pete's arm.

"Give me your keys." Pete shrugged his father off. "I need to get out."

"What about Carrie?" Mum said. "She'll need you."

"They won't let me see her, will they? I just need to get out and breathe some fresh air."

"All right, son, I'll come with you." Dad pulled his keys from his pocket and began to walk out. Pete followed. He didn't look back towards Carrie's family or his mother. He had to get outside and breathe.

Dad led the way to the car parking area, held up his key fob and pressed to unlock the doors. Pete saw the lights flash on his father's late model sedan.

"Shall we just walk out here for a bit?" Dad asked. "We could walk along the riverbank."

"Do you mind if you give me some time alone?" Pete said. He held out his hand for the keys. "I just want to drive and think."

"Do you think that's wise?"

"Dad."

His father sighed and handed his keys over. "Don't be long," he said. "When Carrie comes out of recovery, you need to be there."

"Don't tell me what I need to do, Dad. I've just lost my daughter."

Dad held up his hands and stepped back. Pete saw that he'd hurt his father, but he couldn't feel regret. He couldn't feel anything but gut-wrenching grief—and rage.

Without taking another moment to consider his father, Pete started the engine of his father's car and pulled it out of the car park. He made his way through the busy streets towards the freeway that headed south away from the city. He couldn't think. His mind was numb. His heart was angry.

It wasn't until he saw flashing lights in his rear-view mirror that he came back to himself and where he was. He glanced down at the speedometer and saw he was traveling at 130 kilometers per hour. He took his foot off the accelerator and immediately slowed down. The police car had pulled out into the lane next to him, and the cop in the passenger seat was waving him to pull over. There was an exit ramp up ahead, so he took it and eventually pulled over to the side on a less busy road. He slumped forward with his arms over the steering wheel. The expected knock on the window forced him to lean back and he pressed the button to lower the automatic window.

"Do you know how fast you were going, sir?" The traffic cop asked.

"About a hundred and thirty."

"You do realize the speed limit in that zone is one hundred kilometers per hour?"

Pete nodded.

"Do you have an excuse?"

"My wife is in hospital and ..." The rest of the sentence choked in his throat and he couldn't talk about the baby.

"Which hospital?" the policeman asked.

"City Central Private."

"You do realize you were traveling in the direction away from the city?"

Pete nodded. His shoulders slumped.

"Could you please show us your license, sir?"

Pete went to get his wallet and couldn't find it. He hadn't got it back from his father.

"I don't have it on me."

"Do you know it is an offense to drive without your license?"

Pete nodded.

"Is this your vehicle?"

"No."

"Have you stolen the vehicle, sir?"

"Look, could you stop with your damn stupid questions. No, I haven't stolen the car. It belongs to my father."

"Would you mind giving us his telephone number?"

Pete looked for his phone, but it wasn't there. He'd left that back at the hospital as well.

"I can't remember his number."

"Your father's number?"

"His number is programmed in my phone."

"And you don't have your phone?"

"No! I don't have my damn phone, and I need to go back to the hospital. My wife is expecting me."

"Could you please step from the vehicle, sir?"

"This is rubbish. Just write me the ticket. I need to get back to the hospital."

"Sir, step out of the vehicle please."

"What for?"

Suddenly the cop pulled the driver's door open and began to look as if he would drag Pete out.

"All right!" Pete unfastened his seat belt and got out of the car. "What is your problem?"

The second cop produced a breath testing whistle. "Please blow into the mouthpiece until I say stop."

"I'm not drunk!" Pete objected.

"Sir, please blow into the mouthpiece—"

Pete felt something break inside. He knocked the breath testing unit from the cop's hand. "This is bloody ridiculous. I'm not drunk!"

Before he could say or do anything else, he found himself spun around and slammed up against the side of his father's car, his arm twisted up behind him. Within seconds his hands were secured in handcuffs. He began to shrug and wriggle to get out of the hold the cop had on him. But the more he tried, the more aggressive the traffic cops became. It wasn't until he was shoved into the back seat of the cop car and they were on the road that Pete realized he'd just been arrested. He threw his head back against the seat.

"I need to get back to the hospital," he said.

The cop seated next to him ignored him.

"She needs me there."

"Then why were you taking a joy ride out away from the city? I'd suggest you keep quiet until we get to the station. We'll test you for blood alcohol and take your statement then."

Chapter Twenty-Five

$\mathcal{W}$hen Carrie emerged from the fog of the anaesthetic, she ignored the nausea. Something heavier was pressing. She could sense it. Where was Pete? What had happened? She vaguely remembered she'd been brought to the hospital and a doctor had said they were going to deliver her baby by emergency caesarean. Where was Pete?

Then they were preparing to move her.

"We'll be transferring you to intensive care," a nurse said.

"My baby? My husband?" Carrie felt her throat was scratchy and dry.

"I've sent word. Your husband will meet you in ICU."

"My baby?" Carrie could feel the baby was no longer within her womb.

The nurse came to her side and looked sadly at her. Why?

"Is my baby all right?"

"I'm sorry, love. Your little girl was stillborn."

Carrie felt a wave of something terrible fall on her, like a heavy blanket. Stillborn. Not alive.

"But where is she?" Carrie asked.

"Once you've been stabilized up in ICU, they'll bring her to you."

"So she's all right?"

"I'm sorry, love."

Carrie's throat felt like it was swelling up. She wanted to get up and shake the nurse. She wanted to make the nurse say something different. It couldn't be true. Where was Pete? She closed her eyes, not just against the nausea, but against the pain that reality seemed intent to push on her. She didn't want to accept it. Where was Pete?

It was some time before Carrie opened her eyes again. She'd heard staff talking in low tones. She heard the words 'second blood transfusion', 'placental abruption', 'stillborn'. She had not opened her eyes. She didn't want to know—as if she ignored it, they would tell her something different later.

"Carrie." The nurse's voice came through her mental fog. "Carrie, your mother and sister are here to see you."

Where was Pete?

"Carrie?" Ellen's voice. She felt someone take her hand. "Carrie. We're here."

Carrie forced her eyes open. "Where's Pete?"

Ellen had tears in her eyes. She cast her gaze across and saw her mother was wiping her nose.

"Where's Pete?" She used a stronger tone. "Why isn't he here?"

"He just went out for a bit," Ellen said. "He'll be here any minute."

"The baby …" But she couldn't talk about it. All her thoughts jumbled and got caught in her throat. She watched Ellen's face. It crumpled, and her chin quivered as tears fell down her cheeks.

"I'm so sorry, Carrie. There was nothing they could do."

Carrie closed her eyes and she heard a groan of anguish. Was that her? It must have been. She could feel the pain being torn from her. She felt hands. Someone had her hand and was stroking the back of it. There was another hand on her shoulder. She opened her eyes, hoping to see Pete. It was her mother, tears streaming down her face.

"Where's Pete? Why isn't he here?"

∗∗∗

Louise was pacing around the sitting room with Russell and Bill. Anne and Ellen had gone up to ICU. Only two visitors at a time, they'd said. Pete should have been the first one there, but no one knew where he'd gone.

"Did he say how long he'd be gone?" Louise asked her husband for the third time.

"He was upset, Louise. He just took off. He'll be back soon, surely."

Surely didn't seem to be a strong enough assurance. He shouldn't have gone off in the first place.

Then the social worker came into the sitting room again. "Mr Brooker?"

Russell stepped forward. "My son, Pete, is the Mr Brooker you're looking for. He's gone out for a bit."

"No, it's Mr Russell Brooker I'm looking for."

Louise looked between her husband and the social worker. "What is it?" she asked.

"There's a telephone call for Mr Russell Brooker. You can take it at the nurses' station."

Louise followed Russell out of the room to where the telephone was.

"Russell Brooker." His tone was short and clipped. She could hear stress.

"What? Why?"

Louise grabbed his arm. "What?" She connected with her husband's eyes. He looked at her but didn't appear to see her.

"Well how did that happen? Good grief." He let out a heavy sigh.

"I don't have my car here, do I! You'll have to wait while I organize something. You should have been more responsible."

Russell hung up the call and turned to Louise.

"He's been arrested and is in the city lockup."

"Arrested? Why?"

"I don't know. He doesn't have his phone or license."

"No, his phone and wallet are here in my handbag," Louise said. "With all the tension, I just kept hold of them for safe keeping."

Russell swore. He began to walk back to the sitting room. Louise hurried to keep up.

"Bill, can I borrow your car?"

Carrie's father looked up at them as they re-entered the room. "Why? What's happened?"

"Pete's gone out and got caught speeding. He just went a little crazy, and now he's rung me from the city lockup. My car has been impounded."

Bill pulled his keys out ready to hand over when Ellen walked back in.

"Where's Pete?" she asked. "Carrie needs him."

Louise intervened before Russell spat the story out again. "I'm going to call Cam."

"Why?" Ellen said. "We need Pete here now."

"Pete went a little crazy and got arrested," Russell said.

Louise got Cam on the first call, thank goodness.

"Hey." Cam sounded friendly. "I heard Carrie's been rushed to hospital."

Emotion strangled Louise for a few moments.

"Is everything all right?" Cam asked.

"No." Louise couldn't get the words to work. She handed the phone to Russell.

"Hey, Cam," Russell said. "Do you think you can meet me at the city lockup and help me sort out whatever trouble Pete has got himself into?"

Louise watched as Russell conducted the conversation. Cam obviously was asking questions.

"He must have lost the plot after he heard about the baby. He's just rung from jail," Russell said. "It's not good news here, Cam, I'm sorry to say. They've lost the baby."

Russell listened a bit more.

"I'll meet you there shortly." He handed the phone back to Louise. "Give me his wallet and phone," he said to Louise. "I'll be back as soon as I can."

***

Pete held his head in his hands, resting his elbows on his knees. Of course there was no blood-alcohol reading. If he hadn't been so stupid and had done the Breathalyzer test when they'd pulled him over, he would have been back at the hospital by now without any of this drama. Now he'd had time to sit and think about it, he realized how much he needed Carrie. He needed her and she needed him. She would be devastated—feeling as bad as he felt, probably worse.

What on earth had he been thinking?

As much as he felt devastated that his baby was stillborn, at this very moment he felt full of regret at not being right next to Carrie. He wanted to cry, but he wanted to cry with her for their loss. He wanted to hold her. He wanted to make sure she was all right, that he wouldn't lose her as well. And yet, he was sitting in a cell in the city lockup because he wouldn't listen to his dad.

There were hundreds of things he would like to have done to express his feelings, but he couldn't do any of them. He could only sit and stew in the overpowering emotions.

"Pete."

Pete looked up to see his brother-in-law, Cam. He was in uniform—another cop.

"Come on, mate. We need to get you organized."

Cam unlocked the cell door. Pete didn't move.

"You wanna stay?" Cam asked.

"I should have been at the hospital with Carrie. What time is it now?"

Cam looked at his watch. "Just past midnight. My wife is pretty upset with you at the moment."

"And Carrie?"

"I'd just as soon sort this out with the sergeant and get you back to the hospital to find out for yourself."

"I was speeding."

"I know."

"I didn't have my license with me."

"I know."

"I got agro with the traffic cops."

"I know."

"So how can you sort it?"

"They'll overlook the agro thing, but you'll have to pay the traffic infringements."

Pete nodded.

"Your dad gave me your wallet. They've recorded everything against your name. You can pretty much get your things from the desk sergeant and go."

"Where is my dad?"

"He's gone to get his car released from the police pound."

Pete sighed. "I stuffed that one up, didn't I?"

"At the moment, there are more important things to worry about."

"Like Carrie."

"Like Carrie. Come on."

Cam waved Pete towards the door. When Pete got close to him Cam grabbed him by the shoulder.

"I'm really sorry about the baby, mate."

Pete felt his throat tighten and tears sting the back of his eyes. He couldn't respond, even if he'd wanted to. The best he could do was nod and keep moving.

***

Carrie lay awake listening to the machines in the ICU ward. So many different sounds. She had her little baby next to her in a special crib. But she didn't make any sound. She was not alive. Carrie's eyes felt like they were full of sand, but she couldn't blink. She just stared into the darkness. Why had Pete run off and left her? She'd heard the story—how he'd been arrested, and Louise had sent Cam to bail him out. But why did he leave in the first place? The answer seemed simple in her mind. There was no baby. No child. No family. That was all he'd wanted from their marriage. He didn't want her. Just children. Carrie felt the wave of emotion swell up in her neck and throat and, yet again, hot tears spilled from her eyes and down her cheeks. She ached all over, not just physically, but emotionally. What if she could never have children? That was the thing at the top of Pete's list. Must want children. She did want children—she wanted this little one who lay silently beside her. Still. Cold. Lifeless. She wanted her. How she wanted her. But the staff would take her away eventually. They had told her she could have a couple of days to bond—for the family to bond—but they had to let her go eventually. Why hadn't Pete stayed?

Ellen, her parents, Pete's mother and sisters had all held their little still baby. They'd all cried over her. They'd taken pictures. They'd hugged her and reassured her that Pete would come. But he hadn't. Not yet anyway.

He shouldn't have left in the first place, no matter how upset he felt. Did he think she wasn't upset? That she didn't want to run away and hide somewhere? Why didn't he stay to see if she was all right?

Then she heard her nurse move. Without lifting her head, she was aware that her nurse had gone to speak to someone. It must be late. Her mother and Ellen hadn't left until after one a.m., and that seemed a while ago. Carrie pricked her ears up when she realized it was Pete. He'd finally come, but it was too late. The baby was dead and Carrie knew he didn't care about her. If he'd cared, he wouldn't have left in the first place.

"She's resting," the nurse said in a low tone. "At this stage, it's best there is very little stimulation."

"Can I see her?" Pete asked.

"If she isn't awake, it would be best you let her try to sleep."

Carrie saw Pete walk up to her bed, but it was dim light. She didn't say anything to him. Could he see she was awake? Then she saw when he noticed the crib for the first time. He went over and stood, looking down at their little dead daughter. He reached out his hand and touched her face. Then she saw his body shake. He was quiet but she knew he was crying. New hot tears flooded her eyes as well. She watched him pull up a chair next to the crib.

"You can hold her, if you want." The nurse was still there, in the dim light. She still spoke in a half-whisper.

Carrie watched while the nurse lifted their baby out of the crib and placed her tightly wrapped body into her father's arms. She knew he was crying. She was crying too. It was too much pain to bear. Carrie closed her eyes against the scene. She didn't want to see it anymore. She didn't want to see him. He didn't love her. Only the baby, and she was gone.

234

Chapter Twenty-Six

$\mathcal{P}$ete was determined to sit the rest of the night in the chair next to Carrie's bed. He held the baby for as long as he could keep his eyes open, but then he was too tired.

"Can you help me put her back in the cradle?" He felt his whispered words must have shattered the atmosphere. The nurse came over and took the baby from him. He felt bereft just giving her up. They had already told him the funeral director would take her when they were ready the next day. He wasn't ready. How could he ever be ready? But he had to be.

"Why don't you go home and try to sleep?" the nurse asked. "I doubt she'll wake up until morning now."

Pete looked across at Carrie. His heart broke for her, but there wasn't anything he could do to make it better.

"Do you think she knew I was here?" he asked.

"I would guess she'll probably be more responsive tomorrow. Perhaps you should take a taxi and go home."

Pete was exhausted and decided it was the sensible thing to do. He leaned over Carrie and kissed her forehead. "I'll be in first thing tomorrow morning," he said.

When he turned, he leaned over the cradle and kissed the baby's forehead. He touched her soft, cold cheek with his work-roughened hand, then quickly walked out of the ward. He took the elevator to the ground floor and asked the woman at the reception if she would call a taxi for him. At least he had his wallet and phone.

The drive through the dark sleepy streets passed quickly and silently. Pete didn't even bother to engage the taxi driver in conversation.

When he got in the house, the dogs barked from the laundry. They'd been shut up there for hours. Pete knew they would probably have made a mess from having been locked indoors without the opportunity to do their business outside. He had to let them out into the back yard even for a little while.

By the time the dogs had come back in and settled on their beds, after he'd cleaned the laundry floor, Pete was ready to collapse. It was nearly five a.m. He didn't want to feel any more and hoped that sleep would act as the anaesthetic his soul needed. He fell into bed and within minutes he was fast asleep.

***

Pete woke with a start, as if he'd just fallen from the ceiling. His heart was racing and he was disorientated. It took a few moments for him to realize it was full on daylight, and he scrambled through his thoughts to remember what day it was. And then it hit him. The full weight of loss pressed on his whole being like a bag of concrete. He thought of the tiny still baby he'd held in his arms for several hours the past evening. Then he thought of Carrie. What time was it? He sat up quickly and fumbled about looking at the bedside alarm clock.

He swore when he saw it was past eleven thirty. He had fully intended to be back at the hospital by the time Carrie woke up. That was probably about four hours ago. He was still in his clothes from the night before and felt uncomfortable and like he needed a shower. But he didn't want to waste more time changing. Picking up his phone, he saw that the battery had run out. What else could go wrong? He was on the edge of losing it again. Taking a deep breath, he quickly plugged the phone in to charge and then saw there were several missed calls. Ellen's number had four missed calls. Then his father and his mother. Because the dogs were scratching at the back door, he knew he'd have to sort them out before he left for the hospital, so he decided he'd have the shower. He had to wait for the phone to charge anyway, and this would give the dogs a bit of time outside. Nothing was going right, and he wondered if Carrie would understand.

***

Carrie had been moved back to an ordinary ward. She was thankful they had private health insurance and so was in a room on her own—with her baby—and other family members who had come in and out. Except Pete.

"Has Pete been in yet at all?" Ellen asked.

"He came in late last night," Carrie said.

"What did you say to him?"

"I pretended I was asleep."

Ellen just glared at her.

"What, Ellen? What should I have said to him?"

"But you haven't talked about the baby, or anything?"

Carrie shook her head.

"Has he been in this morning?"

"No, and I don't expect he'll come in."

"What? Why would you say that?"

"Please, Ellen. You of all people should know why."

"I don't understand."

"According to his list, this marriage was about having children. Now the baby has gone, I don't expect he'll be hurrying in to see me."

"Carrie, I know you're hurting, but I've seen the way you and Pete are together. He loves you."

"Does he? He's never told me so."

"But I've seen how he is with you."

"Yes, well I saw how he was with his old girlfriend and let me tell you, it was not like the way he is with me."

Ellen frowned at her. "What are you saying?"

"His old girlfriend has returned from Germany, newly widowed, and Pete was all over her. I go into surgery, and he disappears and doesn't turn up for hours."

"Carrie, you're hurting from your loss. Don't push Pete away too."

"I don't have to push him away. You'll notice he's not here, is he?"

"Carrie …"

Just at that moment, Pete walked into the ward. Carrie could hardly look at him. She was so hurt by his absence. Ellen didn't say anything.

"I'm glad you're looking better this morning," Pete said.

Carrie didn't respond. Pete looked across to the baby.

"When will they come to take her?" he asked.

Carrie couldn't answer, even if she'd wanted to.

"The funeral director will come as soon as you and Carrie have said your goodbyes," Ellen said.

Carrie's eyes filled with tears and her cheeks went wobbly. She didn't want to say goodbye, but she knew it was inevitable. She watched Pete. Once again, he didn't go to her, only to the baby. He put his hand on the baby's head.

Carrie looked to her sister. Ellen's eyes were full of tears too.

"Would you take a picture of us?" Pete asked Ellen.

It took a few moments while Ellen helped Pete pick the baby up. Ellen took his phone and shot several photos of him holding the baby.

"Do you want me to take one of the three of you together?" Ellen asked.

Carrie watched as Pete came over to her bed, the baby still in his arms.

"You hold her," Pete said. "I'll put my arm around you both."

Carrie just did as she was told. The pain from holding her child for the final time assaulted her from one side, and the anger she felt at Pete as he put his arm around her assaulted her from the other. She was in turmoil. Thankfully Ellen didn't ask them to smile. That would have been too much.

"I'll step outside for a bit while you say your goodbyes," Ellen said. She handed Pete's phone back to him.

Suddenly she was alone with her husband. Carrie wanted to hit him. She was angry with him and was angry with what had happened. She wanted to blame him but knew it wasn't his fault the baby had been stillborn.

But it was his fault he hadn't been there when she needed him, and it was well past lunchtime now. Where had he been all morning?

"Are you happy to still call her the name we decided on?" Pete asked. His arm was still around her and he was gazing over her shoulder, she assumed at the baby.

Carrie nodded. Charlotte Grace.

"I'm so sorry, Carrie."

Still she did not speak. They sat there for a long while, the three of them. Or was it only two of them? Carrie didn't know. In her heart Charlotte was a real person, one whom she loved dearly, and this tearing away was a terrible pain. Eventually, a nurse came into the room. She stood quietly for a moment until Pete spoke to her.

"I guess it's time," he said.

The nurse nodded and came across to take the baby. Carrie clung to Charlotte tighter and broke down sobbing. She wasn't aware of anyone else, just her own terrible pain.

"We need to say goodbye." Pete's voice eventually cut through the fog.

Carrie nodded and loosened her hold. Pete took the baby from her and she watched the tears stream down his face as he kissed their child on the forehead. Then he handed the baby to the nurse who put her in the crib and wheeled her out of the room. As the door closed, Carrie lay back on the pillows and closed her eyes. She didn't want to talk to Pete or Ellen or anyone. She just wanted to be alone.

*****

Pete hadn't known he could feel such grief. None of the pain he'd felt in the past with his failed relationships even vaguely resembled what he was feeling now. Once they were alone together he looked towards Carrie, but she had effectively shut him out. He knew she was hurting as much as he was, but he wanted to find comfort together.

"Carrie?"

She didn't answer, her eyes closed.

"Carrie?" he tried again, placing his hand softly on her shoulder. "Can we talk?"

Carrie shook her head without opening her eyes. "Just go, Pete."

Her words were like salt in an already inflamed wound. He didn't have the emotional energy to find a way to break through. He looked at her for another minute to see if she might change her mind, but she didn't.

Picking up his phone and keys he walked out of the private room, almost bumping into Ellen in the hallway.

"Are you leaving already?" Ellen asked.

"She won't talk to me," Pete said. "She told me to go."

"She's convinced you don't love her," Ellen said. "Something about an old girlfriend."

Pete sighed. "It was a chance meeting yesterday." Was it only yesterday? "Rianne has always been demonstrative and affectionate."

"What Carrie saw was affection, all right, but not towards her. She's convinced that your only worry is the baby—that she doesn't mean anything to you at all."

"That's rubbish, Ellen. I hope you told her that."

"Why don't you tell her that?"

"She isn't in a listening place at the moment. We're both reeling after saying goodbye to Charlotte."

"You named her Charlotte?"

Pete nodded. "Charlotte Grace."

Ellen wiped her nose with a tissue. "I'm so sorry this has happened, Pete. I know you and Carrie would have made wonderful parents."

"We will still."

Ellen looked at him seriously.

"What?" he asked.

"That's the problem, Pete. She's worried she might not be able to have another baby, given what happened with Charlotte, and she knows—or at least she believes—the only reason you are with her is because she was willing to bear children for you."

Pete closed his eyes and allowed his head to drop backward.

"That stupid list again."

"It was a good list, at the time."

"Yes, but because I had the point about being tall enough, she is convinced that I love Rianne more than her."

"Do you?"

"What?"

"Love Rianne?"

"I *loved* Rianne, and I still care about her—I mean, I was concerned for her when I heard about her husband's death."

"How do you love Carrie?"

"If I'd lost her …"

"What?"

"She's my wife."

"That doesn't necessarily follow that you love her. You haven't told her that you do, apparently."

"No, I haven't. I'm not good with words like that."

"Do you think you might like to give it a try, or is she right, and you don't actually love her?"

"I do. I didn't when we first met. I appreciated her. I enjoyed her company, and she turned me on … you know."

"Yes, I don't need all the details."

"But somewhere along the line, I've learned to love her. When the doctors were talking about a haemorrhage and blood transfusion, I realized I might lose her too."

"And how did that make you feel?"

"Desperate. Terrified. Crazy."

"Crazy enough to get yourself arrested."

Pete nodded. "But I don't think Carrie appreciated that demonstration of my feelings."

"No, I think you might have to rework your presentation."

"She's not in listening mode today. I'll come back a bit later and see how it goes."

"Don't give up on her, Pete. You and she were meant to be together and seeing you both like this is horrible."

"For me too."

Ellen stepped forward and drew Pete into a hug. His sister-in-law was not a lot taller than his wife and it reminded him that it was Carrie he wanted to hold, and it was Carrie he wanted to hold him. As he watched Ellen go back into Carrie's room, Pete struggled with what he should do. He felt numb inside—no emotional energy to do anything, let alone go and make a wild profession of undying love and passion. He had nothing. It would be pointless trying to make Carrie understand now. She was hurting. He was hurting. He needed to go home and be alone.

Chapter Twenty-Seven

Pete didn't come back to the hospital. Well, he had come back just the once, but he hadn't stayed. He'd sat for about five minutes, then got up and left. All Carrie's emotional energy was being deflected into anger at her husband. She didn't want to think about anything else.

"Is Pete coming to pick you up?" Mum asked.

"I doubt it." Carrie moved gingerly as she pulled things from the side locker and stuffed them in her small bag.

"Carrie." There was warning in Ellen's tone, but Carrie wasn't in the mood to hear her sister's defense of her husband.

"Leave it, Ellen," she snapped.

"You're being unfair and unkind, and you know it."

"I've just lost a child, and my so-called husband hasn't even tried to be supportive."

"You've pushed him away every time he's tried to reach out to you."

"If he'd been here when I really needed him …"

"You need to forgive him. You're being—"

"What? What am I being?"

"Hard to get on with. Pete is hurting too, you know."

"He has his family, and he can always call Rianne for support."

"Carrie!"

"I don't want to talk about it, Ellen. I just want to go home and die."

"You're not going to die, honey," Mum said.

"I'd like to die."

Carrie caught the look of panic her mother shot towards her sister. And she saw Ellen's facial response and the slight shake of her head. Good, they were going to stop badgering her.

Mum drove while Ellen sat in the back seat. Thank goodness Ellen hadn't brought Lucy. Carrie didn't think she wanted to see a child ever again. When they pulled up in the driveway of her home— *her* home, the one she legally owned in her name, mortgage paid for by her years of wage earning—she saw there was no vehicle in the driveway. Pete wasn't there. Why on earth did her stomach drop with disappointment? She didn't want him to be there. Did she?

"Ellen, you take Carrie's things in, and I'll make some tea." Mum was not going to talk to her either. Good. She had nothing more to say.

Carrie shuffled inside. She had recovered well, apparently, but the sutures from the caesarean wound still hurt. The moment she entered the house, the pain hit her again. Her dogs were at her feet longing for attention, but it was the boxes in the hallway, deliveries from the baby store, that pierced her heart again. Pete hadn't unpacked them. Why would he? They had no use for prams and cots and other baby furniture. Carrie pushed past them, on her way towards her bedroom.

The room was a mess. Pete's dirty clothes were tossed near the laundry basket—not in, but close. The bed was unmade, the bedding twirled into a mess of sheets and blankets, as if he'd done nothing but toss and turn all night. She didn't want to care. She wanted to be angry with him.

"Why don't you go and have a cup of tea, and I'll tidy this mess up so you can lie down?" Ellen spoke over her shoulder.

Carrie turned around and moved slowly back to the kitchen. It was just as bad in here. Empty dog food tins near the rubbish bin.

They couldn't go in. It was too full. Empty mugs and plates stacked on the sink. Food crumbs all over the counter. Why hadn't he cleaned anything?

"He's been working every waking hour," Mum said, as if reading her thoughts. "He just comes home to sleep."

"He could have tried to tidy up."

"Honey, he has to drive over an hour each way in rush hour traffic. After a long day's work, he's tired."

Carrie didn't soften her attitude. He could have tried.

"He's hurting too, Carrie," Mum said.

Carrie took the mug of tea her mother had made and went to sit in the loungeroom. Even there she saw signs of things that were bound to upset her. Before being rushed to hospital she'd begun to pack boxes and there were several stacked in the corner next to the TV. They had planned to move to a small rental place closer to Pete's work until he finished their house. Now she didn't care if he finished the house or not. He didn't want her. There wouldn't be any more children, so why bother?

Carrie sipped her tea and tried to pretend it didn't hurt as much as it did. Then she heard Ellen's voice. She was talking on the phone, and it was obvious who she was talking to.

"I don't know, Pete. She's pretty low at the moment … I'm not sure she's ready yet … If I were you, I'd just stay over at your folks' house and come back on the weekend … I'm thinking that Mum and I will take turns staying with her. It will be two weeks by the time you get back on the weekend. Hopefully that will have given her enough time to … You can come if you want, I just can't guarantee how she'll respond to you, or if she'll respond to you … I know. I'm sorry. This is so unlike Carrie, I'm sure it's grief. We all need time … yes, I'll tell her."

Carrie leaned her head back against the lounge chair and closed her eyes. Did she want to hear what Pete had said?

"Carrie?"

She didn't want to respond to her sister, but Ellen was persistent.

"Pete is going to stay at his folks' place until the weekend."

Carrie showed no sign she'd heard, but her heart broke a little bit. She wanted him to fight past the wall she'd thrown up. Why couldn't he see that?

"He says he loves you."

"If he loved me, he'd be here."

"What, so you can attack him, or ignore him, or blame him?"

Carrie didn't respond. Some of Ellen's words hit the mark.

"Mum is going to stay with you for a couple of days, then I'll come for a couple."

"I don't want you to bring Lucy here."

Ellen went quiet, and Carrie opened her eyes. "It hurts too much, Ellen. Please."

Though the look on Ellen's face was one of restrained anger, she nodded.

"I'm sorry. I know I'm being a real …" she didn't say the word bitch. It was a horrible word, and she didn't want to hear it. But she was aware her behavior probably deserved a word like that.

"Perhaps in a couple of days I'll be better. I'm sorry."

"You should say sorry to your husband. He needs you and you need him."

"I can't. Not just yet. I'm not strong enough to play the game knowing how much I've failed him."

"You haven't failed him, not with the baby anyway. That wasn't your fault. But if you keep pushing him away, and if his ex-girlfriend is around and showing him sympathy, you might be sorry you've shut him out."

"Ellen." Mum had come into the room. "That's not fair. Carrie has enough to work through without throwing the threat of an ex-girlfriend at her. Give her a couple of days, and I'm sure things will work out. I'm sure Pete will be back, honey. Don't give Rianne another thought."

It was all very well for her mother to scold Ellen, and tell her not to think of Rianne, but they'd both said her name. She still hung in the background like a threat. But did Carrie care? If Pete decided it was all too hard and went back to Rianne, would she really care? By the amount of dread that settled in her stomach like a block of cold steel, she realized she cared all right. How she wished Pete would just come and fight past her pain and indifference.

***

Back to square one. Pete didn't call his mate, Andy, this time. He couldn't bear to see his three children. It was too painful just yet. Even Megan was sensitive enough to not bring her baby around. They all let him have his space, for the time being. He worked long hours. After he finished on site, he'd go around to his own new house build and continue working there. He didn't get back to his parents' place until late every night.

"You're avoiding the issue," Mum said, when he walked in the door late one night.

"I know, Mum."

"Would you like some advice?"

Pete stopped and looked at her. "Yes, Mum. I would like some advice." She appeared surprised that he'd asked. "Tell me how to make things right, because I really don't know what to do."

Rather than launching into a full-scale lecture, Mum put her arms around him and pulled him into a hug. It felt good. He needed this comfort, and he felt the tears—tears that were never far from the surface—overflow his eyes again.

"Go and have a shower, then come and sit down. I'll warm up some dinner, and we can talk."

Pete didn't argue but dragged his tired body to the bathroom. He let the stream of hot water run unchecked over his sore muscles, trying to imagine the water could wash away his pain. It helped a bit.

"Are you going to go back home on Saturday?" Mum asked as she placed the warmed dinner plate in front of him.

"I said I would."

"Have you spoken to her on the phone?"

Pete shook his head, then picked up his fork and began eating.

"Why haven't you called?"

"I tried a number of times before she left the hospital, but she let them all go through to voicemail and she never returned any of them."

"But you should keep trying."

"Ellen told me she's in a bad frame of mind at the moment."

"Which will only get worse if you don't go to her and tell her how you feel."

"How do I feel?"

Mum let her gaze bore into Pete, even though he concentrated on his meal and pretended he couldn't see her.

"You need to go see a counselor," Mum said.

Pete just kept eating.

"Will you go see a counselor?"

"What for, Mum? Is this you feeling guilty for having pushed us together in the first place?"

Pete held her gaze now, and he saw her face fall. She didn't say anything, but he could tell he'd hurt her with his comment.

"I'm sorry," he said. "I'm just tired and confused right now. I don't know that marriage counseling would really help."

"I meant grief counseling," Mum said.

Pete looked up at her again. "Grief counseling? Why?"

"Aren't you grieving?"

Was he? Is that what he was feeling? Confused, guilty, angry maybe, but grief?

"Do people grieve over a child they never knew?" Pete asked.

Mum nodded. "I lost a child, Pete."

"What? When? I didn't know that."

"He was stillborn at 19 weeks gestation."

"How come I didn't know that?"

"It was before you were born. He would have been our eldest son."

"Did you name him?"

"Not officially. His birth was considered a miscarriage, and we weren't encouraged to bond with the baby, like they do now days."

"How did you and Dad cope?"

"A bit like you, I guess. I cried a lot and didn't want to see anybody. Dad was angry, and just buried himself in his work."

"Did you get through it … well obviously you did, as here we all are, but … how did you get through it?"

"I think someone wise forced me to see a counselor. I didn't realize the symptoms I was experiencing were grief, but once we began to talk about it, it was obvious. We lost our baby—whom we both wanted very much—and we could have lost our whole family if we'd stayed in that place of deep despondency. We needed help. You need help, Pete."

✳✳✳

Pete stayed the Friday night at his folks' house so he could work late on the new house. He wanted to get it finished as soon as possible. He wanted to move Carrie and all their hopes for a future into the new place and get past this terrible time of loss and grief. He realized now it was grief. Dr Google had been very helpful in showing him he was quite typical in the way he'd responded to the loss of Charlotte Grace. Carrie too. His own heart softened towards her when he realized what her behavior really was. He'd looked up a counseling center that dealt specifically with grief and had made an appointment for the next week. Now he had a diagnosis, he wanted the cure. He hoped Carrie would come with him—that together they would be able to walk through the valley of the shadow of death and emerge into the green pastures beside the still waters.

His high hopes faltered however, when he pulled into the driveway of Carrie's home—his home. He'd expected Ellen would still be there. They'd discussed it to make sure Carrie wasn't left on her own, with her not being allowed to lift anything and with recommended rest. But Ellen wasn't there.

Pete got out of his work vehicle and strode up to the front door. It only took a moment to open the door for him to realize the house was empty. She wasn't there. The place was much tidier than it had been last time he'd walked through the door, but it was empty. The boxes that had been delivered from the baby store were still in the hallway and there was a note taped to them.

Please take these away.

Pete slid his phone open and called Carrie's number. It rang through to voicemail.

Where is she?

He tried Ellen's number. His sister-in-law answered at least.

"Hi Pete," she said.

"Where's Carrie?"

"She's at Mum's house."

"Why? She knew I was coming back this morning. I text her to let her know."

"She doesn't want to see you, Pete. I'm sorry."

Pete felt something like a rock fall in the pit of his stomach.

"How can we work things out, if she won't see me?" He knew he sounded angry and desperate, but he couldn't help it.

"I can't seem to talk any sense into her, Pete. It's like she's completely shut down. It's so unlike her."

Suddenly, Pete remembered the list of symptoms he'd seen displayed when he'd done his internet search on grief. Detachment and isolating oneself were typical. But what could he do to shake her out of it?

"I'll talk to her again," Ellen said. She sounded tired. "I guess we just need to be patient."

"I'm not feeling very patient at the moment," he said.

"I'm sorry. Please forgive her, Pete. She really isn't like this normally."

Pete sighed. He'd lived with her for nine months. He knew she wasn't normally like this. But he wanted the old Carrie back.

"Can you tell her something for me?" Pete asked.

"Sure."

"Tell her I love her and am missing her like crazy."

"I'm glad to hear it, Pete."

"Yeah, well, I also want to give her a good shake, but don't tell her that."

"We're all praying for you," Ellen said.

"Thanks," Pete said. "At this stage I'm guessing there isn't much else we can do."

"Possibly not, but prayer is known to be effective."

He finished the call and looked around the house. He couldn't stay here on his own, and with all the work he had to do on their house he didn't want to spend precious hours traveling. He flipped open his phone again and sent a text.

Carrie,

I'm going to go back to my folks and give you the space you seem to need. Just letting you know you can come back to your home whenever you like, and I won't be here. But do come back, as someone needs to look after the dogs.

Love Pete

He reviewed the message before pressing send and wondered if he should take the 'love' part out. He didn't feel very loving at the moment. He felt hurt and angry too. He left it in and pressed send.

Chapter Twenty-Eight

When Carrie arrived back home she had to fight the internal conflict that rose up in her. *Why didn't he wait? Why doesn't he try harder?* But then she argued the other emotion that seemed to have the upper hand. *What would be the point? It's only duty? He doesn't really love me.*

She was tired of this conflict—a conflict that seemed to be controlling her. Why couldn't she just let it go? She wanted Pete here, not her mother or sister. *What is wrong with me?*

She put the kettle on.

"Do you want a cup of tea?" She called out to her mother, who was still dragging heavy bags of groceries through the front door.

"Coffee, please."

Carrie knew she could at least do light household duties. As the kettle boiled, she began to put away some groceries that didn't weigh much and in places where she didn't have to reach or bend. She had to get back into life. Sitting around feeling sorry for herself was excruciating. She wished she had a classroom full of kids to distract her, but she had given up her position. She was meant to have a newborn baby to keep her busy. The pain overwhelmed her again.

"Honey, I wish you had met up with Pete," Mum said as she hefted the last bag of groceries onto the kitchen bench.

"I can't, Mum."

"Why?"

"I don't know. I guess I'm scared."

"Scared of what?"

Carrie shrugged.

"I've spoken to Louise. She tells me that Pete is in a fair state himself."

"Over the baby, perhaps. I doubt he's lost any sleep over me. I was just a means to an end."

Mum paused as if she were searching for a defense but couldn't find one.

"You see! Even you don't believe he cares—I mean really cares—about me. That wasn't what was arranged. I was supposed to produce children."

"There was more to it than that, Carrie. Otherwise you wouldn't have gone through with the marriage in the first place."

"We were supposed to enjoy the footy together and keep each other company."

"Are you telling me that in the last ten months you and Pete didn't form any sort of attachment other than getting pregnant together?"

Carrie pressed her lips close together and gave a long sigh.

"There must have been more," Mum pressed.

"From my part, I thought I loved him. On so many different levels."

"As a soul mate?"

Carrie nodded.

"Well ...?"

"But then I saw him with Rianne. It was like he'd come alive."

"Are you sure? Or is it just your insecurity talking?"

"I'm not insecure."

"So you're perfectly happy with your height, and your weight, and your fly-away hair?"

"Mum! Why are you asking me that? I thought you loved me the way I am."

"I do, but I'm not so sure that you love yourself as you are."

"Well, look at me. Even nearly three weeks later and I'm still fat and tubby, and there's nothing to be done about my height. That ship sailed when I was fourteen."

Carrie saw her mother suppress a wry smile as she raised her eyebrows.

"Well, I wouldn't have said I was the insecure sort," Carrie said.

"Neither would I, but apparently seeing Rianne brought something to the surface."

"She's nearly six foot, perfectly coiffed hair, make-up, legs up to her armpits. I don't even know why Pete agreed to his mother's ridiculous matchmaking scheme in the first place when he could have had Rianne."

"But he couldn't have had Rianne. She went off to Germany and married over there without giving Pete a second thought."

"Which makes me what? A rebound? A last resort?"

"Carrie, you knew all this before you agreed to marry. Didn't Pete tell you he was emotionally unavailable?"

"Yes, he did! And that's my point. He was happy to marry for companionship and family—that meant children …" Suddenly Carrie's throat thickened and tears burned her eyes. She took a breath. "That's … not going … to …" She couldn't say it, as the emotion blocked her speech. But she thought it. *It's not going to happen. I lost Charlotte Grace. I couldn't hold her long enough to be born safely. I nearly died. There won't be any more.*

Without saying anything else, she got up from the kitchen table and continued putting groceries away. *I have to focus on something else. I can't keep breaking into tears.*

Carrie kept at the task until she found herself with a three-kilo bag of potatoes in her hand and her mother bearing down on her.

"That's enough, Carrie. I'll finish the groceries. You go outside and sit with the dogs for a bit."

It shouldn't have mattered, but it did. She was recovering from a caesarean section, and the doctors specified she wasn't allowed to lift heavy things, and she would have been happy to follow his orders if—if she'd had her baby here to nurse, and to kiss and to sing a lullaby to. But she didn't. No baby. No husband. Both gone. She broke down crying again and went, not outside, but to her room. She lay down on the bed and grabbed Pete's pillow. She held it to her chest and sobbed into it. Why couldn't he just love her like she loved him?

***

Louise slammed her computer shut. Why had she called her main character Charlotte? Every time she opened the document and tried to keep writing she would stall the minute she saw her main character's name. But she couldn't change it. She'd lost a precious grand-child, Charlotte Grace, and even grandmothers grieved. She recognized it and let her publisher know about the tragedy. She had to give herself some time to strengthen before she could face Charlotte and Benjamin again. They would keep. In the meantime, was there something she could do for her son and daughter-in-law?

Louise was not stupid. She knew about the precarious relationship that often existed between young women and their mothers-in-law. She'd observed it many times and she'd written about it. Her own daughters were a bit clueless when it came to their mothers-in-law. Now that Megan had a baby, Cam's mother, Janine, showed all the signs of desperately wanting to be involved, but Megan put her off and deferred instead to Louise. Louise guessed Cam's mother would like to feel the same welcome as she did. Now she was experiencing it from the other side.

Carrie had her mother and sister to support her. She didn't need a mother-in-law. But Louise couldn't sit back anymore and watch from a distance. Carrie was hurting in a way Louise understood. Losing a child was something she empathized with. The pain and the desire to hide away.

"I'm going to visit Carrie," Louise said to Russell as she picked up her keys from the kitchen bench.

"Really? Is that wise at the moment?"

Louise let out a lungful of air. "I don't know, but I have to try. You and I both know what it is to lose a baby."

Russell nodded. There was a gleam of moisture in his eyes. Bless him. He remembered the pain as well.

The dogs barked from the backyard as Louise approached the front door. She saw Anne's car in the driveway and was glad Carrie wasn't alone.

"Louise!" Anne sounded surprised when she opened the front door. "Come in. We weren't expecting you."

"How is Carrie?" Louise asked.

Anne's face fell a bit and she blew out a short breath that sounded like frustration. "I can't make her see sense."

"She's grieving," Louise said. "It takes time."

Anne gave a weak smile. "Come in and have a cup of tea. I'll tell Carrie you're here."

Louise didn't feel comfortable to sit. She would have put the kettle on if she'd been visiting her daughter's house, but this was her son's house. It was Carrie's domestic domain. She didn't feel so free here. Neither Carrie nor Anne came immediately, and Louise felt the time drag by. Perhaps she shouldn't have come. It was obvious Anne was having to talk Carrie into coming into the lounge room to greet her mother-in-law. Louise wasn't an insecure sort of person but she felt insecure at the moment. Carrie had apparently rejected Pete. Would she now reject Louise as well? The time ticked by until Louise couldn't just stand by any more.

"Anne?" She called in a soft tone, as she approached the bedroom door where she knew they were. "Perhaps I better call in another time."

Anne opened the bedroom door and Louise could see the frustration written on her face. "Go in and talk to her, if you're game," Anne said. "I'm about ready to give up."

Louise watched, just a little anxious, as she saw Anne head back to the kitchen. She looked back at the open door and decided she was game. She understood what Carrie was going through.

"Carrie?" she said softly. "I'm so sorry, honey. The pain must be awful." She stood and watched her daughter-in-law clutching a pillow close to her chest as if she was clinging to it for life. Carrie didn't acknowledge her but Louise had come this far and figured it was now or never. She sat on the bed near Carrie's head and brushed stray hair away from her face.

"You know, honey, what you're feeling is perfectly normal. You're supposed to feel anger and loss and pain."

"I should get over it, though, shouldn't I?"

"It's not the time for getting over it, Carrie. You've lost your child, and you need to feel this pain."

"I don't think you understand how much it hurts," Carrie said. She still didn't look up at her visitor.

"I do understand, Carrie. I lost my first child too."

At this, Carrie turned questioning eyes in Louise's direction. "You had another child before Pete?"

Louise nodded. "A boy. We didn't name him, as … well, it wasn't really the practice in those days."

"How many weeks were you?" Carrie sounded desperate to know the answer.

"I was nineteen weeks when he was born prematurely. They called it a miscarriage, but we saw the tiny little body. I knew he was my son. I felt as if my world had fallen apart."

Carrie broke down sobbing, and Louise just stroked her hair. "I'm sorry, Carrie. The loss is awful."

"Nobody understands," she said through her tears.

"I do. It's all right for you to grieve."

"I'm angry at Pete too."

"I know."

"He should have been there, and he took off."

"I know."

"I'm scared he'll go back to Rianne. She'll probably have babies without losing them."

"He won't go back to Rianne, Carrie. Pete loves you, and he's grieving the loss of his child too."

"I'm not sure he does love me. I saw how he lit up when he saw Rianne. She is so beautiful."

"She has a model kind of beauty, but she was vain and shallow when she was with Pete before. Pete knows that. He loves what he has with you, your depth and personality."

"But he doesn't love the way I look."

"Honey, you may be assured that he does love the way you look, or you would never have gotten pregnant in the first place."

Carrie shook her head. "I'm just … I'm not sure."

"I know, and that's all right. You need time to work through how you feel, and you don't need any of us pushing you on a schedule."

"Why did Charlotte have to die? That's all Pete wanted from me—to have a baby. I wanted to give him a child, but I couldn't keep her alive long enough." Carrie burst into tears again.

Louise just sat with her and stroked her hair. She didn't have answers to the big 'why' questions. She doubted that anyone did. Even if someone did know the answer, it wouldn't help take away the pain.

Chapter Twenty-Nine

"Reassure your wife that she is allowed to grieve, and that she is allowed to be angry."

Pete heard the counselor's words. He didn't want Carrie to be angry with him.

"You do understand why she's angry, don't you?"

Pete nodded. That stupid meeting with Rianne, and then his ill-timed flight from the hospital. Both of them were being perceived as betrayal and rejection. He understood, but he wanted to make it right with her.

"You understand that her shutting me out hurts me also?" Pete asked.

"Yes, of course. And you feeling your anger is important too. But it's important you don't use your anger as a weapon. It would be easy to cause more damage."

Pete nodded. He could see that.

"Keep your heart open to God as well," the counselor said.

Pete didn't say anything. He couldn't understand why God had allowed this to happen to them.

"We have two choices in times of pain." The counselor continued without waiting for any response. "We can shake our fist at God—angry and demanding answers—or we can run into his arms and allow him to comfort us. I recommend the second."

Pete let out a breath he'd been holding. The idea of resting in God's strong embrace was appealing. He didn't understand why Charlotte

Grace had died, but being angry and trying to cope all alone was exhausting.

"When your wife is ready, I hope she will come to counseling as well, and begin to rebuild the trust you once shared."

"I'd like her to come now, but she doesn't want to."

"Have you spoken to her?"

"Not in recent weeks. I pass messages back and forth through her mother and sister."

"Be patient with her, and in the meanwhile, allow yourself to process your own pain. Build some coping strategies so when you do see her you won't be tempted to lapse into angry words."

Pete left the counseling appointment wishing there was a bottle of pills he could take and make all the pain and anger go away. That would be so much easier, but if he'd understood correctly, this was going to take time and patience. It was a journey and a process.

One thing the counselor had suggested was creating something meaningful for Charlotte Grace that reflected their love and loss. He was creative and he felt both the love and the loss keenly. It didn't take much for him to come up with a meaningful memorial for her.

The weeks of separation had been stressful on one hand, but Pete had poured himself physically into their new house. It was nearing completion and only lacked some decor. Pete didn't want to make those decisions on his own. He wanted Carrie to make those decisions with him. He wanted her to be there when it was all finally put together. But he still hadn't seen her. He decided, that notwithstanding the counsel to let her have her space to grieve, he wanted to make a deliberate invitation to take that first step together as a couple on the road to rebuilding their marriage.

It was time to enlist help.

"Pete! Hi! I haven't heard from you in ages." Amanda's voice came over the phone with loud enthusiasm.

"We've had some stuff to sort out," Pete replied.

"I'm sorry how things turned out," she said.

"They haven't turned out, yet. In fact I have a plan to get the show on the road again."

"As in …?"

"As in our marriage—mine and Carrie's." He rushed to clarify. He would never underestimate Amanda and some of the crazy ideas she got in her head sometimes.

"And you've called me, why?"

"I need Carrie to come and see the new house, but I'm a little scared to ask her in case she says no."

"It's got really bad for you guys, huh?"

"It hasn't been great. But I have plans to make it better."

"What exactly do you think I can do?" Amanda asked.

"I thought perhaps you could take her out for the day—treat her to a day spa, the pair of you together, and then after take a detour by the new house just to take a look."

"And you'll what? Just happen to be there?"

"Of course. I just want her to come and spend some time here with me, and let's see how things turn out from there."

"I dunno, Pete. That sounds like you're wanting me to lie for you."

"Amanda Keenan! You owe me big time after that stunt you pulled luring me to your place and trying to get me to be unfaithful to Carrie."

"I wouldn't have let you go through with it."

"Still. That was really awkward, and think what would have happened if I'd fallen for it."

"It was not a big deal. I needed to test you out."

"You still owe me."

"But this is Carrie we're talking about."

"You owe her too, after your wedding present fiasco."

"Oh, come on, Pete. Don't tell me you didn't enjoy it."

"I didn't! How could I? You embarrassed your best friend almost to death."

"All right, all right. Don't nag. I'll do the favor for you. I don't like seeing Carrie like this, and I know you guys were great together. But I can't take responsibility if it doesn't work out."

"You just have to get her here. I'll take responsibility for what happens afterward."

"So you say, Pete Brooker. I'll need your assurance, though, that we are now square and there will be no more referring to past misdemeanours."

"You have my word."

***

Carrie hadn't been out much in the weeks since the loss of Charlotte Grace. Now she had let herself be talked into a day of pampering at a day spa. Amanda was hard to say no to.

"You'll love this place," Amanda chatted as they drove. "I've booked us in for the full package."

"I'm not sure I can afford the full package, not being employed at the moment."

"My treat. Besides, I figure I owe you."

"For what?"

There was an awkward pause, which made Carrie zero in on Amanda's thoughts. Amanda never had an awkward pause.

"What do you owe me for?"

"Never mind."

"What have you done?" Carrie asked.

"Oh, you know …"

"I don't know."

"Your wedding present, which apparently neither of you enjoyed."

Carrie went quiet and turned her gaze out of the passenger side window. She didn't want to think about Pete, and especially not about their honeymoon. Too late. The thoughts were there. It had been some honeymoon where they'd soon warmed up to each other, and they hadn't needed Amanda's wedding gift to spice things up. Once they got started, the whole thing was simmering with passion. Carrie shook her head. What had happened? How had she convinced herself that Pete wasn't attracted to her? Remembering their honeymoon, she came to the conclusion Pete was either a really good actor, or he—

"So what are your plans for this coming new year?" Amanda broke into her thoughts.

"I haven't really thought about it," Carrie replied. She hadn't been able to think about anything but her grief for the past three months.

"Do you have plans for Christmas?"

"That's still weeks away."

"What about your anniversary? That's coming up the first week of January."

"Manda, please. Don't push me."

"Sorry."

Amanda went quiet for some time. At first Carrie didn't notice as she descended into her own thoughts again, but after a long time she realized her best friend, who usually never shut up, had not talked for a while.

"I'm sorry, Amanda. I'm trying to work through things. I really appreciate you organizing this day, and luckily, all I'll have to do is lie quietly and listen to running water and birdcalls. But I'm not sure I'm ready to think about ..."

"Pete?" Amanda guessed.

"I think about him, but it's deteriorated so much, I'm not sure we're going to make our first anniversary."

"OK. Let's not talk about it."

Carrie was surprised Amanda just cut the subject off. She was tempted to think something was going on, but her own thoughts dragged quickly back to the pain of loss—not just Charlotte Grace, but also the loss of her marriage. She needed this time of quiet reflection while she enjoyed the soothing sounds and relaxing massage. Whatever Amanda was up to, she decided to let it slide. She wasn't ready for confrontation.

It wasn't until they were back in Amanda's car and set to head home when Carrie realized they weren't heading home at all.

"Where are you going?" she asked.

"Since we're in the area, I thought it might be good to drive by your new place and see how it's shaping up."

Suddenly Carrie saw what Amanda was up to.

"Amanda, is this a set up?"

"What do you mean?" If Carrie hadn't known her friend better, she would have sworn she was innocent. But she knew her friend.

"Is this why you booked the day spa way over this side of town instead of one closer?"

"This one came highly recommended."

"By whom? Louise? Chloe? Megan?"

"Does it matter?"

"Are they trying to get me and Pete back together again?"

"Do you want me to be honest?"

"I wish you would."

"No. This has nothing to do with Pete's mother or sisters."

Carrie stayed quiet but kept her pointed gaze on Amanda. Carrie knew Amanda could see her with her peripheral vision, even while she was driving.

"Don't raise your eyebrows at me like that," Amanda objected. "We are five minutes from your new home and I'd like to see it. In fact, you should have invited me over to see it before now and let me be excited about it, along with you."

"I don't know if I am excited about it," Carrie said. She sighed. "Amanda, I'm not sure Pete and I are going to work out."

"What makes you say that?"

"It's been three months, Amanda. I haven't seen him since we lost the baby."

"You haven't wanted to see him. You've avoided him, and kept him away."

"Who told you that?"

Guilt was written all over Amanda's face, but she clamped her lips tight together.

"Who, Amanda?"

"Oh look! This is your street."

Carrie looked up. She hadn't been along this street since she and Pete had first come to inspect the foundation after it had been laid. She'd been excited then. Pete had put his arm around her and kissed her head. She had walked over the whole slab and they'd talked about which rooms would go where, according to the plan. She hadn't been out again, first because of her busy schedule and then tiredness had prevented the trip. And then—Charlotte Grace.

Amanda pulled the car up into the driveway and Carrie's thoughts were snapped back to focus. He'd finished it. A beautiful house, white rendering, with light gray moldings around the windows. There were fences, a letter box and even some lawn had been rolled out. Tears flooded Carrie's eyes, and she couldn't stop the sobbing that came over her.

"Hey, what's that for?" Amanda softened her tone and put her hand on Carrie's arm. "Come on, Carrie. Shhh. This is your home."

Carrie shook her head. "It's Pete's home. I don't know if he'll want me back after—"

"After what?"

"I lost our baby. He wanted a baby, Amanda. I couldn't give it to him. He could do so much better than me."

"You talk a lot of nonsense." Amanda released her seatbelt. "Come on. I'm going to look around the place."

Carrie didn't move.

"Are you coming?"

"Is he here?"

"Well I'm sure I don't know."

"I'm sure you do. Is he here, Amanda?"

"You stay in the car if you must. I'm not going to waste the trip. I want to have a look around."

Amanda closed her car door and flung her bag over her shoulder. She made a great show of inspecting everything as she went, peering in at the windows, opening the side gate, and turning back to wave as she went down the side of the house.

Carrie sat firm. She was overwhelmed with sadness and regret, and a terrible longing to be able to feel happy again. She closed her eyes and leaned her head back against the head rest of the car, allowing all her jumbled emotions to grab hold of thoughts and spin through her mind. Then the car door opened. Carrie figured Amanda was returned from her inspection of the back yard, but the moment he pushed the lever to set the seat back, Carrie knew it was Pete who had got into the driver's seat. She kept her eyes closed. She was afraid to open them.

"Hey." His voice was soft and gentle, and he lay his large hand on her knee. "Carrie?"

She knew she couldn't shut him out forever. She didn't want to. Slowly she opened her eyes and looked at him through a sheen of tears.

"I'm sorry, Pete. I wish I could have done better for you."

She didn't know how it happened but, somehow, she found herself pulled into an embrace and they were both sobbing. It was only because it was so awkward and uncomfortable in the front seat of Amanda's car that they pulled back.

"Will you come inside?" he asked.

Carrie nodded. She couldn't speak. Her throat was swollen with a lump of emotion.

Pete came around, opened her door and helped her out. Before they could move, he had her in an embrace again, his long arms enveloping her. She just lay her face against his chest. More tears. So many tears. When would they stop?

Taking her hand, Pete led her over the porch and in through the front door. Amanda was there. Carrie saw her smile. She smiled back.

"Guys, listen, I'm sorry to be in a rush, but I've got another appointment to go to. Can you drive Carrie home?" she asked Pete.

"As if," Carrie said. "I know you set this up."

"You can thank me later." She kissed Carrie on the cheek and was out the front door before either of them could say a thing.

Carrie took a deep breath trying to calm her emotions down. She stood in the entry hall and took in the formal lounge that opened up from there. The walls were painted, and there was a wood floating floor, just as they had discussed. But there were no curtains or light fittings.

"I wanted to wait for you to choose," Pete said.

"It looks great, Pete. You've done a wonderful job."

"Before we inspect the rest of the house, I want to show you something first."

Carrie looked up at him.

"Come on." He took her hand and they walked down the hallway to one of the rooms Carrie knew they had designated as the baby's room.

"Pete?" She pulled to a stop. "I can't. You know what we'd planned for this room."

Pete nodded. "I know. Let me show you. Please?"

He put his arm around her shoulders and guided her in. It was no use trying to calm her emotions. They were out of control, and so, apparently, were his. Her chin ached and her lips quivered as she saw what he'd done. Tears ran down her cheeks as she saw the room completely finished, with all the baby furniture set up. On the wall was a series of photographs framed in white frames, each photo showing pictures of Charlotte Grace—with Pete, with her, with them both, and beneath the frame was a carved plaque.

Charlotte Grace

Our beautiful daughter, gone but not forgotten.

Beneath that was the date of her birth—and her death.

Carrie turned into Pete and they held each other in their grief, crying until they could cry no more. Eventually, Pete kissed her head and began to pull away. Carrie felt bereft. She just wanted to stay wrapped in his warm embrace, physically close, their hearts beating the same rhythm of comfort in their sorrow. But he broke that connection, and before Carrie knew it, he was on one knee before her. He'd taken both her hands in his and was gazing up into her eyes. His kneeling posture brought him closer to her than when they were both standing. She wanted to kiss him and re-establish that connection, but waited.

"I love you, Carrie."

Those words she had wanted to hear for months. Her eyes overflowed again, but this time, she had a wobbly smile to go with it.

"I love you, and I can't live without you. Will you be my wife, not just my companion, but my soul-mate and lover? For better or worse, in sickness and in health. And forsaking all others. There's no-one I'd rather be with than you, Carrie. You are my one true love."

Despite the watery eyes, Carrie's smile expanded into a grin and she nodded her head.

"Yes. Please. I love you and want to be with you too, Pete. And I'm so sorry about the last few months. I'm sorry about Charlotte..."

Pete put his fingers on her lips. "Shh. Charlotte's death was not your fault."

"But what if I can't ..."

"I just want you. If it's just you and me for the rest of our lives, I will be a happy man."

"Do you mean that?"

Pete nodded. Carrie thought through a hundred more problems that came to mind.

"I love you, Carrie. I want you. Will you have me as your husband?"

Carrie put her hands either side of his face, since it was so accessible, and kissed him. He threw his arms around her waist and she fell forward, unbalancing him on his one knee. Together they fell sideways, then rolled so Carrie was on top of Pete, but she didn't care. He loved her. She loved him. That was all that mattered. Then it was back again. The passion. The urgency. The desire. All released by the healing power of forgiveness and reconciliation.

Chapter Thirty

"*Is that what you thought?*" Benjamin was aghast at what he'd just learned.

"*Why else would you have consented to a marriage to someone you didn't love?*" Charlotte kept her gaze down, uncertain.

"*Why did you assume I did not love you?*"

"*You never spoke of love. It was understood from the beginning that you were marrying for my money.*"

Benjamin closed the distance between him and his wife.

"*But surely, you must have realized … when we came together …*"

"*I knew you had to produce an heir. Why else would you have come to my bedchamber?*"

Confound it. How could she have so misunderstood him?

"*Did you never suspect that I came because I loved my wife?*"

"*No.*"

"*Not ever?*"

"*I knew you loved Kitty Coleborn. I knew you needed my inheritance to shore up your estate. I knew you needed an heir. How was I supposed to know that you cared for me?*"

Benjamin thought on the question. What did a man have to do to communicate such sentiments?

"*And you never stayed,*" she continued, "*Always you left for London the day after.*"

"*I have business in London and, as a member of the House of Lords, responsibilities in parliament.*"

"I know, but how was I supposed to know how you felt?"

"My dear, I see I have been remiss in my attentions as a husband and lover."

He watched Charlotte's face pink prettily.

"I love you deeply, my dear, and I wish you to travel with me in future. I detest being in that house in London all alone."

Charlotte raised her eyebrows. Did she not believe him?

"I have my valet, butler and housekeeper, but they are nothing to the company you provide."

"No one else to keep you company?"

Good heavens! Her doubt of him had run deeper than he'd imagined. What a fool he'd been to keep his emotions so guarded.

"I desire only your company."

"Only mine? Is there no room in your heart for another?"

"None. I swear!" What was she smiling about? She picked up his hand and placed it on her abdomen. What was she saying?

"Not even for your son and heir?"

He was aghast for a second time in a half-hour.

"You're increasing?"

"Yes, my darling man. And I would like it to be clear, I love you deeply."

He drew her into his embrace and kissed her. Surely she could interpret that.

Confound it, the phone was ringing and at an inopportune time.

"Who on earth is calling at this hour?"

Louise woke from her dream, disorientated. It took a while for her to find the handset and connect the call.

"Hello." She tried to inject wakefulness into her tone, though she knew it was ridiculous. She wasn't really awake.

"Mum! We're in delivery. Can you pray for us?" It was Pete.

A shot of adrenaline sharpened Louise's senses and she sat upright in the bed, feeling around in the dark for the light switch. With the bright light, Russell began to make noises as well.

"Is everything all right?" she asked.

"So far."

"Has she gone into labor?" Louise asked.

"Yes, on her own, naturally."

Louise knew Carrie had been hospitalized for the last month as the doctors monitored her blood pressure. They were expecting another three weeks before due date, unless an emergency arose.

"Carrie's blood pressure?" Louise asked.

"All good at this stage. And the baby's heartbeat. They're not alarmed. I think it's going to be OK."

"Do you want us to come in?" Louise asked.

"It's three in the morning. I guess you'll want to sleep."

Fat chance of that now.

"We'll come if you want."

"No, leave this one to us, Mum. I think we've got it covered. I just thought you and Dad would like to know."

"Thanks, love. We're praying for everything to go well this time."

Louise hung up the phone and turned towards her husband.

"Baby coming?" Russell said in a groggy tone.

"They're in the delivery ward. Let's hope everything goes OK this time."

"Did he say there was anything to worry about?"

Louise shook her head.

"Then I dare say we can finish the night, and catch up with the news in the morning."

"Honestly, Russell, you have no imagination."

"No, I leave that up to you. You're the writer."

Louise settled back in her bed, but couldn't go to sleep. She was so glad Carrie and Pete had gotten pregnant again. She was even more glad they'd got back together again. It was a lot of pressure having played the matchmaker, and when it looked like it had all fallen apart, Louise had scolded herself for having ever interfered in the first place. She'd made a vow she would never interfere like that again. What had she been thinking?

But then she had reflected on how much she and the whole family loved Carrie. She was a perfect fit for all of them, especially Pete. And once they'd got through their grieving time, and had moved back in together, she'd breathed a sigh of relief and decided she'd done a good job after all. Despite Carrie's fears she might never have children, the doctor had cleared her to try again, though he wanted to monitor her much more closely than last time, given the previous disastrous outcome.

Louise enjoyed imagining situations and scenarios. She'd done it for all her children, and though she'd had three happy-ever-after endings, the journey had never quite matched the glorious plot and narrative she'd had in her mind when she'd set out. Pete and Carrie's narrative had had entirely too much drama for her liking, and now she was happy for them to settle back to normal and uneventful. She decided she would reserve her plotting for her next series of novels. She got paid for that, and nobody's life and love were affected.

∗∗∗

It was one thing to go into labor, another for the baby to appear in short order. It was now nearly lunchtime and Carrie had been in the delivery ward for just on eleven hours. The family had gathered in one of the waiting rooms, and all the mothers in the room were swapping labor stories. Louise smiled. It was funny watching the men huddle in a corner away from all the gory details. They just couldn't relate.

When the door to the delivery suite opened, Pete emerged. He looked kind of bedraggled.

"Any news?" Russell asked the question they all wanted to ask.

Pete smiled. "He's here. A healthy seven-pound two-ounce boy."

"And Carrie?" Anne asked. Her concern was obvious.

"She's good, Mum," Pete said. "She managed the labor all on her own, even though it took a while."

"Thank you, Lord." Louise couldn't help but offer a prayer of thanks.

"So, who wants to come see the baby?" Pete asked.

Louise could have told him that was the wrong question to ask. It would have been simpler to ask who didn't want to see the baby.

"OK. Perhaps I'll see if I can bring him out here for a bit."

"Can I come in and see Carrie?" Anne asked.

"Sure." Pete held his arm out to his mother-in-law and they went into the delivery suite together.

Louise watched it all, a little bit detached from what was going on. Anne, Bill, Ellen and even Carrie's brother, Mark, fit together with her family, Russell, Chloe, Megan, herself. It was as if they'd always been family.

"Mum," Chloe interrupted her thoughts, snapping her fingers. "Head out of the clouds."

"What?"

Chloe cast her eyes in the direction of the delivery suite. Pete was wheeling a hospital crib out with his son inside. Louise's heart melted. She'd always known that Pete would make a wonderful father, and he was off to a good start.

"Ellen, I'm putting you in charge," Pete said. "You've got five minutes to goo and gah and introduce yourselves."

"Why? Where are you going?"

"To be with my wife, of course. I'll be back for our son shortly."

Louise smiled as she watched him go back inside the door. Chloe came right next to her and threaded her arm through hers.

"So, you did a good job in the finish, didn't you?"

"Do you think so?" Louise asked.

"All the scheming and organizing. And this is the result. I guess you must be fairly proud of yourself."

"I'm just glad it worked out."

"It worked out all right. It's beautiful, even if I do say so myself. It would make a good plot line for one of your novels."

Louise smiled. *Yes. Yes it would.*

Before you go:

If you enjoyed this story, would you mind taking a few minutes to pop a review on the site where you purchased *All Arranged*, or on the Good Reads website. Every review helps me, as an author, to get new readers involved. Thank you for spending the time with me and my Luella Linley family.

Meredith ☺

Have you read the other books in the Luella Linley – License to Meddle series?

Book #1 in the Luella Linley – License to Meddle series

<u>Organized Backup</u>

By Meredith Resce

Regency romance author, Luella Linley, arranges her characters' lives, making sure that they weather all storms and live happily-ever-after. Her characters are putty in her hands, but her 21st Century adult children are not so easily organized. When her daughter, Megan, asks for support with an inappropriate situation at work, Luella decides Megan should get a boyfriend to intimidate her boss. The cop who just pulled Luella over for speeding is a likely candidate.

Cam Fletcher is expecting to be interviewed by a famous author. Instead of sharing insights into his job working in the police force, he is sharing a meal with the famous author and her daughter, Megan. When left alone with Megan, Cam wonders when the interview will begin. The parents' extended absence gives him a clue, which Megan confirms. Luella Linley is playing matchmaker, but is he willing to play the game.

Also by Meredith Resce

The Heart of Green Valley series

(Period drama romance set in Colonial Australia)

Book 1 – The Manse

Book 2 – Green Valley

Book 3 – Through the Valley of Shadows

Book 4 – Wallace Hill

Book 5 – Beyond the Valley

Book 6 - Echoes in the Valley

The Schoolmaster's Bride (Period drama romance)

The Schoolmaster's Daughter (Period drama romance)

Mellington Hall (Murder mystery)

Cora Villa (Period drama romance)

For All Time (A time slip novel)

How Sweet the Sound (Fantasy Allegory)

The Greenfield Legacy (Contemporary romance)

Falling for Maddie Grace (Contemporary romance novella)

Where there's Smoke (Contemporary romance novella)

Four Short Stories (paperback of four novellas)

Mortal Insight (Contemporary political crime under pen-name E.B. James)

Thank you

Thanks to you, the reader, for engaging in this story. I hope you have enjoyed it and will get an opportunity to read the other two books in the *Luella Linley – License to Meddle* series.

All Arranged, while it is released as the third in this series was actually written first. I wrote it a number of years ago when my children were in that single, young-adult phase of life, and perhaps Luella Linley might resemble something of how I used to plan possible romantic encounters. But a word of advice for mothers in this stage, or approaching it: meddling in your adult children's lives is not usually met with a friendly eye, and should only be attempted with the utmost caution and consent of said children. Luella Linley is fun fiction—good for a laugh, but I wouldn't pattern your life after her antics.

Thanks to my children, who all managed to get married without any assistance from me, and who love me despite my hints and nudges. Thanks to my husband for sticking with me during the twenty something years of writing and publishing. He still maintains he is the inspiration for all my romantic heroes. (insert eye-roll here).

Thanks to Kate and Rodg Mackereth who went to some trouble to assist with cover images. Good job, guys.

Thanks to those readers who take the extra time to review. It is encouraging to an author, and it helps to tickle the algorithms to do something useful.

Thank you, God, Creator, Saviour, Healer and King – who is the genius behind anything that is particularly brilliant. I pray that something of his grace and peace is infused into these stories, and that they will bring inspiration and encouragement.

About the Author

South Australian Author, Meredith Resce, has been writing since 1991, and has had books in the Australian market since 1997.

Following the Australian success of her *Heart of Green Valley* series, they were released in the UK.

All Arranged is Meredith's 22nd published title.

Apart from writing, Meredith teaches high school students. She is an avid reader, particularly Christian fiction. She is a fan of British costume-drama television series, and British murder mystery shows. Jane Austen, L.M. Montgomery and Charles Dickens are favorite classic authors. Meredith is a country-girl at heart, and takes every opportunity to visit the farm where she grew-up.

Aussie rules football and cricket are her choice when following televised sport. Come on Aussies!

Meredith often speaks to groups on issues relevant to relationships and emotional and spiritual growth.

Meredith has also been co-writer and co-producer in the 2007 feature film production, *Twin Rivers* now available on Amazon Prime.

With her husband, Nick, Meredith has worked in Christian ministry since 1983.

Meredith and Nick have three adult children.

www.meredithresce.com

www.facebook.com/MeredithResceAuthor